SHADOW'S SECRET

SHADOW ISLAND SERIES: BOOK ONE

MARY STONE
LORI RHODES

Sometimes the past can come back to haunt you, and sometimes it can lead you to exactly what you need. This is to all those who need the ocean waves and sea salt to piece together the mystery and heal.

DESCRIPTION

Hidden secrets lead to deadly lies...

Following the incident that brought justice to her parents'
killers but ended her career, former FBI Special Agent
Rebecca West needs a fresh start. Hoping to find peace, she
decides to spend a few months in the sleepy beach town of
Shadow Island, where she spent idyllic summers as a kid.

However, her vacation is cut short when a seventeen-year-
old goes missing with no leads or clues. When the girl's body
is found in a nearby marsh with strangulation marks around
her neck, Rebecca can't say no when the overworked sheriff
asks her to help investigate.

Rebecca's gut tells her that on the small island, the murder
hadn't been a chance encounter. But who would want the
likeable teen in a seemingly sweet and innocent relationship
with her boyfriend dead? And why?

Rebecca soon discovers something bigger is going on around Shadow Island, something involving an enigmatic Yacht Club that no one will talk about...but that just might hold the keys to solving the girl's murder. But who are they willing to kill to keep their secrets buried?

From its enigmatic beginning to the twisted ending you won't see coming, Shadow's Secret—the first book in the Shadow Island Series by Mary Stone and Lori Rhodes—is a stark reminder that two people can keep a secret...if one of them dies.

1

Pressing a hand over her mouth, Cassie Leigh attempted to hold back the sobs fighting to escape her throat. She had to be quiet. If she made a sound, she knew she wouldn't survive this night.

And she needed to survive.

How had this happened?

With no time to even consider the question, Cassie ran as fast as she could. She didn't realize she'd made it into the marshes until her bare feet splashed into the slimy mire. With a soft gasp, she barely managed to strangle her startled yelp as decaying plants, mud, and silt squelched between her toes.

Holding the red dress she'd bought just for him closed in the front, Cassie was exposed to the rawness of the swamplands hiding in the sharp grasses and hidden pools of water. That was just a couple of the many reasons she should have tried to avoid them, but when she'd started running, there hadn't been time for choices. The only thing that mattered was to get away. She needed to keep moving.

Lightning flashed, providing Cassie with a glimpse of her

current location and saving her from running into an old, abandoned boat half buried in the muck. The marshes stood out during the day, an oddly satisfying addition to the island landscape. If she hadn't spent so much time looking over her shoulder, she still might have seen them, even in the dark of night. It was too late to change her path now.

Marsh muck would be the least of her problems if he caught her.

No!

She couldn't think like that.

Cassie's lungs burned, and her mind raced, stirred by panic and the very sudden and real understanding that she had royally screwed up. Cassie had never seen him like this before.

"You lying bitch!"

Spittle had flown from his lips as he'd shouted into her face, and that hadn't even been the worst of it. The way he had screamed at her, the names he'd called her, even the way he moved, none of it was like the man she thought she had known so well.

It wasn't until he'd slapped her that she knew he wasn't going to calm down. She'd had only one choice after that... run. He'd pursued her, though, still raging and screaming, so she had kept running, trying to keep ahead of him.

Cassie wasn't sure if she was more scared or heartbroken as she tore through the mud...if it was tears or the stink of the marsh trickling down her cheeks. She sloshed forward as the first drops of rain pelted her skin. The stagnant, muddy water coming up to her ankles and then her knees. Each step was accentuated by the swish and splash as she groped forward blindly. She tried to ignore the things that were sticking to her bare flesh as she prayed it didn't get any deeper.

I'm making too much noise.

She stopped for a moment, holding her breath and listening, then jumped when lightning struck again. Maybe she could hide from him instead? Though the storm was terrifying, it might even be her friend. Its sound would cover her shaking breaths, and if she hunkered down in the tall grass, maybe he'd walk right by her. It wasn't like he had a flashlight, and the moon was covered by clouds.

Maybe he'd give up. Or maybe he'd calm down, and they could—

Splashing footfalls came from behind her, and she gasped as the world was lit from yet another strike of fire. Did he see her?

"Cassie!"

The word roared over the sound of the rain, and she'd never had anyone speak to her in such rage. Less than an hour before, Cassie had loved listening to his labored breathing as he called out her name during the throes of passion, but there was something unmistakably different about it now. In the darkness, standing in the mud and pelting rain, it sounded desperate. It was the sound of an enraged animal on the hunt, not someone she'd willingly spent so many happy times with.

From what she could tell, he seemed to be somewhere off to her right. Keeping low in case lightning lit up the sky again, she slunk off to the left, angling herself so she'd come out closer to the beach. She only had fifty yards or so to cross, a distance she felt sure she could make. All she had to do was be quiet, to keep panic from slowing her legs.

They'd been pushing this mad dash ever since they'd left the old witch's cottage that had become their meeting spot. She'd been tempted to climb the steps to the lighthouse but knew she'd be trapped there if he spotted her before she could get to the top.

If she could make it to the beach, she could run much

easier. Even out in the open and visible, she could still get away. And go where? Where could she go that was safe from him? There was nothing close by, she knew.

This hadn't been the plan.

She'd been so careful...so picky! They'd never argued before tonight, and it was the first time she'd ever experienced his violent side. Sure, she'd heard others talk about him losing his temper and knew what he was like when he was frustrated.

But tonight was different.

Tonight, she'd refused to do what he wanted, and she'd seen it in his eyes—some sort of fissure or break. The man who revealed himself at that moment was a stranger. Not the loving, gentle man she'd grown to care for.

Crash!

She screamed as a bolt of lightning hit the island several hundred yards away. She had to get out of there...for more than one reason.

The water was shallower now, only to her ankles. If she allowed herself to run, maybe she could escape. The beach was visible through the weeds and salt grass. She could outrun him for a while, but if she didn't find safety within a minute or so, he'd find her for sure.

She hated the idea of running from him. He'd been a place of safety. Even the mere thought of him had made her feel secure. That's why she had chosen him in the first place. But what she'd seen in his eyes before she bolted from the bedroom...she gagged as a wave of nausea snuck up on her.

She didn't trust herself.

Didn't trust him.

Not anymore. She had to make it out of here and get help.

Or maybe it was better to hide? But where?

Crash!

Maybe he'd simply give up or come to his senses. She could talk with him about this tomor—

A hand came down on her shoulder with a viselike grip. A scream rose, but only a whimper escaped as his other hand clamped around her throat. Before she could claw at his arm or fight in any way, Cassie was lifted from the ground. Her feet came free of the muck, but only for a moment before she was slammed down onto her back.

Mud and brine combined with the rain to splash into her eyes, but even through that and the darkness, the face above hers was clear. The water was deep enough to cover her face as he shoved her down into the soft ground. Mud crept into her ears, muffling his harsh breathing.

Silt kicked up as she shook her head, both in denial of what was happening to her and in silent communication with her attacker.

No. Please don't do this. Please.

As the storm waged a war with the land, Cassie fought against her lover, but he was too strong. As she grew desperate for air, instinct forced her mouth open, but her breath had nowhere to go. The hands wrapped around her throat were too tight.

Crash!

She gagged as the bitter taste of the marsh coated her tongue. And her lungs screamed, as if they knew they would never draw in air again. Cassie tried with all her might to communicate with him, to say the words she knew he needed to hear.

I'll never tell. I can fix this! I'll do whatever you want!

That was what she wanted to say. He didn't have to do this. She'd have kept this secret forever. They could go back to how it had been. Her perfect life with the perfect man.

I love you. I need you.

Sheltered from the rain by the body above hers, Cassie

poured everything she felt for him into her eyes, trying to make him see that she was sorry. With her expression, she pleaded with him to give her a second chance.

It wasn't working.

Knowing she had only one last chance to communicate her feelings to him, she dragged her trembling fingers off his wrists where they'd clutched on in fear and lifted them to his face, caressing his cheek.

Just the way he liked.

His hand batted hers away, then joined the one at her throat, squeezing harder. The pain in her neck was almost as bad as the pain in her chest.

In Cassie's final moments, she closed her eyes, not wanting to look at his face. She wanted to hate him, but her hand found his cheek one last time.

She didn't know why. He'd betrayed her, was killing her, ripping their future to shreds. How she wished her fear of him had followed her down into the waiting darkness instead of the pain from her broken heart and crushed throat.

2

A thin sliver of moon was barely visible in the midmorning sky, but the pale crescent was a reminder of how clear the air was away from the city.

How peaceful.

And how very necessary.

Former Special Agent Rebecca West breathed in the salty air, raising her face to the warm sun. Smiling for the first time in what seemed like years, the knots in her shoulder muscles loosened a bit.

Yes...this was exactly what she needed. Exactly *where* she needed to be.

At thirty-four, Rebecca was pleasantly surprised to see just how much of Shadow Island looked exactly the same as the last time she'd been there. Rebecca had been in her twenties then, and she and her parents had walked around the town, checking out the shops and attractions.

During the few visits she'd made while in college, most of her time had been spent on the back deck of the family's cottage or on the beach. Still, those memories from the past were clearer than she would have expected.

The island was somehow a perfect blend of old and new. She was especially thrilled to see that some of her favorite childhood spots were still standing. There was I Scream You Scream, the pink and blue parlor where she'd consumed innumerable scoops of chocolate mint, along with numerous sandwich shops and little cafés her family used to frequent.

Hugh's Surf Shop was still open, but time and the elements had roughed it up a bit. The weeds in the cracked parking lot showed that Hugh's was struggling to keep up with some of the newer, more modern surf shops in town. And then, through gaps between the shops and businesses on Cottage Street, was the lighthouse. Its name escaped her, but she had been enamored with it as a kid.

Rebecca took Coastal Drive to Cottage Street, again spotting the lighthouse peeking up over the horizon. She'd only visited the structure a single time in her childhood and barely remembered it. She did remember the story, though, because she'd always found it fascinating.

When the island was discovered in 1822, the land had been uninhabited and empty of life, with the exception of birds and turtles...and a single family who lived in a cottage on the western shore. Other than the single cottage, there was nothing else on the island—no evidence of other settlers, no other buildings, no developed land for many years.

Over time, though, people came, drawn by the sea, and rich developers sought to turn the small island into a tourist destination. But the cottage held pride of place, and its owners refused to sell.

When a ship crashed into the rocky shore of the island, officials decided a lighthouse was necessary. It was then that the townsmen got their revenge.

Rather than perch the fifty-foot structure on the island's highest peak, they chose to build the lighthouse in front of the little cottage, blocking the owners' view of the sunrise and casting a shadow over the little home.

The lady of the cottage, a witch as lore tells the story, cursed the lighthouse and all who stepped into its shadow. As a child, Rebecca had been terrified of that part of the island, even though the beaches there were the best by far.

She wasn't afraid of it now.

As she crossed over Main Street, she was happy to see that the Shadow Island Museum was still up and running. She was pretty sure it had gotten a paint job and new picture windows since her childhood. It was a prime example of how it all looked the same but felt different.

She supposed it was true of most things remembered from childhood and then viewed through the eyes of an adult. Hell, even the ocean and the beach itself changed when studied through that lens. The play and adventure of youth were gone, replaced by the irritation of sand in uncomfortable places and the worry of sunburn and skin damage.

Taking the next few turns from memory, she pulled up in front of the house she'd stayed in so many years ago. When she had come here with her parents, the house had been called Sand Dollar Shores, though the sign on the archway above the porch steps was now gone. Still, it was the same old place.

Very little had been remodeled. The only real change she noticed at first glance was the updated patio furniture on the back deck that she could just barely see from the road. The new outdoor suite was sleek and modern, a far cry from the nearly neon Adirondacks that had sat out there in years past.

Not too far beyond the new outdoor living setup was the brilliant strip of blue she'd been so enamored with as a girl. The Atlantic Ocean sat less than eighty yards away from the deck, the two broken apart by a sparse backyard, low-lying dunes, and unblemished beach.

Parking her blue Toyota Tacoma in the driveway, she wasted no time in gathering her first load to take inside. Rebecca pulled the gun safe from the passenger floorboard and headed up the little pebble walkway to the front porch. Unlocking the front door was a struggle, but after a bit of fumbling, she made it inside.

It was odd to be back in the old house. Though heart-warming in a way she hadn't expected, the experience of standing here could only be defined as out-of-body, as if she was transported back in time. She hadn't even been close to this place in the past thirteen years. To know she'd be living here for three months was hard to process.

Sand Dollar Shores wasn't one of those mammoth three-story deals that lined beaches in Nags Head or Myrtle Beach since few party crowds and spring breakers visited the island. Instead, it was a basic beach cottage, one-story with a wraparound porch that merged with an extended deck over-looking the beach.

To her left, the living room was connected to the kitchen, separated by a small bar area. The two rooms shared a long picture window that looked out onto the patio, giving a picture-perfect view of the beach beyond, which would be perfect for the sunrise.

To her right, a hallway led to the two bedrooms as well as the single bathroom and laundry nook. The entire place was painted a pale teal, and though there were beach-themed decorations placed here and there, it was quaint and not overdone.

Thank goodness. She couldn't stand beach homes that looked like they were shitting seashells or berthing for a pirate crew.

Heading down the hallway, she dropped her safe off in the master bedroom, storing it in the closet. Once it was settled, she entered her password and opened it. Pulling the

Springfield Armory 1911 from her holster, she added it to the small stack of firearms already there. Concealed carry was possibly a bit much for the first day of her vacation.

A Ruger 22 and a Glock 40 rounded out her collection, each wrapped in a cleaning cloth. The fabric was just there to keep them from getting scratched up, just like the small desiccant pack was in the back of the safe to keep the humidity and rust in check.

She pushed the Glock to the back of the case. It was the most she had touched the weapon since the last time she had fired it, but she couldn't bring herself to dispose of the tool. It wasn't the gun's fault those actions had killed her career, though she hadn't felt comfortable carrying it since then either.

Touching it now, when she was trying to start over, felt like an omen. Good or bad, she couldn't know. Relics of the past had a way of addling mind and memory. Sealing the safe, she stood and headed back to her truck.

The house was a rental, so it came furnished with all the basics and linens. Back home, she'd sold the little bit of furniture she'd had in her Georgetown apartment, giving her an extra twelve hundred dollars for the summer—which was half of what the house would cost her for one month here.

She spent the next half hour hauling in boxes, totes, and bags, dropping them in the foyer. Stepping back, she jammed her fists on her hips.

"You, Rebecca West, are pathetic."

Her life shouldn't have fit so easily in such a small room. In her move from D.C. to Shadow Island, she hadn't even needed a U-Haul or one of those small flatbed trailers to move all her belongings. Due to her preference for a minimalist lifestyle, her possessions had all fit in the bed of her truck.

There was something sad about that, but at the same

time, she was glad. At least there wouldn't be much to unpack.

She had never been the type to hold on to clothing, furniture, or even sentimental objects. Once those were removed from the equation, all she really had were her clothes, library, and important documents. And of course, her guns and ammo, sentimentality be damned. Which all fit neatly into her new accommodations.

As Rebecca set down the final box, she couldn't decide if she wanted to unpack everything now or walk down to the beach. She knew there were happy memories waiting for her down there, just as there were here in this house...if she was ready to face them.

"Well, shit." She blew out a breath.

Standing just inside the door, she examined the place that would be her home for the next couple months while the Ramones serenaded her new life from her phone.

"Sedate me too," she crooned her own version of the lyrics along with the band. Actually, sedation via a nap didn't sound too bad. Maybe if she just ignored the boxes, she could lie down for an hour or so and...

Just as she'd very nearly talked herself into curling up on the couch, Rebecca's Spotify station changed over to "Holidays in the Sun."

Seriously?

Had the Sex Pistols transitioned from punk rock to motivational speakers?

Since it seemed she was getting a universal prod from her playlist to keep moving, Rebecca forced herself to pick up a box. "Just empty this one," she bargained with herself, "and then go sit on the beach for a while."

The box she'd chosen was filled with beach towels and toiletries and took very little time to empty out. Rebecca admired the sparkling chrome in the small bathroom. A sunken tub looked inviting, and the seahorse shower curtain made her smile.

After she'd booked the cabin for the month, Rebecca had been told that a cleaning service would have it in tip-top shape. They certainly had. She could tell the house had been cleaned recently, but she could also pick up some of the trace smells she remembered of the place. Faint teak wood, stale ocean air, and a crisp tanginess she always assumed came from traces of salt on the breeze.

She'd seen the ocean on her way in, particularly during the drive over Shadow Way Bridge, the one and a quarter mile long expanse connecting Shadow Island to the mainland. But that was different. With the beach bordering the little Cape Cod structure and hearing the gentle crashing of waves through the recently cleaned windows, it seemed to be calling to her—to come dip her toes in, to stare aimlessly out to the horizon and lose herself for a bit.

As a girl staying here with her parents all those years ago, Rebecca imagined the waves were whispering as they slapped against the shore. She'd thought of it as a secret language she didn't understand. They hadn't spoken to her but to someone or something else on the island.

She heard it now and smiled.

Glancing back into the foyer at the bins and boxes, she shrugged and walked to the kitchen adjoined to the living room and opened the fridge. The contents inside were nonexistent, save for an open box of baking soda. She'd go on a grocery run later, once she was finally unpacked. For now, though, it was time for a break. The secret whispering of the waves told her the errand could wait.

Rebecca took a beer out of a cooler she'd brought along, and after a second or two of deliberation, decided to get a second one as well. It wasn't her favorite coffee stout, but it was better than nothing. It was also the best of a poor selection at the gas station.

Beggars couldn't be choosers.

And yeah, it might be too early to officially be drinking, it was Saturday morning on the beach, so she could do whatever the hell she wanted.

She carried them both outside, making her way across the patio and down the stairs to the backyard. The grass was dry and somewhat dead, but that was the case over most of Shadow Island—a result of all the salt and heat. She crossed over the dunes, and when she came to the stretch of beach she'd explored as a girl, the sudden surge of nostalgia pulled at her heart.

Grief burned her eyes, but she blinked it away. As she hunkered down in the sand, not caring about getting it on her shorts, Rebecca imagined her family sitting here. Her father would be reading some nonfiction book about the Revolutionary War or the creation of the atomic bomb. Her mother would be sitting just close enough to the ocean so that the waves would rush up to her feet, a magazine draped across her chest as she snoozed in the sun.

And Rebecca would have been bodysurfing or looking for conch shells. She could see it all a little too clearly as she popped the top on her first beer and drank deep, almost half of the contents gone in a forced gulp. The alcohol warmed her belly as she gazed out at the ocean, then closed her eyes to focus on her other senses.

The waves crashed, the sweeping gulls cried out, the coastal breeze swirled around her. Her thoughts turned once again to her mother and father, of what their reactions might be to know she was here, back at Shadow Island to live the summer in solitude.

Sadly, she'd never know their reactions because they'd been dead for the better part of five years. Though Rebecca had been the FBI agent responsible for bringing their killers to justice, she still felt as if nothing had been accomplished. It was naive, she knew, but the fact that her success would never bring her parents back made everything that had followed hurt even more.

After dealing with all of that, after fighting for so long, there should have been some kind of payoff, something good to come from it. With no one to turn to, no place to call home, she had felt as if she was drowning in grief. As if sucked out to sea in a riptide.

The family home had been put up for sale because there'd been too many memories there for her to want to keep it. That was what had made her think about this place again. She'd been compelled to come back here. Her hope was that Shadow Island would help her sort it all out. A sense of home without being overwhelming. Only the good memories lived here, not the ones now filled with sorrow.

And no memories of blood-splattered walls.

Rebecca blew out a breath, then finished beer number one. This was supposed to be about finding a new life, not wading back into the problems from her past. She'd be damned if she was going to let the events of the last few years ruin it. Wrinkling her nose, she tried to usher those thoughts away.

Twisting the cap from the second beer, Rebecca only took a sip this time, forcing herself to slow down. Not that she cared. She wasn't much of a drinker aside from a glass of red wine from time to time, but when she did allow herself to indulge, she'd never been too worried about limitations. This summer might very well be the epicenter of one such moment.

She knew there was a liquor store somewhere on the island, but she couldn't remember where. That was going to be a key location if she planned to drink her cares away on the beach every day.

"Note to self...find liquor store soon."

Her quiet mumblings came to a halt when she spotted a woman walking a dog down the beach. The canine was one of the most gorgeous golden retrievers Rebecca had ever seen. All her dark thoughts evaporated as she watched the dog sniffing at the sea foam as it washed in and out on the waves.

When he sneezed so hard his nose dipped into the sand, she couldn't help but laugh. Startled, the dog looked around. When he spotted Rebecca, the hairy beast gave a tug on his leash in her direction.

"No, Brody!" The woman's voice was filled with exasperation, and she gave that little apologetic wave people of her parents' generation did.

"It's okay, really." Rebecca had always loved dogs, though she wasn't the type to ever own one. She wasn't home enough, and she'd only end up feeling guilty leaving the pup alone so much. Her family once had a golden retriever as a pet, a dog named Goldie who died at the ripe old age of fifteen. Heartbroken by his loss, Rebecca wasn't sure she ever wanted to outlive a beloved pet again. "Mind if I pet him?"

"Sure." Brody's mom walked over, allowing the beautiful animal to receive the petting and attention he knew he deserved.

Rebecca scratched behind his ears, and his tongue lolled out as he gave her a goofy grin. "He's adorable."

"Shh. Don't let it go to his head. Because, oh boy, will it." She cocked her head to the side, her wavy dark hair swaying as she studied Rebecca closely. "Are you vacationing here?"

"Sort of. I'm renting out the house for the summer." Rebecca hitched a thumb over her shoulder to indicate the little Cape Cod directly behind them.

"Oh, exciting! I live just down the beach a bit." She pointed behind her. "About half a mile back that way." She stepped forward, nudging Brody aside for a moment. "I'm Kelly Hunt. And this, of course, is Brody."

Brody's tail stirred up a breeze at the mention of his name, and he looked over his shoulder at his mom.

"Brody, shake."

Like the good boy he was, Brody sat back and waggled one paw at Rebecca. She reached out and shook it before adopting a formal tone that came out more British sounding than she'd intended. "Pleased to meet you both. I'm Rebecca West."

Kelly laughed, and Brody gave her a goofy, tongue lolling grin. "Forgive the nosy questions of a local, but are you new to the island?"

Nostalgia threatened to clog Rebecca's throat, but she swallowed it away and smiled. "Not really. My family used to come here every summer when I was a little girl. I guess I'm trying to recapture the mindset of my younger self...if that's even possible."

"Absolutely." Kelly inhaled deeply, lifting her face to the sun. "Half the reason I decided to move out here seven years ago was because I wanted to remember what it was like when I was a kid."

I'm not the only one.

Warmed by the thought, Rebecca found herself even more curious about the woman. "Did you grow up around here?"

"No, I'm from just outside of Daytona, Florida. And even though my parents might disown me for saying so, I think the ocean up here is much nicer. Cleaner and...I don't know. Wilder, maybe?"

Rebecca looked out to the ocean, sipped her beer, and nodded. "Yeah, wilder. I think that's fitting."

She wasn't sure about the cleaner part, though. This stretch of the ocean was also known as the Graveyard of the Atlantic due to the piles of wrecked ships just below the surface. Partly due to pirates and the sea battles they caused, but mostly the result of shifting sand dunes between the different islands and peninsulas. Kelly might be a local now, but she certainly hadn't grown up raised on the stories of the past.

A gull landed nearby, catching the dog's attention and nearly toppling Kelly over when he lunged for the bird. Kelly laughed. "Well, Rebecca, it was nice meeting you. I'm sure we'll run into one another again."

"I hope so. Take care." They exchanged polite waves as Kelly tried to keep up with Brody's quest for another new scent.

Rebecca watched as the pair continued down the beach, toward a bend in the sand where the island gradually curved around to create its rough crescent shape. Turning her attention back to the sea, Rebecca mulled over Kelly's description of the ocean lapping at the shore just ten feet from her.

The almost pleasant sting of little bits of seashells digging into the bottoms of her feet made her wonder if she still had that one single pair of sandals she'd been holding on to forever. She'd tossed all her shoes and clothes in boxes so haphazardly she hadn't even noticed.

Curling her toes into the sand, Rebecca thought about what Kelly had said...

Cleaner. Wilder.

Two attributes entirely different from one another but that seemed to fit perfectly. The ocean covered up and hid all the remnants of its past while slowly eroding them. That concept provided a tiny spark of hope. Maybe she could come out of this summer a little cleaner, her mind settled and finally focused.

As for the wilder part, Rebecca had experienced enough of that to last a lifetime as far as she was concerned. Perhaps the ocean would help her redefine the term as her summer on Shadow Island wore on.

Turning away from the view and her memories, Rebecca went back inside. There were still several boxes to unpack before she could get some rest.

3

Sheriff Alden Wallace chewed his lip as he reluctantly drove through town. With over forty years on the force under his belt, he loathed the look of incompetence. Which was exactly what he was afraid he may have already done today.

He'd just taken a report of a missing girl an hour ago and had hated like hell to admit to her parents that he didn't have enough staff to go out looking for their daughter. Then he'd nearly fallen as he got out of the chair they'd offered. That embarrassing stumble had reminded him that he felt every minute of his sixty-seven years and that he didn't have much gas left in his tank.

It was time to retire. Dammit.

Wallace came to the intersection of Ash and Main Streets. A young boy holding his mother's hand pointed to the sheriff's vehicle in awe, a bright smile on his face. Alden's late wife had always pointed out that was what he loved most about his job. Sure, there was protecting and serving, and that was all good. But to see the light in a child's eyes when they saw him was something to always be treasured.

Jesus, he missed Rita. What a gem she was.

He wondered what she'd think of his decision to ask an outsider for help. Alden was fairly certain Rebecca West was going to say no, but he still had to ask. And it wasn't like she was a true outsider. Her family had spent a month here every summer when the girl was a child. They were more like snowbirds than regular tourists.

Rita'd probably think it was a good idea and make some comment about how the presence of a woman at the station might be just what the sheriff's office needed. It was either that or suck it up and ask the mainland for assistance. The thought of having to do that again left a sour taste in his throat. No, first he would ask the almost-local with much better credentials.

No one wanted to see cruisers with a different city name on them crawling around town when trying to enjoy the beach. It was a terrible way to think, but when your town's revenue was heavily based on summer tourism, these were the aspects in need of consideration.

Alden accepted the situation was going to be miserable, but he couldn't do it on his own. He had to convince her to help him out.

Alden parked the Explorer and got out. He took two steps forward, and a wash of dizziness came over him. He fixed his gaze on a stationary object and reached out to steady himself against the SUV. His world swayed, his head teetering and tottering like a drunkard half in the barrel.

"Shit."

It was probably the vertigo his doctor warned him about, though the weakness pulling at his body, making it hard to stay upright, seemed worse than a spell of dizziness. During his last checkup, the doc had mentioned something about orthostatic hypotension. Maybe that's what this was. He wasn't sure.

At his age, it seemed like there were too many medical terms he needed to learn, and it honestly pissed him off. Getting old was harder than it needed to be, and vertigo was just another symptom, he reckoned.

Alden took a few deep breaths and stood there until the world stopped tilting and spinning. On legs that felt far too uncertain, he looked around to make sure no one had noticed his frailty. Seeing it was clear, he adjusted his hat and focused on the door ahead of him.

He needed to make a good impression on Rebecca West.

4

The ache in Rebecca's right shoulder was deep and irritating, a constant reminder of what happened in the D.C. parking garage less than two months ago. Both the doctors and her old partner, Benji Huang, had reminded her how lucky she'd been. She just needed to keep telling herself of that when the pain got to her.

The gunshot had been clean, passing all the way through. The bullet had been half an inch from completely severing a tendon and about an inch from shattering her collarbone. In other words, she should be happy she could move her right arm at all.

Happy my ass. It still hurts like hell every time I lay down. Cramping like it's going to rip my shoulder out of the socket.

Putting on a pot of coffee to help defeat the afternoon slump she knew would be coming, she finally started to take a real crack at truly unpacking. Her plan was to be done by two in the afternoon so she could take the remainder of the day to drive around the area.

She'd spent most of her teenage and adult life building Shadow Island up as this almost mythical destination in her mind. She needed to get a good grasp on the place—both of the local feel and the more tourist-oriented edges—if she planned to spend three months here.

Pouring a cup of coffee and choosing to forego music in favor of the sound of crashing waves and gulls through the windows, Rebecca started with her clothes. She didn't have much, so it didn't take long, which was great as the closet in the master bedroom was only a little bigger than a telephone booth. She had the closet and bureau filled within forty-five minutes and then turned her attention to several boxes of books.

Built-in bookshelves took up the majority of the wall between the stairway just off the foyer and the entrance to the kitchen but were sparsely decorated with trinkets. She packed these shelves with her books on the practice of criminal law, serial killer biographies, and perhaps far too many colorful covers on Bigfoot and UFOs.

These were topics she'd found fascinating since the age of twelve, when she saw what she still insisted was an unidentified flying object. While she usually kept these peculiar interests quiet, she had to admit they did look sort of cool on just about any bookshelf. Because she was not the sort to regularly entertain, they were titles and spines usually only seen by her.

She was shelving a thick volume on Bigfoot sightings in the Pacific Northwest when someone knocked on her front door. Since no one knew she was here, she figured it must be a curious local kid who noticed the truck parked out front and was hoping to make a new friend. Or maybe it was Kelly Hunt coming by with Brody for a neighborly visit.

When she opened the door, it was neither. She took a moment to make sure the coffee had kicked in, and she was seeing things right. Sure enough, an older man wearing a sheriff's uniform stood on the porch. On the shorter side, he had the beginnings of what might be a beer belly. His scraggly beard could have been a style choice, but considering how tired he appeared to be, Rebecca had a feeling he hadn't wanted to waste time with shaving the past couple of days.

"Can I help you?"

The visitor eyed Rebecca with great interest, his eyes sparkling with curiosity. "I'm not sure, exactly. I'm Sheriff Alden Wallace. I was hoping to come by and have a word with you if you have a few minutes."

Confused, Rebecca nodded and stood aside to let him in. She offered her hand. "I'm Rebecca West."

He ducked his head to take off his uniform hat as he entered the doorway, so she missed any expression he might have at the mention of her name. "Yes, I know. It's a fairly small town, so news tends to travel pretty fast."

Interesting.

"That is fast. Just got in. I'm unpacking, so it's a bit of a mess. I do have some coffee on, though, if you'd like a cup."

"Oh, no, thank you." He patted his belly. "I don't let myself touch the stuff after nine."

"That sounds...awful." Every cop she'd ever known had basically lived on coffee or energy drinks. It was the only way to stay awake when sitting on stakeouts or sifting through piles of paperwork. Maybe things were different in a town this small.

Sheriff Wallace looked around the living room, placing his hands on his hips. "How long do you plan on staying?"

She answered as his eyes continued to roam, taking in the small personal touches she'd added to the rental house. "Three months. I'll head out around the beginning of October."

"Heading back to D.C.?"

Rebecca had to give the man credit. He'd not only done

his research but apparently had a knack for steering a conversation in the direction he wanted it to go.

"I'm not quite sure yet, actually." She did her best to remain polite. "Forgive me for asking, but how did you know I'm from D.C.?"

"License plate on that good-lookin' truck outside." When he smiled, she decided she liked him. He had the sort of look that a mall Santa often possessed. Friendly without really trying, with an edge of warmth. "Being a former FBI agent, I thought that might be obvious."

"Well, you could have run my plates or googled me. Either would have worked." She sat down on the edge of the couch, kicking her feet up on one of the few remaining boxes. "Is that why you've come to pay me a visit? Wanting to make sure I don't cause trouble while I'm here?"

Wallace sighed, and his gaze settled on her for the first time since entering the house. "I did both, actually. Believe it or not, your last name rang a bell when I read that news article. I was a deputy back when your parents used to come during the summers. I can remember your father fairly well, though we spoke only two or three times in simple passing conversations."

This alarmed Rebecca for reasons she couldn't immediately identify. While it was sort of comforting to know this man had known her father, it was a bit strange to know he also was aware of recent events in her life.

"I'm sorry for your loss. Your folks seemed like good people."

"Thank you." She swallowed a wave of emotion. "I appreciate that, but I'm sure you didn't come by to offer condolences."

"You're right." His chuckle was deep and rumbly. "Let me get to the point. I think you may have come to Shadow

Island at an opportune time. Well…an opportune time for me, anyway."

Rebecca frowned. "How so?"

The sheriff scratched his chin, and Rebecca's gut began to churn with the onset of worry before he finally dropped his hand. "I find myself with a case that I'm currently not very well-equipped for. There's a seventeen-year-old girl missing, and I have no leads, no clues, nothing."

"That's terrible." Rebecca waited a moment to see if he was going to add anything else. When it was clear he wasn't, Rebecca finally caved. "What, exactly, makes this an opportune time?"

It was like getting the truth out of a child, but she almost found it endearing. He was clearly not happy about having to say what was on his mind, which she appreciated.

"My primary deputy is at home recovering from surgery. He's supposed to be out another few weeks at least. Another deputy is out on paternity leave after his wife gave birth to their first child just a couple weeks ago—a beautiful baby girl. As for me…well, I keep getting these damned spells of vertigo." He tapped his temple. "The doc says the type I have isn't dangerous, but I need to take it easy for a while." He sighed again, maybe a little more dramatically than necessary. "In other words, I could use your help."

"Shit." The word popped out of her mouth before she could force her lips closed. When he didn't respond to her harshness, she took a deep breath to get her knee-jerk emotional response under control. "You mean to tell me you only have two officers working under you?" Rebecca had to work to keep her face calm but couldn't help the twitch that jerked her eyebrow up. She'd be a shit poker player. Her face always gave her away.

Wallace fidgeted with the hat in his hands. "Technically, they're deputies, since we run a sheriff station out of

Shadow, not a police department. And while I do have more than those two men on the payroll, the others aren't the sort I'd take out to help with a missing persons case."

Rebecca read between the lines of the polite and unhelpful explanation, trying to sort it all out. She'd been on the island for less than a day and was now faced with a very unorthodox situation. While the FBI did help in some missing person cases, she was no longer FBI.

"I don't understand." She flailed for an excuse...any reason to say no. "I mean...would it even be legal?"

"Of course it would." Hope sparked in Wallace's eyes. "I could hire you on as a consultant, or I could deputize you as an emergency measure. There's a form for that and everything. You'd be paid, obviously. Full benefits while working too. Just like the rest of us."

Stunned to her core, Rebecca wasn't sure what to do. "Well, Sheriff, it seems like you have me in a bit of a bind. What sort of bitch would I be if I said no? Not helping a girl in need." He had her in a situation there was no polite way out of, no matter how she answered.

If she said no, she would be refusing to help find a missing local. If she said yes, she would be taking the job of a local deputy away from two men out on medical. Plus, she was looking forward to some time to herself. Had that been too much to ask for?

"I know my coming to you puts you on the spot. I nearly talked myself out of coming to ask you, but after visiting with the family and knowing the statistics of recovering a missing person after those first couple hours, I figured it couldn't hurt. And this girl isn't the sort to just get tired of island life and run away. From what I can tell, she's a good kid, and her parents are adamant she wouldn't skip town."

Even more curious now, Rebecca couldn't stop from learning more. "How long has she been missing?"

"Honestly, we're not sure. Her parents have been out of town 'til late last night. She's old enough they didn't think to check in on her before they went to bed. The girl had nothing planned, so she wasn't missing from anything. Her boyfriend last spoke to her early Friday evening, but she's a seventeen-year-old, and her phone is at her house. How many teen girls do you know that leave the house for hours without their phone?"

A missing teen in a small town rarely ended up being a crime. More often than not, it was a kid running away, looking for a better life in "the big city," or just staying out too long partying with friends. But something about the way Wallace had gone about presenting it to her had her hooked.

The sheriff was right about one thing, at least. For him to come to someone like Rebecca, someone he didn't know at all outside of a news article and had only a vague memory of her family visiting the island, he had to be in a tough spot. The town was small, but not so small a single cop could track down someone on his own.

She pushed her hair back from her face. "What specifics are there at this point?"

"Very little. Her name is Cassie Leigh, she's a senior in high school, and she's never been in any trouble. I haven't yet run an entire circuit of friends and extended family. Honestly, with being so understaffed, the whole thing is overwhelming. I almost called in the State PD, but I hate going to them for anything. More often than not, they come out here and push their weight around, making things harder and show shit for results." Wallace threw up his hands, clearly frustrated.

"So, you decided to call on me."

"Yeah." He shifted from one foot to another. "I just need some help doing the legwork, asking questions, and talking to people. Hopefully, we can find her holed up with one of her friends or camping on the beach somewhere."

Rebecca's mind was already sorting out the very limited information, trying to form a story with it. Still, the last thing on her mind in coming out to Shadow Island was work.

"Give me a few hours to think it over." She hated to sound so flippant in the face of a missing girl, but she wasn't about to jump in without processing her thoughts. It also didn't help that Wallace was unable to hide the look of disappointment on his face, and she felt the need to defend herself. Something she was tired of having to do. "I know very little about this island and its people. And, as you mentioned yourself, she could just be running late and out with new friends. Or she got a flat somewhere."

Wallace nodded, and when he did, his blue eyes looked very tired. "True. Her car's missing, so I get what you're saying. Tell you what." He checked his watch and frowned. "It's a little after noon right now. If I haven't heard from you by two, I'll go ahead and call the state boys. And no matter your answer, no hard feelings. I'm sure you've been through the wringer the last few months. Believe me...I truly did hate coming by here with this favor, but if you keep the star player on the bench, you can't cry when you never win."

Rebecca tried to keep the sour look that comment evoked off her face. "That's a fair deal. Two o'clock."

Sheriff Wallace gave her a curt little nod as he started back to the door. She saw him scanning some of her books, making a small laughing noise under his breath. Rebecca hurried him along to the door and shook his hand one more time.

"It was good to meet you, Sheriff."

The corners of his lips pulled up a bit. "No need to lie about it. I came by with an impossible favor. It couldn't have been that good to meet me."

Rebecca couldn't stop from smiling. Yes, she liked Sheriff Wallace a lot. And even as she watched him walk down the porch steps to a white and tan Ford Explorer with "Sheriff" emblazoned down each side, she was already wondering what it might be like to work with him. Maybe there was a way to find out if she could be of any help.

Ignoring the few remaining boxes yet again, she dug into her cooler and pulled out the meager makings for a ham and cheese sandwich. In a few minutes, she'd made a simple meal consisting of the sandwich and an apple. She ate on the patio, relishing the warmth of the sun, which made the meager lunch a bit more enjoyable.

Waves meandered to the shore only to destroy themselves and complain loudly about it. The sound was surprisingly soothing, allowing her to focus on the surreal conversation she'd had with Sheriff Wallace.

The entire situation brought to mind those terrible prank shows where there were hidden cameras at every corner. Or maybe it was some sort of weird hazing, just trying to get a good laugh in on the disgraced FBI agent who'd come out here looking for some solitude after all the blood's been washed away.

Only she'd seen the hesitation and discomfort on Wallace's face when he'd spoken to her. He'd not been thrilled with the idea of coming out to ask for the favor. More than that, he'd been the sheriff long enough to know the island well. He'd likely have a very good radar as to which teens would not be prone to simply run away from home.

It was that bit of information that kept nagging her. He knew the island and the locals, and he thought he would need help on this case. Even from someone who could barely find the grocery store.

Rebecca assumed going missing on a small island like

Shadow—full size somewhere around a total area of twenty-eight miles and a population of just over 1,900—was a tricky business. If someone was missing for more than several hours, it would be a safe assumption they were no longer on the island. Or dead. Once that could be assumed, the search became much more difficult, as law enforcement then had an entire coast to search.

The mere idea of such a terrible tragedy on Shadow Island was odd, especially while looking out at the ocean from a back porch that rivaled something out of a magazine on island living or home designs.

Curious, and feeling more than just a tug toward this case, Rebecca took out her phone. She tried googling for articles on recent disappearances on the island, but there was not yet a news story concerning Cassie Leigh. No one was even talking about it. And when she looked over the few results available, the last result came from six years ago, a nine-year-old boy who was eventually found alive out on a private dock.

Rebecca tried another tactic. She opened Facebook and typed in "Shadow Island VA missing" into the search bar. It didn't take much scrolling before she found a few posts from the past twelve hours or so. One was from the Shadow Island Sheriff's Department Facebook page. The other two had been posted by well-meaning locals. One woman described herself as being a "friend to this precious, worried family."

All the posts told the same story—a story with few details. Seventeen-year-old Cassie Leigh hadn't been in her room when her mother had checked in on her. The bed hadn't been slept in, either. And none of her belongings seemed to be gone.

With summer vacation just starting for the school district, Cassie had been taking full advantage of the lazy summer days and sleeping in. Because of that, neither of her parents bothered checking her room until almost ten in the morning. When she wasn't there, they contacted her boyfriend and friends. Everyone seemed just as shocked as they were that Cassie wasn't home.

The comments in the Facebook posts offered prayers, and some people seemed to suggest even mobilizing a neighborhood search to go out looking for the missing teen. But according to comments as recent as fourteen minutes ago, there had been no luck. One comment stood out above all the others to Rebecca.

It was from Belinda Leigh, Cassie's mother. She'd replied to one of the people thinking of organizing a neighborhood effort. The message wrenched at Rebecca's heart.

Thanks so much, everyone. We're honestly at a loss and don't know what to do. If we can get enough people to help us, maybe we can find her.

Thinking of Sheriff Wallace, severely understaffed and paranoid about mainland interference muddying his local waters, made the comment even more heartbreaking. Rebecca knew what it felt like to be working a high-pressure case with no one to help. Calling for leads, asking difficult questions of hesitant people, facing truths that grew uglier when exposed to the light. The difference here was Wallace had an island full of locals eager to help.

But did any of them know how to set up a proper search? If not, they were all just driving around in circles and asking each other questions.

Letting out a long sigh, she looked to the beach. She was surprised to find that she wasn't too upset about the idea of upending her vacation time. More concerning was being the outsider trying to fit in and help where she could. There would be no supervisor, no director, and outside of a stressed-out small-town sheriff, no partner.

The waves crashed, and a group of herons flew low to the

water, almost skimming the surface. Elsewhere on this island, a mother and father sat in a house, their hearts torn apart with worry. Rebecca figured helping them find their daughter was a bit more important than starting her three-month long escape from the troubles in D.C. Hell, maybe this would even be a nice distraction from all of that.

"Son of a bitch."

She'd made it halfway through another box before she came to the conclusion she wanted to work the case. She'd told Wallace she knew the structure of these cases well—that the longer they waited, the smaller the chance of finding the missing person became. So, to sit idly by to make sure her decision was based on solid logic rather than emotion could be endangering Cassie Leigh.

"Fine." Her voice was soft, almost playful, as she headed for the door.

Unpacking be damned.

Pulling open a box of clothes, Rebecca pulled off the shorts and t-shirt she'd been wearing and stepped into a pair of khakis. A plain navy shirt would have to be good enough for her makeshift uniform.

By the time she was behind the wheel of her truck, she was already trying to think about places a seventeen-year-old who had lived her entire life on an island might have gone.

5

When she pulled into the parking lot of the Shadow Island Sheriff Department, Rebecca felt like she was crossing a line. Once she stepped foot into the building, the scope of her summer might change. Even if the case was closed in a day and Cassie Leigh was reunited with her family, the remainder of Rebecca's summer would be anchored by this moment. More than that, she would be getting intimately involved in the lives of the Leigh parents as well as Sheriff Wallace himself.

Surprisingly, she was fine with that. She'd gone into the FBI to protect and serve her country and its people. This was no different.

And even if it did turn out to be slightly uncomfortable due to her status as an outsider, what the hell else was she going to do with the summer? Feel sorry for herself while resting? Wondering what could have happened if she had stepped up? No matter how things turned out, she would be pestered by the girl's fate if she sat on the sidelines. There'd be no avoiding it now. She did not need more "what if" questions plaguing her.

That was what she kept in the center of her mind as she crossed the parking lot and entered the station.

It was smaller than she thought it would be and felt more like some sort of lounge than any sheriff's department she'd ever been in. While they'd, fortunately, decided not to incorporate the beach theme found everywhere else in town except for the painted horse statue outside, there was a light and breezy feel to the place. It was not stuffy or crowded, not stagnant or boring. The light carpet, soft lighting, and clean, white walls were almost relaxing. It made her want to sit down and have a cup of coffee. She nearly expected soft jazz or reggae music to be playing in overhead speakers.

The little foyer housed a curved desk that spread from wall to wall, broken only by a small swinging half-door that led to the rest of the building. A woman of about Rebecca's own thirty-five years sat at the desk, typing on a laptop with a very serious look on her face. Her shoulder-length black hair and deep, dark eyes were a stark comparison to Rebecca's blonde hair and fair features.

"Hey there." When the receptionist looked up to Rebecca and grinned, the smile made her look easily five years younger. It might have been ten years had they been outside and standing in the island sun. Not a single wrinkle marred her smooth chocolate skin. "Can I help you?"

"I need to speak with Sheriff Wallace."

"Okay." At the mention of her boss, the woman sat up straighter. "He's in right now, but he's very tied up. Do you have an appointment?"

Rebecca did her best not to peek over the woman's shoulder to see if the station was truly as empty as it seemed. "Sort of. He visited me earlier today. My name is Rebecca West."

The woman's face lit up as she jumped to her feet. "Oh, yes, he was hoping you'd come by."

She clicked a little latch on the backside of the swinging half-door and pulled it open. "I'm Viviane Darby, by the way. It's really nice to meet you."

"Likewise." Rebecca did her best to keep a professional smile on, but the cheer and sudden burst of excitement from Viviane Darby had her feeling a little uneasy. She wasn't sure what this crew was expecting out of her, and Rebecca wondered just what other stories Wallace might have heard about her and her family.

Rebecca had something of a stellar reputation back in D.C.—or, rather, she once had a stellar reputation in D.C. before she tore down a few untouchables from the American government. But she didn't think that sort of news would have spread outside the Bureau. Usually, it was just the nasty stuff, the things that made for juicy headline fodder.

"His office is down the first hallway on the right, all the way at the end." Viviane waved a hand in that direction, the silky material of her yellow blouse catching the wind of the movement.

Yeah. Rebecca liked Viviane on sight. "Thank you."

As Rebecca walked behind the desk and into the larger part of the Shadow Island Sheriff's Department, it seemed unnaturally quiet. She supposed it made sense, though, if Sheriff Wallace was currently severely understaffed. Walking down the hallway, she scanned the artfully done topographical maps, some of which were complete with ornate tide charts.

At the back wall, she came across a door that was partially open, allowing her to see Wallace before she knocked. He sat behind his desk, hunkered over a thin stack of forms and papers. It looked like it was taking him a great deal of effort to focus on any of it.

One hand was pressed flat on the table, his fingers spread wide as if he was bracing himself. Which, if he was suffering from vertigo, might be what he was doing. When Rebecca knocked on the doorframe, his head jerked up, but his startled expression softened into a relieved smile the moment their eyes met.

"Agent West." He slammed a palm over his heart. "Good god, am I glad to see you."

"Just Rebecca, please."

"Sure, sure." He got to his feet and extended his hand as if they hadn't already gone over these introductions. "Rebecca, please have a seat."

She did as he asked, sitting down in one of two very uncomfortable-looking chairs positioned in front of his desk. He gave her about three seconds to get acclimated before leaning partially across the scratched wood and issuing a heavy sigh.

"No sense in creeping around things, I reckon. Have you come to me with an answer?"

She nodded, finding it harder than she'd expected to verbally offer her assistance. Was she really ready for this? Could she actually help? Worse…what if she failed?

Before she jumped from the chair and ran from the room, she nodded. "Yes. I want to help. And based on the dead silence of this place in the wake of a missing persons case, it seems you weren't exaggerating."

"Sadly, I was not." The sheriff's chuckle held no humor this time. "Of course, the two men out on medical right now aren't all I have. I have two more, and they're currently out questioning family and running basic daily traffic routines. As you can imagine, that becomes more of a pressing matter when summer falls on us."

"How many officers in all?"

He leaned back in his chair with a grunt. "Four, including myself. Well, five if you include an older gentleman I keep on the books as a reserve of sorts…but he's rarely called in."

Rebecca couldn't imagine those numbers. "And this is the first time you've considered yourself understaffed?"

"It is. It's a quiet little island. In the nearly forty years I've served here, there have been only six murders, and two of those were perpetrated by tourists. There has been a grand total of three missing persons cases, and they were all wrapped and resolved within two days. And now there's this thing with Cassie Leigh, which could not have come at a worse time."

Rebecca stared at him, unable to believe those numbers. They didn't seem real, even for a small town. But she wasn't able to argue with the older man about his statistics. They had a girl to find.

"That's why I'm here." She rubbed her clammy hands together. "How do we make this official?"

With a wry grin, the sheriff slid the paperwork he'd been perusing over to her. It was a form making her a deputy of Shadow Island. Rebecca glanced down and saw that everything was already filled out except for her signature.

She scanned the paper, ignoring the payroll section since she wasn't going to be working long enough to worry about that. Wallace called Viviane to his office to act as a witness, and a few minutes later, Rebecca was sworn in. Viviane whisked the paperwork away with a cheerful, "Welcome aboard!"

Rebecca blew out a breath after the flurry of activity and gestured to the only remaining stack of papers on the sheriff's desk, guessing at the contents. "Can I see the case file?"

Wallace handed a folder over. It was very thin, having only been printed off that very morning. The two papers inside the file only echoed what Wallace had already told her. The parents were insisting their daughter had been kidnapped or worse.

One of the officers under Wallace, a man named Trent

Locke, had questioned Cassie's boyfriend, and everything the boyfriend told him had checked out so far. There were a few additional names Locke was looking into, but according to the report, there was nothing sinister going on.

"This Deputy Locke…is he good?"

Wallace's nod appeared to be a little hesitant. "He's very good with people, yes."

Rebecca noticed what he did and didn't say. Good with people didn't always mean he was a good cop. But it did mean he could get people to talk to him. "And you know for sure the boyfriend was the last person to see Cassie?"

"As far as we can tell, yes. And while I understand a case like this pretty much makes the boyfriend our prime suspect, I doubt that's the case here. He looked absolutely lost. Maybe a little angry too."

Rebecca shrugged that off. "Could be a good actor."

"Could be."

Rebecca closed the file and handed it back to Wallace. "What do we do next? If you want my help, I'll need access to all your resources and the authority to use them. And that includes your deputies."

"That won't be an issue. If you can get this thing wrapped so we don't have to turn to the State boys, everyone'll bend over backward to help you."

"Do you know how long we—"

The phone on his desk rang. Rebecca smiled, not sure when she'd last heard the too-loud yet somehow warm jangling of a landline phone. Wallace lifted a finger and picked up the receiver that was wrapped with several layers of silver tape. "This is Sheriff Wallace."

Rebecca watched as a dark cloud fell over the sheriff's face. It was abundantly clear the news was bad. She'd answered similar calls during her career, so she was pretty sure she knew what the news was. Still, rather than jump to conclusions, Rebecca listened to the sheriff's side of the call.

"Christ…you're sure?" Wallace closed his eyes and massaged his forehead with his free hand. "Yeah, okay. Thanks."

He hung up the phone and got to his feet. The sheriff appeared to have aged another ten years as he rested his hands on his desk. "Looks like you came with an answer just in time."

Rebecca's stomach roiled. "Bad news?"

"A fisherman gathering mud minnows in the marshes found a body. A blonde teenage girl."

With what appeared to be the weight of the world sitting on his shoulders, the sheriff headed out of the office without another word.

Rebecca followed without hesitation.

6

"This has to be a pretty shitty homecoming, huh?" Wallace steered with one hand while the other hung out the open window where he occasionally flicked a finger up in response to people they passed.

Rebecca understood how the mind of a law enforcement officer worked. While they all processed bad news and terrible cases differently, it was important to vent somehow. LEOs that couldn't do that typically had shorter careers due to mental anguish and stress.

"I don't know that I'd call it that. I mean, it's familiar, and there are great memories from my childhood. So, I guess it does feel like home, but the sort of home where someone is always rearranging the furniture, if that makes sense."

"Makes perfect sense. There are parts of Shadow that feel and look like they've been trapped in time, while others moved on. It was gradual, you know?" Wallace lifted all five fingers to an elderly couple. "Even living here my whole life, a lot of the changes snuck up on me. And this Cassie Leigh thing...that snuck up on me too. This sort of thing just doesn't happen here. It never has."

Doeth the good sheriff protest too much? Is his island really so squeaky clean?

They fell into silence after that, and Rebecca chose not to question the man. Every community, no matter how small, had its demons.

And witches.

Smiling at her clever inclusion, Rebecca focused on the route Sheriff Wallace was taking, committing each turn to memory. The marshes sat on the southernmost tip of the island. Rebecca barely remembered them. While they looked a little strange and almost exotic, they had never really felt beachy to her younger self. And like the kind of place that was filled with snakes. She hated snakes.

Wallace took them away from the beach-themed streets and down into the very small stretch of undeveloped land. Not even the most ambitious developers dared attempt to build on the unstable marshlands.

An unmarked road led them alongside the marshes, a strip of about half a mile or so that meandered in and out of the shoreline along a thin strip of beach. Halfway down this road, Wallace brought the SUV to a stop behind a beat-up old Chevy pickup. A few football fields behind the truck, the lighthouse stood tall and proud.

A tall man stood against the side of the truck, looking nervously toward the marshes while smoking a cigarette. Before getting out, Wallace took a digital camera from the glove compartment. It wasn't much larger than a current iPhone but was clearly much older. It showed signs of excessive use, making her wonder how long it had been in the Explorer.

Rebecca waited for Wallace to get out and followed behind him. She wanted to make sure she didn't come off as overbearing. Even though he'd come to her asking for help, he was still the sheriff and in charge of the case.

Wallace approached the man as he pocketed the camera. Rebecca assumed this was the same guy who'd been looking for mud minnows and found something entirely different.

Wallace lifted a hand. "Hey there, Gary."

"Hey, Sheriff." The man looked both ways up the street and flicked his ash with shaky fingers.

Wallace raised an eyebrow. "You good? You okay?"

Gary chuckled nervously and took a deep drag from his cigarette. "Yeah. It just gave me one hell of a scare is all. She's about forty feet in and just a bit to our left." He pointed with his cigarette, and his hand shook before coming back up to his face to take another long drag.

Wallace nodded before turning back to Rebecca. "Hope you got the right shoes for this."

She didn't, so she shrugged and shook her head. Her runners were the furthest thing from her mind. It wouldn't be the first pair of shoes she'd ruined at a crime scene.

Gary nodded to the back of his truck. "Got some waders in the bed if you wanna borrow 'em. Hip waders."

Rebecca lifted a hand. "That's kind of you, but—"

"We'll get them back to you once we're done here." Wallace accepted the offer for her.

Rebecca, knowing better than to question a local about what was needed for the terrain, nodded her thanks. "I'd appreciate that. I wasn't expecting to work while I was down here."

"I hear that. This wasn't what I was expecting to do today either." Gary ended his words with another swallow and turned around to haul the rubber waders out of the truck for her. They looked like black rubber thigh highs, and for a moment, she wondered if she was being pranked. "Just... just make sure you wash 'em off before you bring 'em back."

Wallace nodded and clapped the man on the shoulder,

bringing him back from whatever scene was playing out in the man's mind. "Will do. You can head up to the station and make your statement with Viviane. She knows how to do that and just put on some fresh coffee. We'll take it from here."

Gary shoved the waders into her hands. "Here ya go. No hurry to get them back."

She took them gratefully. "Thank you."

With a wave, Gary took his time getting back on the road heading to town.

Rebecca was already struggling to pull up the too-big waders when Wallace finally spoke again.

"Poor Gary's got a girl just a few years younger than Cassie." He turned back to the SUV and started hauling out cases she assumed held their crime scene gear. "Part of me hopes this isn't Cassie Leigh."

Rebecca understood the man's wishes, and for his sake, hoped the dead teen wasn't one of his own. But personally, she hoped it was. Otherwise, they would have one dead and one missing. Not a good combination. The body was out there, and she wasn't shoving her legs in rubber to hope on wishful thinking. She kept those thoughts to herself and followed him into the marsh.

Wallace parted the weeds and tall grasses ahead of her, following the trail Gary had made only a short time ago, making her own passage easier. The soggy ground wasn't quite as bad as she'd expected, though some of the stagnant water moved in ways that let her know there was something swimming just underneath the surface.

The swish of the tall grass was a bit eerie. It made a soft scratching sound against her waders that reminded her of construction paper being torn. The silence of the area made her feel as if she might be walking through some deep swamp in search of Bigfoot. The warm sun and the smell of saltwater did little to alter this. She couldn't deny the little stirring of excitement at this thought.

After a few more steps, Wallace came to a stop. "Ah, Jesus." His voice was little more than a whisper.

Rebecca drew up to his right side, careful of the placement of her feet among the marsh grass. She followed Wallace's line of sight, and there she was...the dead girl. Her face was pointed skyward, her blonde hair enmeshed with mud and grime, her mouth closed. Her long red dress was completely unbuttoned down the front, revealing she wore no underwear.

Her feet were bare, caked in the mud and dirt. The pallor of her skin and slight bloating indicated she hadn't been there too terribly long. It was hard to tell with her upper body half encased in mud.

Rebecca asked the question she already knew the answer to. "Is that Cassie Leigh?"

"Yeah, that's her."

Looking like a man who'd aged a good ten years, Wallace took the camera out of his pocket and started taking pictures of the scene. Watching him aim and click was a reminder of just how small his department was. Here he was, the sheriff, having to take crime scene photos, though she knew a more formal forensic department must be on their way. Viviane had been calling them in as they had left the station.

While she waited, she opened the case he had brought and dug through it. Tape measures, evidence bags, gloves, wipes, snakebite kit. That last one made her shiver. Taking a deep breath, she pulled out a set of gloves and focused on the work at hand.

Rebecca walked forward and examined the victim, careful not to interfere in Wallace's pictures or touch the body even though she was gloved up now. There were no obvious signs of a violent altercation along the girl's front side. No stab wounds, no gunshots, no blood that she could see.

There might be defensive marks on her arms, but they were already discolored so it was hard to tell. They could also be scratches from walking through the sharp, waist-high grasses. Of course, it could be a different story along the girl's back. Thankfully, the bloating was minimal, as was the scavenging.

Crouching low, Rebecca noticed the darker marks around the girl's neck. One of the bruises had gone an ugly shade of purple; it was on the right side, just to the side of Cassie's windpipe. Rebecca leaned in closer and noticed other bruise marks—reddish bruises in fractured U-shapes all around her throat.

Spreading her knees, she squatted as low as she could, peering at the fingernails, trying to see if there was anything trapped there. The muck she was precariously balanced in oozed up over the sides of her shoes, and she was grateful for the waders she had borrowed.

Tiny fish of some kind, or maybe they were tadpoles, scattered as her shadow covered them, running away from the body and their meal. Tiny dots of what appeared to be blue-green algae were sprinkled on the ground like minuscule pieces of confetti. She made a note to make sure the forensic techs took a sample.

Rebecca pushed to her feet. "Pretty sure she was strangled."

Wallace nodded and looked to the marshy area in front of them. Farther on, where the marshes came to an end, a shaggy hill gave way to a small strip of field. Beyond that was the road they'd taken down to the little unmarked path alongside the marsh. "At least it will be easy for the M.E. and forensics to find us. And no one else."

Rebecca examined the tall grass and weeds and thought

she could indeed see an area where someone had passed through. Maybe Cassie Leigh and her killer. "You get many animals on the island?"

The sheriff rubbed the back of his neck. "None that are going to leave behind a track through these marshes. We had two foxes around here a few years back. The game warden out of Pea Island guessed they just made their brave little way over Shadow Way Bridge from the mainland one night. But no...if anything beat a path through this grass, it wasn't an animal. Most of our critters are in the air or water. Crabs and gulls are what go for the bodies first."

"Looks like they've hardly touched her."

"Thank God." Wallace continued taking pictures, this time of the area around them. "Crabs would have gone for her lips first, then her toes and fingers. But we're a bit far from the surf here, so there's not many. M.E. will check her out, though. Can you take a water temp and get a sample? We also had a pretty bad storm last night, so make a note for us to get those details."

Rebecca pulled those tools from the bag as he finished up the pictures. She took the samples and jotted down her findings, adding the ambient air temperature as well. Hunkering down again, this time not looking at the girl, she took a soil sample. The marshy ground was tricky business.

Already, the tracks they had made walking in had started to fill with water. She had no idea how long it might take to erase them, but she guessed it wouldn't be any more than a few hours. Six at most. In other words, if Cassie and her killer had left footprints in the marsh, the chances that they were still visible were slim to none. Still, she picked up a stack of the little flags to mark evidence in watery terrain.

Rebecca walked slowly, tracing a line to the body. It was the direction toward the small breaks and disturbance she thought she saw in the grass. The weeds were so tall that some of them came all the way up to Rebecca's chest, yet there were some areas where they were no taller than her knees. The breaks in the grass she had her eyes on were about waist high. She kept her focus on the ground, making sure she didn't step on any existing tracks. She saw none, though. The ground was just as muddy and marshy as the rest of the area.

She had nearly reached the slightly bent grass when she saw something out of the ordinary. Off to her left, and in a straight trajectory with the disturbance in the grass, was what looked like a long drag mark in the muck. If it was the print of a shoe, it indicated a place where someone had slipped a bit, maybe almost falling. This could very well be the killer's print, as Cassie had been barefooted.

Even if it was the killer's print, though, it would only help in narrowing the pool of suspects. No tread of any kind was evident. Just an overall size and shape of someone's hurried foot. It warranted a snap from Wallace's old camera, so she placed a flag.

Rebecca glanced up to take in the barely there path trod down through the grass. It bent slightly right and then hard to the left, where it disappeared completely. But if Rebecca was reading the direction of it clearly, it was heading toward a small strip of beach about a quarter of a mile away. Rebecca could barely see it from where she stood, little more than a small tan U-shape being swallowed up by the ocean.

She followed the partially beaten path closer to the light-house, leaving flags as the direction changed or beside bent tufts of grass, until she couldn't see a clear indentation. By now, she had progressed close enough to that stretch of beach to believe that's where Cassie had entered. She turned back to see Wallace coming her way, making sure to carefully step in the same impacted areas she had already stepped through. He took the briefest of moments to look at Rebecca as he came to her, shaking his head.

"I think Cassie and her killer came in off of this beach." Bending low, she started searching for signs of tracks on the windblown sand. High tide didn't quite reach the dune, as evidenced by the line of debris that was left below where the grasses grow line began. Moving carefully in her footsteps, Wallace followed with the camera ready. She was a little uneasy with him being the one following her now, but she didn't say anything about it.

The little stretch of beach was unremarkable. It wasn't the sort of place you'd stretch out for a tan or hope to catch some bodysurfing waves. A little forgotten corner of the island, the sand littered with small pieces of driftwood and an abundance of tiny, fragmented shells. With the exception of the sand right along the edge of the grass that gave way to the marshes, the sand was packed firm.

"The trail going through the marsh tells me they came running through here, but I guess they could have come running in from anywhere, really." Rebecca chewed on this for a moment. "But why come to the marshes at all? Was she cutting through here to try getting to somewhere else? Or was she just hiding from the killer?"

"Maybe he killed her somewhere else and dragged her here?" Wallace suggested.

She shook her head, checking the line between dry sand and where the tide was still moving out. "I think the trail through the marsh would be a lot clearer if that was the case. Dragging anything through here would have torn up the grasses, and if he'd carried her, the shoe indentions would have been deeper. But she might have run up the beach lower, so we won't find any tracks."

Glancing around, she spotted another strip of open grass, and beyond that, the road that led back into town. And immediately beyond that road, a row of houses began. She wondered if any of those houses were where Cassie Leigh had grown up. More than that, she wondered if the killer lived in any of them or if someone may have seen the murder had they looked out their windows at just the right time. Then again, she didn't think they were close enough that anyone looking would see her and Wallace peering up toward them.

Still looking at the houses, Rebecca knew she was in deep now. This one little venture to the marshes and seeing the body of Cassie Leigh solidified her decision. The sheriff needed the help, and the girl's family deserved the closure.

7

P eering out to the vast darkness of the ocean at night was always calming. On darker nights, there was no clear horizon line between the sea and the sky. Everything merged into one smooth piece. As a boy who had been drawn to sci-fi epics and space operas, I often stared out into that endless pitch of night and imagined I gazed into some massive black hole where creatures of unfathomable rage and intention lurked.

There's a bit of that out there tonight.

Just enough moon in the sky to break that black hole illusion. The caps of meandering waves crept to the boat dock on which I sat. A gentle rocking under my foldable lawn chair soothed me. It was peaceful.

Peeling the label off the beer in my hand, I knew drinking was a mistake. The three empties sitting in the little cooler I brought down to the dock showed I wasn't thinking clearly. I had acted on impulse when I'd grabbed the stocked cooler to come down here tonight, sneaking out of the house.

I needed to focus. Beer wasn't going to help with that.

I couldn't get caught.

Peering into that thick darkness farther out at sea, a part of me wondered if that was what Cassie was seeing. I believed the dead were just that...dead. Firm and reliable. After death, there was only darkness...no matter what.

And I'd been the one to toss her into that never-ending darkness.

What have I done?

I never had any intention of killing her...not really. But she clawed at me, fought me. I knew I couldn't trust her anymore. Not after what she'd said, no matter how scared she appeared.

No. Don't think about that.

I couldn't think about how it had felt.

A monster lived inside me, I realized. It came without warning, and it was scary for a moment—but ended up feeling...normal. I'd been thinking so clearly after. Covered my tracks well. Taken care of everything needed. All of it.

It had been so easy. The lies rolled flawlessly off my tongue. My expression gave away nothing. Concerned, confused, but not too worried. And everyone bought it.

I didn't feel a hint of regret. Something inside me shifted and was finally working the way it was supposed to. She gave me no choice.

The fantasy-like dream Cassie and I had been living was shattered, and nothing would have been the same. No, I had not meant to kill her, but I had done what was right.

It was her fault, after all.

She was the one who'd wanted to meet in the old witch's cottage, telling me how exciting having sex there would be.

It had been exciting all right. Up to the moment it wasn't. Until...

I blinked. Maybe the witch's curse was true. Maybe that was why I did what I did.

Or maybe not.

What had first bothered me most—besides losing her, of course—was that I had made the switch from mournful to figuring out how to cover my ass in less than a night. Calling 911 and letting them know what I'd done had never even crossed my mind, but I had thought about making an anonymous call or writing a note. Anything to move suspicion in a different direction. Never toward me. Now, my only concern was making sure I didn't get caught and could keep living my life the way I wanted.

But I couldn't come up with a good enough lie, so I said nothing at all.

I didn't think it would be much of an issue. I'd lived on this island long enough to know the sheriff's department was pretty much a joke. Hell, one of the two real deputies was out for some sort of surgery, or so I'd heard. The timing couldn't have been better.

I figured by the time anyone found her body, the tide would have settled any traces I might have left behind. That was the one good thing about Cassie running through the marshes to get away from me, I supposed. Finding evidence as to who might have killed her was going to be damn near impossible. If they ever found her body buried in all that muck.

Still, the idea of leaving town for a while was tempting. I wanted to get the hell out of this place. I'd been looking for an excuse to get away from Shadow for a while now, but for the past couple months, I pictured Cassie going with me. With her dead, the prospect of leaving was less appealing.

Or am I just being lazy...maybe even paranoid?

I couldn't tell anymore.

Draining the last of my beer, I tossed the empty bottle into the cooler with the others. I reached for another but thought better of it. If I got sloppy, that would be bad. I was already fighting the urge to get back out to the marsh to make sure there was nothing incriminating. Enough beer in my system, I might give in to the urge, and in doing so, leave even more evidence behind.

With a heavy sigh and one last glance out to the near void of the night ocean, I put the sounds of crashing waves behind me, whispering and breaking.

Don't get caught. You can't get caught.

My phone buzzed, and I pulled it from my pocket.

It was a text from an unknown number.

Unlocking the device, I glanced at the screen and froze.

I know what you did.

And in that instant, I knew I'd need to get my hands bloody once again.

8

Sheriff Wallace pulled his Subaru Outback into the driveway of his favorite deputy's house at a little after ten that evening. He knew that, as the sheriff, he shouldn't have a favorite, but that's the way it was.

Hoyt Frost was a damn fine officer, and as it happened, the only true friend Alden had left. Which was why he was certain his friend wouldn't mind the late-night visit.

He had *friends*, sure, but those were all just friendly faces that knew him for the badge. None of them were *real* friends...not the kind he could tell dirty jokes with or to bitch about how bad the Nationals were playing. Also, at fifty-one years of age, Hoyt at least knew some of the pains and challenges that Alden dealt with on a weekly basis.

The sun was already set, but somehow, this day wasn't over yet. Maybe a visit with Hoyt and Angie would give it at least some degree of warmth. He hoped his visit would serve as a morale boost for Hoyt as well. Alden knew he was itching to get back to work—even though he'd pretend not to.

He knocked on the screen door, and Angie Frost appeared with her usual warm smile.

Angie patted his arm. "He's been expecting you."

"That so?"

"Yeah." She opened the door wider and let him in. "He's been tracking the story about Cassie Leigh on Facebook. He's griping more about social media than he is the actual news of her death."

Alden smiled. The thought of Hoyt Frost navigating any of those platforms to get his news was beyond comical. He knew Hoyt had a Facebook page, but it was just so they could look up the profiles of suspects. As far as Alden knew, Hoyt had only ever updated his profile picture a few times and nothing else. Not a single status update or post of any kind.

Angie guided him through the hallway and into the kitchen where onions and garlic sizzled in a pan. It both warmed and saddened Alden in equal measure that the Frost house felt like his second home, especially after Rita died. Their profound friendship meant that he'd always have some sort of family here on Shadow Island.

"Late dinner, huh?"

Angie rolled her eyes. "I thought babies were the only ones to get their days and nights mixed up, but leave it to my Hoyt to sleep all day and howl at the moon most of the night."

That got a chuckle out of Alden, the first in many hours. "That's Hoyt for you. Ass-backwards."

He nodded toward Hoyt's usual spot at the kitchen table. Since it was empty, he figured his friend would be at his *other* usual spot. Angie confirmed this when she opened the refrigerator and took two sodas out of the bottom drawer. She handed them to Alden and gestured to the back door.

"He's out on the porch, pouting that he can't have beer.

He can't drink while he's taking his painkillers, so convince him this is good enough."

"You're a smart woman, Angie Frost."

"Damn right." She turned back to the pan on the stove, causing Alden's stomach to growl. He headed outside before his empty belly tried to invite itself to their late dinner.

Just as he'd expected, Alden found his good friend sitting in an old lawn chair that had to be at least thirty years old. He'd been sitting in that same chair for as long as Alden could remember.

Hoyt glanced up as he came through the door. "Looks like I'm not the only night owl around here."

Despite his days and nights being flipped, Hoyt looked well-rested, something Alden wasn't used to seeing. He was clean-shaven, and his eyes were bright. His skin was rough, but that was always the case. Hoyt had always shown the wear and tear of island living, but it suited him.

Hoyt spotted the sodas Alden was holding and held his hand out for one. Alden sat in the old Adirondack chair next to him.

"Damn shame what happened to that Leigh girl." Hoyt's gaze didn't leave his backyard. The half-acre of land was bordered by scraggly woodlands that blocked off a good part of the ocean view, but the sound of it was still present, pushing through the trees.

"How much do you know?"

Hoyt shrugged and twisted the top off his drink. "I may have called Viviane and persuaded her to fill me in. She says you found the body and went to tell the family. How'd that go?"

Alden closed his eyes, wishing the simple gesture would shut out the memory of that visit. "Terribly. Belinda Leigh was pretty much catatonic when I left. I called the health center to have someone go check on her. And Robert Leigh...

I think he's looking to the bottom of a bottle for the foreseeable future."

"She was murdered? Viviane said strangulation."

So, Hoyt hadn't looked up the report or the pictures Alden had loaded from the crime scene. Good. The man needed to be resting, not working.

"Looks like it. The medical examiner thinks so at least, but the report won't get to me until early in the morning."

"Well, no one on Facebook seems to know it was a murder. I just saw someone posting about how her body was found fifteen minutes before you showed up. Most of the talk is about you working with that woman out of D.C. Her name's West, right?"

"Yeah, that's right." Alden had known it would come up and wasn't quite sure how Hoyt would react. He supposed he was about to find out. "Got any thoughts on that?"

"A few. Did you even interview her?"

"Not officially, no."

One side of Hoyt's mouth curled up before he covered the grin with another sip of his drink. "You have to beg?"

"Nope, no begging." Alden thumbed the edge of the bottle's label as he gazed out at the scraggly growth of woodland, the ocean providing a soothing soundtrack on the other side. "I told her the situation at the station right now, with you and Hudson being out and then getting this missing persons case tossed in my lap. Told her I could use some help because I didn't want to get the boys from Wilmington involved. She showed up at the station a few hours later and started asking questions about the case."

Hoyt rocked back in his chair. "She went to the marshes with you?"

Alden nodded, smoothing his uniform trousers and brushing away nonexistent dirt. "She did, and she's pretty intuitive. She spotted the bruises on Cassie Leigh's neck and staked out the entry and exit points Cassie and her killer might have taken. Set the M.E. to check the fingernails. If she'll stick it out with me on this for the next day or so, I think we'll get our killer."

For a few moments, the only sound was the ebb and flow of the ocean before Hoyt grunted and sat his chair back onto all four legs. "She's not all screwed up from what happened down in D.C., is she?" Hoyt twirled a finger near his ear.

Alden thought that through. He hadn't told Rebecca just how much he knew about what she had done in her final days at the FBI. "I don't think so. There's something...I don't know...*hard* about her. You can see it in her eyes, the way she studies everything around her."

"You think she might stick around even after this case is closed?"

"On the job or on the island?" The label ripped under Alden's fingers. "Well, I think she had an explicit purpose for coming here, and I'm pretty sure solving small-town island crimes was not on that list. But she loves the island. You can see *that* in her eyes too. She's got something of a past here." He swallowed and looked over to his friend. "You think I've made a mistake by asking her to come along, don't you?"

"Not a mistake, no." Hoyt's answer came without any hesitation. "I just don't understand why you were so quick to ask for outside help before you even got a good grip on the case yourself."

Hating like hell to admit any shortcomings, Alden knew he needed to come clean about what was happening to him. He tapped his temple. "The vertigo's getting worse. The docs don't think it's anything serious, but when it hits me, it's... scary. Disorienting. Puts me out of commission, sometimes for a whole day. And god help me if it ever decides to kick in when I'm driving."

Face a mask of concern, Hoyt turned in his chair,

squinting as he studied him. "You sure there's nothing more serious going on? Vertigo can—"

The back door opened, and Angie poked her head out. "Dinner's on. I got a plate out for you too, Alden."

Saved by the dinner bell.

"I appreciate that, Angie, but I better get going."

Fists jamming on her hips, Angie's fierce scowl wiped away her bright smile. "The hell you say?"

"Listen to your betters." Hoyt pushed to his feet and patted Alden on the shoulder. "Stay for dinner."

"Fine." As much as he didn't want to talk about his health concerns, Alden wouldn't pass up a fine meal and good company, even this late at night. "But it's going to have to be an eat and run situation. I've got a grieving family and a dead girl...and god only knows how many calls coming in at the station. Concerned locals, people with far-flung tips...good-meaning people jamming everything up."

"Whatever." Angie opened the door for him. "Eat and run. That's fine. Hoyt has a check-up tomorrow, you know. If all goes well, he should be back on light duty in a few days to make sure you're not drowning all on your own. But in the meantime, get your ass inside and grab a hot meal. You're going to need it."

Alden knew better than to argue with Angie, so he joined the Frosts for dinner as he had countless times in the past before he headed back to the station. A few moments of peace would go a long way in his mind.

The peace wouldn't last long.

9

Rebecca pulled into the employee parking lot the following morning and her stomach twisted low in her gut. She wasn't nervous, per se, but she couldn't shake the feeling she might be making a mistake.

There was always the anxiety of starting a new job and a new case. Under normal circumstances, she would have been prepared for this. Of course, nothing about this was normal. This was supposed to be her downtime so she could think about her future.

Running her hands down the front of her pants, she opened the door and started across the parking lot. She'd been forced to wash the navy t-shirt and khakis last night and had pulled them on again this morning. The outfit was a long way from looking like an official deputy, but it was the best "uniform" she had with her.

It's not about you right now. The voice in her head sounded a lot like Benji's. *It's about finding Cassie Leigh's killer.*

Inside, she was greeted by Viviane Darby again. It was just shy of eight in the morning, and the station seemed a bit different. It smelled of strong coffee, and the mood coming off Viviane seemed to fill the entire place. She was beaming as bright as the morning sun coming through the front windows, clearly excited to see Rebecca.

"Good morning, Viviane. Is Sheriff Wallace in yet?"

"He is. You know where to go. And I..." She pressed her pale pink lips together, clearly unsure if she should go on.

"What?" Rebecca leaned closer. "What is it?"

Viviane looked around, then leaned closer too. "I just wanted to say thanks for coming on to help. He won't come out and say it, but Alden has been beyond stressed over this. He's been stressed ever since Hoyt had to step out for his surgery. It came on suddenly and caught us all off guard. Thankfully, they caught it before it got too bad."

"Sure. I'm happy to help." The lie slipped easily from her lips in the face of such appreciation, though it was more of a half-truth than anything.

Viviane beamed at her and opened the swinging half-door. On her way down the hall to Wallace's office, she passed a deputy carrying two cups of coffee. The little name tag over his left breast read *Locke*. Rebecca guessed him to be forty, give or take a year.

He wasn't overweight, but beefy—the sort of guy who looked like he might be a few pounds over a healthy weight, but it was mostly muscle. The bottom half of his face was covered with a well-groomed beard. It, like his hair, was black and just starting to show signs of gray, but the sort of gray that looked refined rather than worn down.

"Can I help you, ma'am?"

Rebecca gave him a warm smile. "Just heading back to see the sheriff."

He seemed about to question her again, but Viviane called back. "She's good."

Locke studied her for a long moment before moving out of her way. "End of the hall."

Rebecca inclined her head. "Thank you."

Just as before, Rebecca found Wallace's door standing wide open. He was on the phone and reading over a piece of paper at the same time. He smiled and waved her in.

"Yes, of course," he said into the phone. "I get that. Uh huh, uh huh. Yes. Okay, thank you." He dropped the receiver into the cradle and let out a heavy sigh that she was starting to think might be his trademark. "That was the medical examiner. You were right. Strangulation."

Rebecca slipped into the chair across from his desk. "Anything else of note?"

"Maybe not of note, but she also pointed out that there is no indication of sexual assault, though she was fairly certain the girl was sexually active. Seminal fluid in the area, swelling. Consistent with intercourse but nothing violent."

Rebecca frowned. "Meaning that the killer could be her lover."

He nodded, looking vaguely uncomfortable. Wallace glanced at the paper in his hands. "They found what appears to be skin under her nails. That's off for testing too. I'm betting our labs are a bit slower than you're used to. It might take a day or two to get results, but they'll update us as they get more information." He opened a bottom drawer of his desk and produced a badge and a holstered gun—a Glock. "You good with a 19?"

Rebecca picked up the weapon, dropped the magazine, checked the barrel, and pointed it at the floor. "Not my favorite." She rubbed her thumb over the trigger, rocking the safety bar to see how sensitive it was.

"Because of the trigger?"

Rebecca shrugged and cupped the gun in her hands, getting the feel of it. "A bit."

"Well, if you were staying, I would give you the option of getting your own gun."

Rebecca immediately brightened. "You allow your deputies to carry personal weapons?"

A slow smirk lifted the corner of his mouth. "Well, yeah, so long as we have ballistics on them, and they're registered."

His eyes widened when she reached into her pocket and pulled out a small manila envelope and tossed it on his desk.

"That should be good enough. Straight from the manufacturer. Serial is on there too." She pulled her 1911 from her side holster, dropping the magazine, locking the slide open, and set them both on his desk. "You can verify the numbers."

Her grin must have been infectious because he chuckled in response. "You really don't like the 19, huh?"

"Glocks are good weapons, and I actually own one too, but I prefer this one. I like a solid safety and having the ability to customize it to fit me better."

Wallace pulled his keyboard in front of him. "We can get that authorized now. I want you in the field today, and you need to be carrying if you're going to drive one of the patrol vehicles. Shoulda known FBI would be bringing in their own concealed loaded with hollow points to work." He ended with an amused grumbling.

"Failing to prepare is preparing to fail." It was her favorite John Wooden quote, and she used it often. "If I couldn't carry it, I could always lock it up here. Or use it as secondary."

She took the paper he slid over to her, scanned the page, then signed the bottom. Once all the paperwork was finished, Wallace slid her gun back to her and picked up the Glock and its magazine.

"Let's go drop this in the armory. After that, I can introduce you to everyone."

"Everyone?" She couldn't keep the sarcasm from her voice.

"Well, everyone that's here, anyway." He beckoned her to follow as he exited the office. He led her to one of the two locked doors in that hallway, and after showing her the key code to unlock it, they ended up at the large area behind Viviane Darby's station. From the setup of the desks, she assumed it served as the bullpen.

Locke, the officer she'd passed in the hallway, sat at one of four desks spread out around the room. In the back, an older gentleman was cleaning up the area around the coffee machine.

"Everyone, I'd like you to meet Rebecca West. She's going to be helping us out for a bit while we're short-staffed. I know there were some rumors going around, so I want to clear it up." Rebecca tensed, sure he was going to talk about her FBI background. "She's a duly sworn deputy, with all that goes with it. I talked her into taking time out of her vacation, so let's give her a warm welcome at the very least."

The two men gave stilted nods while Viviane applauded. Her colorful bracelets jingled along with the sound.

Locke was the first to walk over.

"This is Deputy Trent Locke. He's been handling the work of two or three men while my other guys are out."

Locke offered his hand. The look he gave Rebecca was one of borderline contempt, and he seemed to be expecting Wallace to tell him this was all a joke. Rebecca was used to such reactions. Twenty-first century or not, a career in the FBI had taught her that sexism was alive and well.

"Good to meet you." Rebecca shook his hand, though he offered little more than a light grip around her knuckles before quickly dropping it.

"Same. Just let me know if you need anything." Locke's tone, though, indicated that he really hoped this never happened.

Wallace led her to the back of the room where the older man had finished tidying up and was now pouring himself a cup of coffee into a mug that read *First Coffee, Then Talkie*. He smiled as he poured a generous scoop of sugar into his mug.

"This here is Deputy Greg Abner. He's the oldest fart on my team, which means he has the most experience."

"See how he spins things?" Greg laughed as he offered his hand. "He's got a couple years on me, and I'm the old one. Right. Playing politics is how he got to be sheriff. I'm really just a consultant now that I've retired, but I'm so bored I come and hang out at the station and keep Viviane company."

"Greg works as our reserve," Wallace explained. "If there happens to be a bad car accident that takes more than two bodies to sort out, Greg will come into the station and field any other calls that might come in. He's been in a few hours a day while Hoyt Frost and Darian Hudson have been out. Hudson is the one whose wife just had the baby, and Frost is the one that just had his appendix removed."

Rebecca nodded, committing the names to memory. Wallace finished his quick round of introductions by taking her to the front desk that separated the lobby from the foyer. "And of course, you've already met Viviane Darby. She's here just about all the time, answering calls and usually running dispatch too. We have another woman, Melody, who runs the after-hours dispatch, but I doubt you'll ever even meet her."

Viviane beamed from behind her desk. "Hello again."

Rebecca couldn't help but beam back. "Hi."

"Viviane started with us four years ago, filling in for her mother after she retired. But the job fit her well, and it just sort of stuck."

"Yep, stuck like a bug in a Venus flytrap." Viviane laughed at her own joke. It was the sort of trait that convinced Rebecca she was going to like Viviane Darby very much.

"Any questions?" Wallace rocked back on his heels.

"Not now. I think I'm good." As she said this, she glanced back toward Trent Locke and noticed that he was eyeing them with a scowl on his face.

"Now that's all out of the way, let's get moving." Wallace grabbed a set of keys. "We've got a boyfriend and some parents to talk to."

10

Diane and Owen Miller lived in a typical beach-style cottage. It didn't have an unobstructed view of the ocean, but as Sheriff Wallace pulled the Explorer into their driveway, Rebecca could just barely see the sparkling tips of small waves over the expanse of their side yard. Walking to the front door, the waves were gentle and calming, almost like white noise.

Wallace knocked, and a pretty blonde woman in her mid-forties answered the door. Her hair was pulled back from a face tight with worry, and she held herself stiffly, her arms wrapped around her thin frame. Her shoulders were elevated from tension, her head hanging down just enough to hide tired brown eyes. She offered a weak smile as she opened the door wider to allow them inside. The bright foyer looked like something straight out of a *Beachside Living* magazine, if such a magazine existed.

"Good morning, Sheriff."

"Good morning, Diane." Wallace stepped out of the way as he introduced the women.

As he did, a man also entered the foyer. He didn't look

stressed, but he did look tired. He was rather tall and handsome, but in a way that snuck up on you. The longer Rebecca studied him, the more his subtle good looks became noticeable behind his stoic façade. Rebecca figured it was in the salt-and-pepper tones of the five o'clock shadow that covered the lower half of his face. Or maybe it was the fact he was wearing a business suit. Rebecca made a mental note to ask about the type of job he worked.

He could be going to church, of course, seeing as it was Sunday. But Diane didn't appear to be joining him based on her attire.

Not that it probably mattered.

Rebecca had an eye for noticing details, even if the details didn't need to be noticed.

"Owen and Diane Miller, I'd like you to meet Deputy West. She has extensive FBI experience, and I think she'll be a real asset. I can assure you, she's here to help in any way she can."

"FBI." Owen's eyes went wide. "Wow, that's fantastic. She's not gunning for Frost's job, is she?" His joke fell flat as his wife frowned at him.

"No, not by any means." Wallace's words were short and clipped. "I was hoping to have a talk with your son this morning. But maybe a word or two with both of you first."

Diane pushed a lock of hair that hadn't been out of place behind her ear. "You know, Sheriff, Deputy Locke was out here to talk to Dillon yesterday, and I think he answered everything then. Do we really need to keep going after my son like this?"

"I'm not *going after* him at all." The sheriff sounded more like a grandfather than law enforcement as he soothed the mother with his kindly act. "When we talked to him, we were looking for a missing teen. Now we're looking for her killer. We need to find who might have done this, and if it's all the same to you, I'd like Deputy West to speak with your son. Now, I can't promise this will be the last time we come by, but I'd very much like for it to be."

The boy's parents had two very different reactions. His mother bristled while his father flinched.

"Surely you don't think our boy had anything to do with that!" Diane stepped in front of the sheriff, as if shielding her house from him.

"Never said I did, Mrs. Miller." He leaned closer and dropped his voice slightly, making her lean in as well. "But yesterday, he was asked about her friends. People she would likely hang out with. Now we need to know if she was in any trouble or had any enemies. It's a totally different line of questioning."

The Millers looked to one another, and after a few seconds, Owen shrugged. "I think that'll be fine."

For a moment, Rebecca couldn't help but marvel at the smooth way Wallace had of quickly getting people on his side. A tiny show of dropping his voice, acting as if he didn't want to say what he was saying, and the parents were instantly reassured.

"And I'd like to speak with him without the two of you present." Rebecca braced herself for an explosive reaction, absent Wallace's charisma.

Diane looked as if she might reach out and try to push Rebecca over. "And what for?"

Wallace raised both hands in a placating manner, stepping in and doing his best to keep the peace. "Let's not get defensive. You know as well as I do that no teenager—much less a teenage *boy*—is going to be honest about certain things in front of his momma. Especially when it comes to his girlfriend."

"Christ almighty." Diane tapped her foot in a rapid staccato. "You really think—?"

"It's okay, Diane." Owen reached out and took his wife's arm. "Let them talk to him, and maybe then we get it all behind us."

"Fine," Diane snapped. "But you wanted to speak with us first, right?"

"Yes, please." Rebecca smiled, but she didn't think it provided quite the same soothing benefits as Wallace's did. "As his mother, you might have noticed something about Cassie Leigh that young love would have blinded him to. Or threats to her that your son would overlook."

Placated by Rebecca's words, she finally relented and stepped back, forcing her husband to step back as well. "Come this way."

Owen led them into a living room adorned with a few beach paintings and a multitude of white and aquamarine decorations. The place was done up in a way Rebecca didn't expect locals to live. Seashell artwork and lighthouse sculptures littered nearly every surface. It made her wonder if the Millers rented the place out as an Airbnb on occasion.

It was everything she found horrifying about vacation homes, and this was their full-time residence. Where they'd chosen to live and selected the decor...on purpose. Rebecca wondered for the briefest of moments if she could make the case that decorating like this was a sign of a mental illness to push for a warrant and confiscate everything. Then lose it in an evidence locker. Or an incinerator.

Only Diane sat, and when she did, it was with a very rigid posture. She looked like she was ready for a job interview. Owen remained standing at his wife's side, his eyes darting back and forth between Rebecca and the sheriff.

Rebecca spoke first, eager to establish a sense of urgency with the Millers. "From a parental perspective, what was your opinion of the relationship between your son and Cassie Leigh?"

The Millers exchanged a look, and Owen shrugged, more or less giving Diane the task of answering. "It sort of came out of nowhere. They were always friends, as far back as grade school. You could see it in the way they interacted. Always playing and teasing, you know? They went from friends to one day being something more. Dillon never really came out and told us. We just noticed, and he *knew* we had noticed, and all of a sudden, they were a couple."

"Did she spend a lot of time here?"

Diane answered this too. Some of the anger from earlier was still there, but it seemed she was starting to understand Rebecca only wanted to learn more about the relationship. There was a softness to her tone and a release of tension from her previously rigid posture. "A good amount, yes. A few evenings after school and a lot of Saturdays."

"What time did Dillon get home Friday night or Saturday morning?"

His mother hesitated. "I'm not sure. I was asleep, and Owen always says I could sleep through a hurricane."

Owen squeezed her shoulder. "Before midnight. I got up just before one for some water, and he was already in his room asleep."

Rebecca made sure to jot some notes down on her pad to show she was taking their answers seriously. "And did you approve of her? Did you think she was a good girlfriend to your son?"

That question seemed to really win the woman over, and even Owen seemed to relax a bit.

"She was a good girl, so yes. Went to church every Sunday. Was active in school. Bright. A little immature, maybe, but her parents did shelter her quite a bit."

Rebecca made sure to take note of that. How could parents who left their child alone for so long also over shelter her? "Did you ever see them arguing at all?"

Owen's chuckle was heavy with sadness. "If Cassie and Dillon ever argued, it was over things like which movie to watch or who got to pick the music when they were in the car together."

"Or which toppings to have on their pizza," Diane added. "Small things."

"And what about their intimacy? Do you happen to know if they were sleeping together?"

The question dropped like a small bomb, and both of the Millers bristled. It was Owen who fielded this question as well, as Diane seemed a bit too distressed over the thought of it. "Diane and I talked about this last night, trying to figure it out. We'd catch them looking at each other sometimes in a way that made you think there was something going on. And lately, they'd seemed much more comfortable around one another. When they were just sitting on the couch or even the way they maneuvered around each other in the kitchen, there was something there. Something different."

Rebecca added a question mark to her notebook. "So, you suspect they *may* have been sleeping together but can't know for sure?"

"That's right." Diane hugged herself tight. "It was mostly in the way Cassie acted. As if she was more sure of herself with my son. Like she was confident when she wasn't before. And forgive me if I seem like I'm being difficult, but what does their sex life have to do with anything?"

"Maybe nothing. But it's my experience in cases like this where there are teenagers involved, the end result is going to come down to either sex or drugs. Has Dillon ever participated in any illicit behavior?"

Diane glared at Rebecca. "None at all."

Beside Rebecca, Wallace nodded. "He's never given me reason to keep an eye on him."

"Are you saying Dillon is a suspect?" A wave of anger

passed through Owen that was almost tangible. He was showing more emotion than he had when they'd arrived.

"He's no stronger a suspect than anyone else in town." Wallace held up both hands. "But you two have to understand. Cassie was Dillon's girlfriend, so yes, there are going to be eyes and speculation pointed his way."

"Until we start finding leads toward the actual killer." Rebecca watched as mixed emotions passed through the Millers. Confusion and fear came first, then acceptance. Rebecca felt she'd handled it well, tying it up with a hint that she and Wallace were not *after* their son and were looking to the parents to direct them elsewhere. Riding on that, she added, "Do you know if Cassie was into any illicit behavior? Drinking or drugs or anything? Hanging out with the wrong crowd?" She phrased it that way to make it seem she was more worried about the girlfriend being a bad influence on their son.

That did not soothe Diane, however. "Of course not. If she was into anything like that, I wouldn't have allowed my son to date her. I don't allow that kind of stuff in my house. I know her parents drink, but we don't."

So, the boy's mother was controlling, just as Rebecca had suspected. "If it's okay, we'd like to speak with Dillon now."

Owen nodded and started for the hallway. "I'll get him. Honey, do you want to meet me out on the back porch?"

Diane didn't bother to respond. She simply gave Rebecca and Wallace a worried look before she left the living room. Rebecca and Wallace shared a glance, and she found the sheriff hard to read. He didn't appear to be worried, scared, or relieved. Like her, he seemed to be trying to process the little bit they'd heard.

Several moments later, Owen came back into the living room with a miserable looking Dillon. The teen's face was pale, and his eyes were red and swollen. He also appeared to be scared to death.

His father placed a reassuring hand on his shoulder, but when he spoke, he was looking directly at Rebecca and Wallace. "If there's a problem, I'll be right out on the porch. Okay, bud?"

As thinly veiled threats went, Rebecca considered it a weak one. Oblivious to what was really going on, Dillon nodded. "Sure, Dad." But he didn't seem sure as he watched his father leave the room to go join his mother on the back porch.

When they were alone, Wallace introduced Dillon and Rebecca to each other before nodding to Rebecca to begin. She spoke gently to put the boy at ease. "Dillon, when was the last time you saw Cassie?"

"Friday. The night she..." he cleared his throat, "died." He turned away, breaking eye contact. He took a deep breath.

Was he building the strength to continue the conversation or craft the proper lies?

Rebecca nodded and softened her tone even more. "What time did you see her? Do you remember?"

Dillon thought about it for a moment. She could see that he was very nervous but doing his best to hide it. The obvious concentration on his face made him look very much like his father. "She came over around six-thirty or so, I guess. After dinner. We didn't really have any plans together because I'd told her I'd be hanging out with my friends. We hung out for a bit. She left here just before I left to hang with my friends, so that would have been a little before nine, I guess."

"Hung out doing what?" Sheriff Wallace asked, leaning back slightly.

The boy's eyes widened again, then flicked to the side where his parents were just out of view on the porch. "Just watching videos. Stuff. Talking about summer. Nothing serious, just...talking."

Rebecca cut in, not lifting her head from her notes. "And was she okay with you hanging out with your friends?"

Dillon's eyes darted over to her. "Yeah, she always has been. Sometimes, she'd get a little annoyed, but it was never anything bad. Just wanted to know what time I would get back. She liked it when I texted her to let her know I was heading home. We would FaceTime after, and she wanted to get ready for it."

Rebecca wondered how exactly the girl would "get ready" for a video call but didn't push that yet. "And did she happen to tell you what she was going to do while you were out?"

Dillon shrugged, then rubbed his hands on the chair like he was drying them. "No. I just assumed she would have gone home. It wasn't until yesterday that Deputy Locke told me that wasn't the case. I texted her, but she never responded." Tears shimmered in his eyes, and he ran a hand under his nose. "I figured she was asleep. With finals being rough and all, she wanted to catch up on sleep."

Tears filled the young man's eyes, and Rebecca didn't know how much longer she'd have him. She wasn't worried about his emotions getting in the way of the questions, but his concerned parents. He seemed more than willing to help out. She supposed if they heard him crying, one of them would come running in and ask her and Wallace to leave.

Wallace spoke up next, keeping his rather gruff voice as low as he could. "What did you and your friends do the night Cassie was murdered?" He hesitated and added a bit more with something very close to sympathy in his tone. "And be honest. I'm not here to trap you or get you into trouble."

Dillon Miller looked down when he answered. He was picking nervously at his fingernails. "We were down on the beach, over near where they sometimes have the firepits by the older docks. We were drinking a little. But it was mostly just playing football on the beach and listening to one of my other friends play his guitar."

"What about sex?" Rebecca was tired of walking around the elephant in the room. "Were you and Cassie sexually active?"

Dillon's face exploded with color, and the poor boy looked at Wallace as if shocked the sheriff had allowed this strange woman to ask such a question. When Wallace's expression didn't change, Dillon gulped before answering. "I don't know how to answer that. We haven't had *actual* sex, but we've done...stuff. Just not *that*. We're still virgins."

Rebecca cocked a mental eyebrow. Frost had told her the M.E. confirmed no sexual assault present with Cassie Leigh but that the girl likely had recent intercourse. She took the mental note and moved on to help push him past the embarrassment of the last question and his own admission. "Just one more thing, Dillon. Can you think of anyone who had argued with Cassie recently or held something against her?"

Dillon looked back up to them, and Rebecca saw true hurt in his eyes. "I've been asking myself the same thing, over and over. But I can't think of a single person that really had anything against Cassie." His tone was pleading, and he once again looked to the sheriff for reassurance.

Clearly, the young man respected authority figures, or at least he personally liked Wallace. Or he was just less scary than the big bad, out-of-towner from the FBI.

"I'm sorry we have to ask you such hard questions." Rebecca really did feel sorry for the kid, but it couldn't stop her from doing her job. "It's never easy to look at people you know and wonder which one of them could have done such a terrible thing, but based on coroner's reports, they believe she was killed somewhere between midnight and one in the morning. Were you home by then?"

A choked sob escaped Dillon's mouth, and he pressed his fist to his lips to keep another one from escaping. "I got home a little before midnight. That's my curfew, and I didn't want to run the risk of being caught with," he slanted a glance at the sheriff, "beer on my breath, so I made sure I wasn't late."

To his credit, Wallace just nodded, avoiding the under-aged drinking admission completely. "Would your friends be able to confirm you were with them the entire time?"

"Yes. And I gave Deputy Locke an entire list of the guys I was hanging out with."

"You came straight home?" Rebecca knew that witnesses and suspects alike both hated to be asked the same question over and over, but it had to be done.

"Yeah. I mean, there's nothing else to do. And like I said, I didn't want to get caug...in trouble. With my mom."

Wallace got to his feet and looked to Rebecca, an "are you ready" eyebrow quirked high. She was. As far as she was concerned, they'd gotten more than enough from Dillon Miller...for now.

Rebecca stood and held out a hand to the young man, trying to get a proper gauge on him. "Thanks, Dillon. Please let us know if you can think of anyone that might suddenly pop into your head...someone who may have had issues with Cassie."

He nodded vigorously, wiping away the tears that had reappeared in his eyes. "I will."

Now for the hard part, talking to her parents.

Rebecca always hated this part, and she hated it even more because she understood the kind of grief these families were dealing with. And how awful it felt to be the one getting questioned by law enforcement when the real bad guys were getting away.

11

Cassie's mother, Belinda Leigh, sported puffy, red eyes and appeared to be summoning all her strength to keep their lids from slamming shut. Still, she seemed appreciative that Rebecca and Wallace came to visit. She'd even seemed to perk up the slightest bit when Wallace had introduced Rebecca the same way he had back at the Millers' home, as someone with FBI experience here to help with the case.

As for Cassie's father, Robert seemed to not really give a damn about who was in his house. He was sitting in the kitchen, drinking bourbon, even though it had just turned ten in the morning. As Rebecca sat in the Leighs' small den with Belinda, she could hear Robert speaking loudly with Sheriff Wallace. Good thing Wallace had already confirmed both parents' alibis for the night of Cassie's disappearance. It made the tough conversations easier knowing she wasn't speaking with a murderer.

"I know you're in a pinch here, Sheriff, but something's gotta be done."

"I know, Robert." Wallace was using that grandfatherly voice Rebecca was quickly growing fond of. "And we're working on that. That's why I've brought Rebecca West in on this. You can—"

"Too many cooks in the kitchen." Robert's voice was slurred. "Too many fucking cooks!"

Rebecca heard every word, even though the kitchen was separated from the den by a rather expansive hallway.

Belinda shot Rebecca a tired *what-are-you-gonna-do* type frown. "I'm so sorry. It's how he's coping. I think he started drinking around six this morning. I tried to get him to stop, but…" She shrugged, as if that simple gesture explained it all. Her voice was rough and haggard. Even as Rebecca spoke with her now, the poor woman sounded closer to crying than speaking.

"It's quite all right." Rebecca squeezed her hand. "Maybe it's best that he isn't in here right now. Do you think you could handle a few questions?"

"Yes." She lifted her chin, nostrils flaring. "Whatever I can do to find the monster responsible."

"We've just come from the Miller residence. We spoke with Dillon, as well as both of his parents. Can you tell me your thoughts on Dillon and Cassie's relationship?"

Belinda blew her nose. "Well, Dillon is a sweetheart, that's for sure. But they'd been getting a little too familiar. I caught them in some pretty passionate kisses in his car and on the front porch when he'd bring her home."

"But in terms of arguments or violence?"

"Oh, lord no. No, Dillon was crazy about Cassie." Tears glimmered in the grieving mother's eyes again. "I don't know that I ever heard a cross word between them…and not a single negative word about Dillon from Cassie."

The mere act of speaking her daughter's name caused

Belinda's face to tighten, and her shoulders scrunched up each time Cassie's name was mentioned.

"The way I understand it, she left here two nights ago and didn't return. Is that right?"

"Yes. She left to go see Dillon. She went to the Millers' a lot, especially on the weekend, so I thought nothing of it. His mom always made sure Cassie left by midnight."

"So, you have no idea what she could have been doing Friday night or early Saturday morning?"

"Not for certain, no. Her bed was still made. She always makes her bed first thing. Her room was spotless too. As if she'd just cleaned it. My little girl was always so responsible. And thoughtful."

Little moans escaped Belinda as she rocked in her chair, her gaze turning into a million-mile stare. Sheriff Wallace came into the room and lowered himself onto the couch next to Rebecca.

"And what about her car?" Rebecca glanced between Belinda and Wallace. "It wasn't at the Miller home, and it isn't here. I assume she had one."

"She did. It was her sixteenth birthday present. I don't know where it is. I didn't even notice it wasn't in the old garage until we couldn't find her. Bob went out to check." Her face crumbled in abject misery. "I should have checked. I should have noticed. How could I not notice something like that?" Her self-blame was evident in every word.

Rebecca reached over and squeezed the mother's hand again. "Don't be hard on yourself. You loved your daughter, and not thinking to check on a car doesn't change that."

Wallace cleared his throat and spoke softly. "We'll put out an APB for her car and let you know when we find it."

Rebecca knew she had to finish getting answers before the mother broke down completely. "Mrs. Leigh, in your opinion, do you think there's any way Dillon Miller did this?"

There was no hesitation at all when she shook her head. "No. If it turned out to be him, I'd be shocked to my core. They were so in love and—"

Her face crumpled, and a wail of grief came out of her, long and deep. As if summoned by the noise, Robert Leigh came into the room. His face drooped at the sight of his wife in such pain. He wobbled toward her, glass of bourbon in hand, and turned to Rebecca and Wallace.

"Nah, Dillon didn't do this." His words were slurred, but he was speaking well enough that Rebecca could make out what he was saying. "But I bet some of those little shits in the Yacht Club might know something about it."

Rebecca did a double take. "Yacht Club?"

"Yeah." Robert tossed back the rest of his drink. "He wasn't *in* it, but some of the rumors I hear are—"

Wallace held up a hand. "Are just rumors."

Rebecca directed a stern glower at Wallace but tamped it down quickly, forcing a lightness into her voice she didn't feel. "What club is this?"

Instead of answering, Wallace got to his feet and gave the Leighs a sympathetic little nod. "We'll leave you to your privacy now. Is there anyone we can call for you?"

Belinda pressed a tissue under her nose. "No. Pastor Wright is coming over in a bit, and he'll..." She was choked by a sob. Robert went to her, and they wept together. He perched awkwardly along the side of the armchair and cradled her head.

Silently, Rebecca followed the sheriff as he left the house. They'd made it down the porch steps when she finally allowed her frustration to come out. "What the hell was that about? You just ignored my question in there. Why wouldn't you let Robert Leigh tell me about this club?"

The sheriff kept walking to his vehicle, and Rebecca thought he was going to ignore her again. Once inside the Explorer, he turned to her with the sort of expression that, at first, made her think he might have stepped in something left behind by a neighborhood dog.

Wallace sighed. "Because it might be better if you heard it from me. Come on. Let's take a ride."

12

They'd been in the SUV for about two minutes when Wallace radioed back to the station. Viviane picked the call up right away, and Rebecca listened to the conversation as she watched the sea disappear on her right, replaced by the narrow two-way streets leading into town.

"Viviane, you know what Locke's up to?"

"Searching for Cassie Leigh's car. I believe he's got Greg out looking too."

"Thanks. I'm heading over to Clam Diggers. You want anything?"

"Seasoned fries with some of their ranch would be good. Thanks, Sheriff."

Rebecca was perplexed by it all. They had a dead girl, her missing car, and no leads. Yet the sheriff was about to go grab lunch while his already depleted force was out searching for the missing car. She bit back these comments, hoping Wallace would choose to explain them without being asked.

But when he parked in front of a small diner with a picture of a clam sitting on top of a hamburger in a large picture window, he'd still said nothing. As he reached for the door handle, Rebecca couldn't take it anymore.

"Sheriff Wallace, with all due respect, I'm finding your methods a little lacking."

Wallace let out a genuine laugh as he opened the door. "You and me both. Come on inside. Let's get some grub, and I'll walk you through everything."

Rebecca examined his expression. If he was about to lie or hold back, she was done playing deputy. If he wasn't going to be straight with her, she was done. Murdered teen or no.

Once they were both out of the vehicle, he finally met her gaze. "I guess I could have done a better job from the start, huh?"

"I absolutely agree."

Of course, she understood why he hadn't. She was only helping for a few days, after all. She was only supposed to help him until they'd hopefully found Cassie Leigh's killer. That meant there were certain things about Shadow Island she hadn't needed to know.

Yet, at the same time, the last thing she wanted was to work on a case with half the facts. Rebecca had decided to help find a missing teen, and now she'd consoled a grieving mother when they found the girl dead.

No more games.

Clam Diggers smelled of shrimp and Old Bay seasoning. A dozen tables and an old-school style wraparound counter with twenty or so stools filled the small diner. The lunch rush wasn't yet in full swing, so there was relative quiet when Wallace and Rebecca were seated and placed their orders with a bored waitress. Wallace ordered a bacon cheeseburger and onion rings, as well as Viviane's order to go. Rebecca got the Cobb salad. She'd already spent several days eating junk food and sandwiches. Veggies were exactly what she wanted now. They sat in silence until their drinks were delivered, Wallace shifting in his seat while Rebecca studied him.

Good. Be nervous.

Wallace sipped from a glass of sweet tea.

Rebecca said nothing, drank nothing, simply sat and waited while Wallace looked everywhere except at her. Just like she knew he would, the old sheriff broke the silence.

"I rushed you out of the Leigh home at the mention of the Yacht Club because that certain club tends to be a hot and rather sticky topic around here."

No, shit.

Rebecca cocked her head. "Why would that matter? If it gives us answers about Cassie Leigh's murder, we should pursue it."

Wallace spun his glass between his thumbs. "In a perfect world, I'd agree with you. But the Yacht Club is the sort of thing you don't mention loosely around here. To even suggest that someone is tied up in it opens a whole can of nasty worms. And a lot of speculation and insinuations too."

He kept his head down, face pointed at the table. Even looking directly at him, a fellow diner might not know the man was talking from a distance. This was all very peculiar. Was he afraid someone might try to read his lips?

Rebecca wasn't going to let his paranoia bother her, though she kept her voice low. "What *is* the Yacht Club? From the way you're dancing around a straight answer, it makes me assume it's much more than boating enthusiasts."

"Yacht Club is just what we call it. It's not like it's official or anything. It's sort of an urban legend around here. The best explanation would be a," he stopped, clearly searching for words, "an exclusive frat for wealthy old men."

Rebecca wasn't buying it. "So, what does the *legend* say these old, rich frat boys are doing?"

That seemed to be the right tactic to take, referring to it

as nothing more than an old myth not to be believed because Wallace relaxed a little.

"The story goes, they use a route around Shadow Island for late-night excursions that are said to be nothing more than sex-and-drug fueled parties."

"So, how has it not been busted?"

"Because so far, that's all it is, rumors. My jurisdiction ends at the waterline. What am I supposed to do about rumors of things that may or may not be happening in the ocean? I can keep an eye out for crimes, but that's about all. I've never had proof of them even buying pot, let alone anything else. And getting drunk in boats isn't illegal unless you're driving. Neither are parties."

Rebecca mulled it all over as the waitress delivered their food. The statements were bullshit, and they both knew it. Coastal jurisdiction extended a few miles out in the water, and alcohol on boats was cause enough to check for underage drinkers. He was shirking his responsibility, but her gut told her this wasn't the focus.

She finally sipped her tea and stabbed a tomato with her fork. "What I'm hearing is that, even if Robert Leigh is right and Dillon Miller might have somehow been connected to this Yacht Club, you don't plan to look into it?"

The sheriff's nostrils flared, but that was the only movement his blank expression provided as he dipped an onion ring into a pile of ketchup as big as a pond. "Not without some hard evidence. And look, I know it sounds conceited, but I've been on the force on this island in some capacity for about forty years. Dillon Miller is not the sort of kid to get wrapped up in that crowd. And even if he was, there's no reason for the club to recruit him."

"Has the influence of this club popped up as a shadow of sorts in any recent investigations?"

Instead of answering right away, Wallace drank half his

glass. "I've had two minor drug busts over the last three years that I believe were the result of the Yacht Club. Then last year, there was a case of a seventeen-year-old girl insisting that she'd been sexually abused. She wouldn't give names but indicated it was related to the Yacht Club. Even the parents got involved in that one. Eventually, we let it go. At the end of the day, she had no hard evidence and because she refused to give names or dates or anything pertinent..." He shrugged, as if that said enough, and attacked his burger with a huge bite.

A girl claimed she was assaulted, and the sheriff dropped it because the victim didn't know the name of her attacker? No wonder there was so little crime here. Nothing was officially written up.

Rebecca swallowed down the words she really wanted to say. If she still had any good contacts with the FBI, she'd start a larger investigation just based on what she'd already found out.

"So, you can't prove anything, but what about the rumors?"

"There are some deep grumblings." Wallace shook his head and wiped his mouth. "Not even rumors but whispered fears at most, I'd say. Anyway, the rumors say that the minor stuff *is* public so that more deplorable stuff could go down. We're talking older men paying teenage girls for sex. Maybe inviting teens from not just the mainland but from our little island too, on their boats as a sort of recruitment."

Rebecca frowned. "And there's no evidence of this?"

"Just speculation. And it's become something of a boogeyman around here." Wallace waved his fingers in the air, mimicking a scary ghost. "'Don't miss curfew, or the Yacht Club will get you.' 'There's graffiti on that wall. It must be because of the Yacht Club.'" He dropped his hands and picked up his burger again. "That kind of thing."

"Seems like there would be enough to get concerned parents behind shutting down the club. Raise enough hell, and at some point, the higher-ups in the state would *have* to do something, right?"

Wallace lifted a shoulder and finished chewing a bite. "Which leads to people making up even more provocative rumors about it. You have to understand that people who live on Shadow Island live here because they expect a certain life-style. Yes, I'm fully aware of how pretentious and elitist that sounds, but it's the plain and simple truth. If there's anything vile or dark—anything that might upend their island life—it usually goes ignored."

"So, a collective blind eye is turned?"

Wallace tapped his nose. "Exactly. Everyone blames the nefarious Yacht Club. Except, it's my job to uphold the law on the island. And I do a decent job of that. When drugs made their way onto the island in the past, we stopped them, and arrests were made. Because I know what happens when it all reaches the state level, I stay out of it after that. I keep the peace here. Out on the ocean, I don't have a leg to stand on. And I can't spend all day chasing rumors."

Rebecca didn't say anything for a long time. She tried to hide the disgust roiling up inside her, but from his expression, she didn't succeed. They both tucked into their meals, though Rebecca had lost much of her appetite.

On occasion, she thought Wallace was going to say something, but he would shake his head and pick at his meal.

"What if I wanted to look into it?" The question came out of Rebecca before she could think everything through. She wiped her mouth. "Just to make sure Dillon Miller absolutely has no links. Even if the accusation did come from a heart-broken father that just lost his daughter, the speculation had to come from *somewhere*."

The waitress came over and slid the check in the center of

the table. Wallace grabbed it right away and reached for his wallet. "I'd ask that you use my protocols. Unless you find very hard and irrefutable evidence, the Yacht Club stays out of it. We don't want to muddy the waters with boogeymen and rumors."

She scowled, but before she could ask another question, they were interrupted.

"Rebecca? Rebecca West?"

The man standing beside their table looked to be about her own age, and as she studied him, she thought his face might look just the slightest bit familiar.

Wallace, apparently happy to take this as a great opportunity to drop the conversation about the Yacht Club, scooped up Viviane's to-go container, and quietly excused himself, leaving Rebecca to puzzle through who the newcomer was.

"You *are* Rebecca West, right?"

"I am." Was this a trap? "How do we know each other?"

He offered his hand in a way that was a little more awkward than polite. She shook it, mainly because he seemed so enthused about doing so.

"Ryker Sawyer. I won't be at all upset if you don't recognize me. It *has* been a pretty long time."

The familiarity of his face and the inclusion of *a pretty long time* finally offered up an answer. It was an answer her brain didn't seem to be too sure about, but she figured she'd at least give it a shot. The name *did* sound familiar, and his face...those dimples.

"Oh my god." Flashes of memories made her smile. "We used to play together on the beach when my family came for the summer!" Relief trickled in, allowing her to relax.

"Whew." Ryker mimed wiping the sweat of worry from his forehead. "You do remember. That's good."

"How are you?"

Ryker ran a hand through his sandy blond hair and

glanced toward the counter, where Wallace was settling the check. "Better than you, it seems. I take it you're either in trouble with the law or are *friends* with the law."

Rebecca laughed, though she was honestly still hung up on the fact she'd run into this figure from her past. It had to be at least twenty years since they'd seen one another, and likely even longer than that.

Ryker was now a far cry from the gangly, thin, rambunctious kid who used to instigate seaweed fights on the beach. When the corners of his mouth turned up, and his tawny eyes practically glistened with joy, he was transformed from rather basic-looking to handsome.

Beneath all of that, he exuded a hint of being mischievous. Had he not made a point to come over to her, she may not have even given him a second look. The five o'clock shadow appeared to be a natural extension of his face, and he still had the same deep tan she remembered. Beach life did have its perks.

"Neither is the case, really. I'm just having a working lunch with Sheriff Wallace. Sort of lending a hand. Short term basis."

He seemed impressed by her admission and half turned to smile at the sheriff, who gave him a little wave. Everyone in town seemed to know and like the sheriff. "Oh, wow. So… you grew up and became a cop?"

"FBI, actually…but that's a long story."

She saw that he took a moment to try to decide if she was joking with him. When it was clear she was not, he looked impressed and a little embarrassed. "Is this a one-day sort of trip, or are you around for a while?"

"At least three months. How about you? Do you live on Shadow?"

It was odd, but talking to him made it much easier to remember him. She caught flashes of memories when she and Ryker had dug holes just above the tide line, hoping to trap little minnows and crabs. She was quite certain there was a lightning bug hunt one Fourth of July too. She'd never been quite sure where his family had lived on the island, but Ryker had always seemed to show up on the same stretch of beach as the West family.

"I do. I nearly moved to Boston after college, but the beach life…she kept calling me."

"What do you do for a living?"

He cringed and shook his head. His sandy blond hair was slightly messy, and he needed a haircut. "No way am I telling you that after you dropped the FBI thing on me."

She smirked. *Cause that had turned out so well.*

"Be a man of mystery, then."

"This is so cool." He rolled his shoulders. "But—and I hate to do this—I need to get back to work."

She raised an eyebrow, trying to appear completely innocent. "Which is where, exactly?"

He wore basic jeans, a plain black t-shirt, and a broken-in pair of sneakers. He could have worked anywhere on the beach based on his clothes.

"Good try." He grinned. "Where are you staying? Maybe if you're here for three months, we can get together for a drink or something."

Did she want to get together with this man? Maybe. She wasn't ready to share her location so she avoided that question.

"Yeah, I think that's possible." And maybe she could learn more about the beach and its goings-on than what Wallace was willing to share. Maybe the good sheriff thought the Yacht Club was just wild rumors, but she'd seen similar situations that turned out to be real. Rumors had to have at least a bit of truth behind them in order to get so big.

Wallace came back to the table, and Ryker used it as a

clean break to end the conversation. "It was nice seeing you, as brief as it was. Take care. And take good care of our sheriff, would you?"

Wallace gave him a mock glare of annoyance that sent Ryker scampering off with a laugh. He gave a final wave and smile as he headed out of Clam Diggers, leaving Rebecca and Wallace alone again.

"How do you know Ryker?"

"I don't really know him, per se. We used to play together on the beach when we were kids."

Wallace chuckled. "It's not too hard to believe. The whole 'It's a Small World' phenomenon takes on an entirely different meaning when you live on an island."

Something about that idea stirred a sudden urge in Rebecca. *It's a small world...and a small island.* She thought of what Dillon Miller had said about coming home the night he'd ditched Cassie for a game of drinking and football with his friends.

"Hey, Sheriff?"

"Yeah?" They were on their way out the door, the summer heat slapping away the coolness of the Clam Diggers' air-conditioning.

"Dillon Miller mentioned a certain beach. What beach was that?"

"Beaman. It's a weird little strip up on the northern tip of the island."

"I'd like to go check it out."

"Good thinking." Wallace tossed the keys to the Explorer to her. "However, I'd like for you to drop me off at the station. I've got a teleconference with the Shadow Preservation Society about security measures for the Noble Lighthouse plans and then some paperwork to fill out for administrative stuff."

Rebecca groaned in sympathy. "Paperwork...the bane of every law enforcement official in the world."

"I'm trying to train Viviane to do more admin, and it'll be a huge help when she finally fills that void." Wallace scratched the back of his neck. "I know it might seem a little irresponsible, but I figured as long as I've got you helping me out, I can get caught up on the office crap while you can peek into the case on your own. No doubt I'd slow you down."

He said it all rather nonchalantly, but it gave her a better glimpse into the chaos of this poor man's life. It made more sense why he'd come to her for help. Outside of the case, he still had to run the station and deal with the less glamorous, behind-the-scenes administrative matters.

It made her want to do her absolute best to help him with this case, if for no other reason than to take some of the weight off his shoulders.

And maybe take down a group of boat loving assholes at the same time.

13

The direction Rebecca had to drive in order to make it to Beaman was almost an answer in and of itself. It was a good distance away from the marshes—almost on the exact opposite side of the island, in fact. With a total land area of somewhere shy of twenty-six miles, a person didn't have to be an experienced local to get a proper lay of the land.

Her route took her into a small, undeveloped stretch that bordered a jagged and rocky-looking portion of the coast. She followed the two-lane road until she came to a small sign posted at a T-intersection just a few yards away from the rocky outcroppings. The sign told her that she'd found Beaman Beach.

Rebecca turned right and found herself entering the small, rectangular parking lot. Judging from its limited footprint, Beaman didn't get a lot of traffic, but most of the spaces were filled. After using one of the numerous dirt trails worn into a tiny strip of wild grass, she saw why.

The beach was rocky and littered with fragments of broken conch shells and innumerable rocks made slippery from moss and sludge. Jagged outcroppings of larger rocks stuck out from the ground here and there, making use of the beach treacherous. This dangerous stretch was about fifty or sixty feet long, and no more than twenty or so feet wide between the place where the sand started and the ocean began. She spotted a single person, an older man standing in the gentle surf with a fishing line cast into the water.

He didn't drive all those cars here. Where's the other people?

An L-shaped embankment to Rebecca's right brought an abrupt end to Beaman Beach. In the distance, she noticed another trail leading north. She picked her way over to the dune covered in weeds. It rose gradually, making it easy to climb its height of about ten feet.

About half a football field away, smooth, golden, and nearly pristine sand like the other beaches around the island stretched away from the embankment, curving slightly to the right to take the shape of the island's northern coast. A perfect, mostly hidden beach just for the locals to enjoy. No wonder she hadn't recognized the name.

Numerous people frolicked in this particular area. More than that, when she looked to the right, she spotted a more populated area of the island, where a few oceanfront developments stood tall.

Rebecca noticed a group of boys among the people out on the beach. Two were currently wading into the water with boogie boards while another rode a small wave in. It was hard to tell from this distance, but they looked to be teenagers—right about Dillon Miller's age. Figuring there was no harm in taking a chance—hadn't Wallace pointed out it was a small world?—Rebecca walked across the embankment and down to the smoother beach.

She passed by two tanning women and a family picnicking on a blanket as she made her way to the boys. They were indeed teenagers. One was swimming back out while the other two bobbed and weaved on the wave they'd chosen to ride in.

Rebecca waited for them to make it to shore. When they did, a kid with half an inch wide gauges in his ears looked up almost apologetically as his board came less than a foot from hitting her ankle. "Sorry!" But his tone indicated that it was really her fault for just standing there like a tree.

"No worries." Rebecca waited as a second boy wearing red trunks came skidding in behind him, casting glances at the weird woman standing in their way. "I was wondering if you guys had time for a few questions."

Both boys got to their feet, holding their boards at their sides. The one who had nearly struck her ankle shrugged and tugged at the hole in his ear. "Sure. I guess. What about?"

"I was wondering if you might know Dillon Miller."

Red Trunks raised his hand. "Yeah." He was rail-thin, and his trunks looked like they might fall off at any moment.

"Would you consider yourself friends?"

"I would. He," Red Trunks backed up a few steps, then froze, "woah...wait. Is this about Cassie?" He eyed Rebecca skeptically and turned to his friend as the third boy wearing orange goggles rode a wave in, falling off a little early. "Are you a cop?"

Rebecca tapped the badge hanging from her waist that should have been evident to the young men, even though she wasn't in uniform. "Deputy West." Just saying that felt weird.

The boys exchanged looks, and the newcomer bent over to better inspect her badge before peering at her face. Clearly, he didn't trust this strange woman. Considering the entire force was made up of five people, she was certain everyone knew the cops by sight. Every cop except her.

"I'm new. Sheriff Wallace asked me to help him with this." Red Trunks looked both concerned and genuinely interested. "I spoke with Dillon earlier today. On the night Cassie went missing, he said he was playing football with some friends. Would any of you three happen to have also been playing?"

Red Trunks and Orange Goggles nodded. "We usually play on Saturday nights," Orange Goggles said. He hitched a thumb behind them, pointing farther down the beach. "We played right back there Friday until Dillon had to leave to make it home by curfew."

Rebecca lifted an eyebrow. "What time was that?"

Orange Goggles shrugged. "Not sure exactly, but before midnight for sure."

"And what's your name?"

"Isaac Smith."

Rebecca pulled out her notepad and checked the notes she'd gotten from Locke back at the station. Sure enough, this was one of the names Dillon had given to explain where he'd been during the time of Cassie's murder, though his curfew wasn't much of an alibi when she looked at the timeline. He'd left his friends with plenty of time to make it to the marshes and kill Cassie, then get home before his dad noticed. "Where is the dock where you guys were drinking?"

It seemed to come as a surprise to the boys that she knew this, and she mentally smirked. Let them wonder how she knew so much. It might keep them on their toes.

The first kid, the one who had almost collided with her leg, didn't seem too bothered by the question. Perhaps it was because he had been the only one not to nod when she'd asked about the football game.

"It's okay. I'm not here to bust you on drinking. I'm just trying to get some answers."

Red Trunks stepped forward an inch, and when he did, he wouldn't look Rebecca in the face. "There's a dock on Oyster Bay. An old fishing one. We use it to just hang out sometimes."

"What's your name?"

He stuck his hands in his pockets so deeply Rebecca was afraid the trunks would fall down his spindly legs. "Jake Jones."

Rebecca decided she may as well go all in. She had their attention, and at least two of them were heavily invested in what was going on in terms of Cassie's disappearance. "Do either of you know if Dillon Miller was in any way affiliated with the Yacht Club?"

All three of them shared a baffled look. Red Trunks, who was either the spokesman for the trio or the one who knew Dillon the best, seemed to take the lead. "No way, not Dillon."

"You say that as if you're certain."

"Well, it's just that, even if Dillon wanted to be with the Yacht Club, they wouldn't take him."

Interesting.

"Why not?"

They all shared a knowing glance before Ear Gauge spoke up. "The Yacht Club doesn't really recruit guys. It's sort of exclusive. He's not rich enough to join them. What else would they want with him?"

"What's your name?"

"Chris Arnold."

"Thank you, Chris. How do you know all this?" Rebecca was starting to wonder if this Yacht Club was nothing more than some sort of small-town myth as Wallace had said or if the secrecy of it had gotten its roots into the entire island.

The kid answered with the tone of someone telling a secret they knew they had no business sharing. "Pretty much everyone on the island knows about it. It's the kind of thing no one actually talks about, but everyone's aware of."

"And what have you three heard about it?"

"It's a floating party," Red Trunks said. "Just one big party for rich dudes. There's drinking and drugs and…girls."

Hearing a kid his age say "girls" let her know just how

young those girls probably were. His age and younger. The thought pissed her off.

"You're sure this isn't just small-town rumors?" She purposefully kept her eyes on her notepad, both to lessen the effect of being questioned by a cop and to make it seem like she was taking this seriously while still watching them out of her peripherals.

Red Trunks and Ear Gauge shrugged, this time sharing a confused and slightly scared glance. After a while, Red Trunks spoke up again, and when he did, his tone was heavy with worry and uncertainty. "They sometimes come pretty close to the island. Some people even swear they'd pulled into Shadow docks to pick up local girls and even some tourists. And also…"

He trailed off, closing his mouth as if sensing he'd said too much.

"It's okay. Nothing you tell me has to be shared with anyone. I'm just trying to find answers about what happened to Cassie." She needed to be careful, not wanting to spook them now that they were talking.

The young man nodded, and when Red Trunks spoke again, he looked a little guilty. "I was just going to say…I know Dillon wasn't involved, but I'd heard a few people mention that Cassie may have been part of the club."

That got him a dirty look from his friends.

Which was how all rumors started. Heard it from a friend who heard it from a friend. "But you don't know for certain?"

"No. But around here, when you're talking about the Yacht Club, that's not the sort of rumor to use *against* someone, you know? If anything, it makes you look cooler than you actually are. Especially for girls, I guess. It makes them really popular…sort of like they're part of some elite club. Which only the hottest girls are. No one is going to lie just to make her look better, right?"

Now to see if this was a rumor that would actually lead somewhere. "Who told you Cassie was involved?"

The trio glanced around without meeting each other's gaze. Rebecca didn't sense guilt but rather a shared knowledge making them uncomfortable. Rebecca thought it might be similar to the mood of a preteen caught in the midst of the birds and the bees talk. In these glances, something shifted among the boys, and Red Trunks no longer looked like the group representative. Instead, Ear Gauge spoke up, and when he did, Rebecca knew the question-and-answer session was close to over.

"The whole Yacht Club thing is touchy. If we gave you names, it's just going to lead to another rumor and another rumor. Plus, our folks are so paranoid about that stupid club that we could get in trouble for even talking about it. Especially if we started just dropping names to a cop." He paused for a moment. "Listen, we're all about helping and feel bad about Cassie. But the damn club's not worth it."

The boy's snarky tone grated at Rebecca, but she let it go. The snark was probably hiding his fear. It was the same reaction when asking teens about local gangs.

Besides, even if what these boys had told her about Cassie and the Yacht Club *wasn't* true, it did give her another avenue to look into. And despite Sheriff Wallace's caution about digging into this seedy organization, Rebecca's intuition told her it was going to resurface during the course of this investigation. She needed to figure out if Cassie was connected. Every lead, no matter how flimsy it seemed, needed to be pursued. It was all a matter of finding the buried dots and then connecting them.

Someone started the rumor about Cassie being invited to the Yacht Club. Even if it was a legend, someone had started the rumor for a reason. Finding out why was just as important now as finding out if it was true.

14

They found my beautiful Cassie.

I knew they'd find her eventually, but I hadn't expected to be so nervous, or for it to happen so soon. How had they found her so soon?

Every moment of that night played over in my head, a repeated loop where I searched for any mistake I might have made. I knew I'd been careful, and the circumstances had made covering up what I'd been forced to do even easier.

When Cassie had chosen to cut through the marshes, it was almost like she wanted me to get away with it—to catch her and make all her troubles go away. That's probably what she'd been hoping for, though I was sure she thought our little chase would end differently.

But there was no other way it could have ended.

I knew as soon as she told me her secret, she needed to die. That's why I went to get my gloves. Nothing could tie me to her. And nothing did.

It felt odd to think such thoughts while sitting in my car on a beautiful, sunny afternoon. I had to get away from the house. I couldn't think there. The place was like a prison, stifling me mentally and physically. Out here, I was myself. Replaying the night over in my head to look for any mistakes or holes in my story, the details knit themselves together perfectly.

Except for that fucking text.

I know what you did.

Was it true? A joke? Or did someone really know what I'd done?

I squeezed the binoculars in my hands. Not possible.

If there was anything on Cassie's body linking me to her, Sherriff Wallace or one of his deputies would pay a visit soon. Or they would have taken me in already, instead of just asking questions around town. Wallace wasn't a threat to me. If anything, her death would probably be what finally broke the old bastard.

But I'd been so careful. Hadn't I? I'd been smart about the whole thing.

I kept circling back to that.

I'd been cautious, true. The gloves and her belongings were burned, the ashes thrown into the sea. The shoes I'd worn had been cleaned of all the caked-on mud.

We'd used condoms, and the only scratch she'd managed was tiny. The water and wind should have cleansed away any stray pieces of hair that I might have left behind. Still…

I know what you did.

The words haunted my every thought…and I was pretty sure I knew who'd sent it to me.

Her.

If there was one person on Shadow Island who knew I was the murderer, she was only forty yards in front of me right now. Lifting the binoculars to my eyes, I watched her closely.

Just like I'd known Cassie's every action, I was getting to know this little nemesis's actions too.

I knew her basic routines...her habits, her go-to spots. I'd been following her for about a month now, and she'd never had any idea. Cassie wasn't the only sweet young thing out here, after all.

And she certainly was a sweet little thing.

Tight little ass practically smiling at me as she sprawled on her stomach next to her friend, letting the sun kiss where my lips should have been. They'd undone their tops to keep from getting a tan line on their backs. The straps dangling by the edges of the chairs sent a thrill through me, like fire sparking to life.

It hit every nerve, every muscle, and my mind was already going to that place—to that very bad place where sin and lust lived. It wasn't the same sort of thrill I used to get whenever I looked at Cassie, but it was close.

With Cassie gone, I might have to learn to settle for this. I wondered what their fronts looked like with those tops unfastened. And my hands around their throats.

For a moment, I lost myself to the fantasy.

No...focus.

Were they wild in bed, or did they just lay there like a dead starfish? Were they plain and boring, or did they like to experiment? Had they ever played with each other? What did their skin feel like? Would they beg...

I lowered the binoculars as a swarm of danger and desire let loose within me. That was how this whole mess had started in the first place. Because I'd been so caught up in watching, I hadn't realized Cassie had noticed me noticing her until the little seductress had called me out.

Look how that had ended.

God, I must keep it together. Maybe I should leave. If I just up and left like I'd originally thought, this would be easier.

Slipping the binoculars back under the seat, I realized

that somewhere during the last minute or so, I'd started to tremble. It had been this same way before things started with Cassie. I knew I should be frightened, but the thrill of it was too much to ignore.

Glancing back out to those small figures, I couldn't help but wonder what they might know...and if I was going to have to put my gloves on to silence them.

15

After leaving Beaman Beach, Rebecca headed south toward the lighthouse and the marshes. She did so by using a few secondary roads that managed to close off the sight of the beach as well as the residential lots that fed into the rest of the town.

For a moment, it was almost as if she were out for a leisurely drive in the country, the two lanes rolling between high grass on one side and a gradual hill on the right. As the hill dropped away, houses appeared in the distance. These were the same houses that would be visible from the marshes, which slowly crept into view just ahead of her. Even with the windows up, she could get a slight whiff of the almost swampy smell the marshes gave off.

Rebecca parked in the same spot she and Wallace had used yesterday and started her trek back toward the location Cassie Leigh's body had been found. Walking through this time, she made a long arc around the area, not wanting to disrupt it any further. The area was still taped off, just as she expected, but the forensic team was long gone. She had no idea what she was looking for, but it felt right to be there.

It was difficult to see where she and Sheriff Wallace had come through yesterday. The grass and weeds had already started to spring back up, and there was no hard evidence of their footprints at all, just a few imprints in the grass. It made her wonder if the killer had purposefully chosen the marshes or if the events leading up to the murder had simply led them to this place.

There was still the possibility the killer had murdered her elsewhere and hauled the body here to hide. That, though, seemed like a stretch. With so much ocean around, why dump a body here?

Rebecca turned back to the houses. If the killer lived in one of those homes, or even just close to where she stood, the marshy land could be a good last-minute hiding place for someone who was panicking. She needed to make sure each of the residents had been questioned.

So much to do.

She tried to imagine the killer and Cassie coming in from every possible angle. With no prints to go on, the marshes were keeping their secrets.

Returning her gaze toward the lighthouse, she focused on the small cottage directly behind it. Smiling, she got into the SUV and headed in that direction rather than back to the station. Her memory had somehow blotted out the notable little building, and she had not thought of it since she'd arrived at Shadow Island.

The building in question was called, quite simply, the old witch's cottage. Rebecca had heard the history countless times, and while she knew it was steeped in truth, she also felt certain locals had exaggerated that truth and added on some fantastical details to make the stories about the cottage even cooler.

Of course, there were rumors the cottage was both haunted

and cursed. There was the local lore about the witchy inhabitant, of course, but Rebecca's favorite tale from her childhood was that the tiny abode had been created by time travelers to make sure the island was discovered and eventually settled.

She wasn't sure if anyone really knew where the small structure had come from or why it had been placed there. There was a very good chance her interest in it had stemmed from the same curiosity that later fueled her interest in Bigfoot and other unexplained mysteries.

All this history cascaded through her head as she pulled into the small parking lot that sat twenty feet or so away from the cottage, in the shadow of the lighthouse. Rebecca shivered, remembering the tale of the witch's curse to all who stepped where she now stood.

Had Cassie run through the lighthouse's shadow?

Forcing those thoughts away, she inspected the simple lone-room shack that sat on a flat piece of land. Rebecca couldn't remember if she'd ever noticed its coloring during her childhood visits with her mother and father, but it stood out now. It had not been painted but coated in some sort of protective sealant that made the original wood look almost gray.

Remarkably, the only means of keeping people out was a single chain hanging from twin posts on both sides of the front doorway. There was no door, just a chipped frame that allowed visitors to look inside. She could only imagine the sort of work and maintenance that went into keeping the cottage clean and stable. No door and no protective additions meant that whenever it rained, rainwater got inside. The meager little chain meant anyone with nerves of steel and a disregard for Shadow Island heritage could traipse right in and deface whatever they wanted.

But as Rebecca peered inside, she saw none of that had

occurred. There were a few dings and dents here and there, but other than that, the cottage was basically untouched.

She was surprised to be alone. Then again, she had to remind herself that true tourist season didn't start until next week. After that, she was sure there would be tourists galore out here. There was something sad about that, something that made her appreciate the little cottage even more. She went to the back of the cottage and saw where the land remained flat for another half an acre or so before dropping off drastically into small dunes that fed onto the beach.

Rebecca watched the sea churn against the sand, putting the scant pieces of this mystery together as best she could. The idea that Cassie might have been linked to this mysterious Yacht Club was an intriguing one and opened all sorts of avenues. Were they just rumors and nothing more? Or were they rumors based on actual events? Or even worse, was it all real and worse than the rumors?

What had Cassie been up to that night after Dillon had gone off to hang out with his friends? Had she been out with her own friends, drinking and partying? No one had come forward yet. But Rebecca hadn't gone looking for any of Cassie's friends yet either. Did she have another boy on the side she ran to whenever she and Dillon weren't quite working? Or was she part of that club?

Were there any drugs or alcohol in Cassie's bloodstream at the time of her death? She thought of a pretty girl like Cassie, on a boat out on the dark water with older men. Could there be other physically incriminating evidence indicating if she'd been with anyone or what she'd been doing?

She needed to talk to the medical examiner.

Turning back to the Explorer, Rebecca took out her cell phone. She called the station, reminding herself she needed to get Wallace's cell number. Viviane answered in her chipper voice and patched Rebecca through to the sheriff.

"Find anything yet?" There wasn't much hope in Wallace's voice, but he tried to inject some cheer into it.

"Not yet." She figured she wouldn't mention the bit she'd learned about Cassie's potential link to the Yacht Club. "But I'd like to speak with the M.E. if that's possible."

"Sure thing. I'll make the call now, so you may as well head on over. I'll do my best to explain our little partnership."

"Where *is* the medical examiner's office, anyway?"

"Ah, it's not on the island. It's right across the bridge in Coastal Ridge, on the backside of the hospital. Want me to come with you? The teleconference is over, and I somehow managed not to fall asleep."

She enjoyed working on her own, and the longer Wallace would allow her to work by herself unhindered, the better. Those kids had already shown her what it was going to be like being the new face in town. She may as well get used to it.

"No thanks. I'll manage. I'll come by the station when I'm done there."

They ended the call, and Rebecca pulled out of the parking lot, taking one last look at the little shack sitting in the lighthouse's shadow.

SHADOW WAY BRIDGE connected Shadow Island to the mainland, specifically the small town of Coastal Ridge. The bridge itself was nothing special, just two lanes that spanned the ocean for one and a half miles. For that matter, Coastal Ridge wasn't much to look at, either.

It consisted of a few mini-malls, tacky beach souvenir shops, a Walmart, a couple of greasy spoon diners, and a few fast-food restaurants that weren't all open. While a thin strip of beach and the ocean served as the backdrop, it was mostly obscured by a few multicolored condos that looked as if they'd been last properly loved somewhere around the late nineties and struggling businesses.

It was also home to Coastal Ridge Hospital, though. The building sat just off a four-lane road, a few miles past the final stretch of beach businesses, including a pirate-themed mini-golf course. Even the hospital attempted to tie into the lazy beach aesthetics. A few scraggly palm trees lined the entryway, but after that, it was all business. As Rebecca turned left to reach the back of the building, she could have easily been in any town in America, far away from the beach.

She found the office exactly where Wallace had said. It was almost like a hidden door, a secret entrance into the lesser-known hallways of the building. Rebecca parked and headed for the door, suddenly wishing she'd taken Wallace up on his offer to come with her. Had the sheriff told the M.E. about her past? And if so, how much? Would the M.E. think she was from the FBI and feel she was trying to puff out her chest and take control?

Well, it was too late for those worries now. She opened the door and entered a small hallway that offered a few different rooms. The first was a check-in desk, the second a blood lab, and the third a small office. As she continued down the hall, a woman appeared farther down, coming in from another hallway. She spotted Rebecca, smiled, and picked up her pace. She looked to be middle-aged and quite pretty.

"Rebecca West?"

"That's me." Rebecca offered her hand. "You're the medical examiner?"

"I am. Bailey Flynn. Sheriff Wallace told me you were on the way over. If you want to see the body, we'll have to go downstairs to the morgue." Her hair was black and fell evenly to both sides of her face. She had thin lips and large, expressive eyes that lit up when she smiled.

Rebecca considered viewing Cassie's body but didn't think it would be necessary. Not unless Bailey Flynn gave her interesting news. "Well, that depends on whether you've found anything of interest."

The M.E. shot Rebecca a knowing grin. "Come on back to my office, and we'll chat."

Bailey led Rebecca to the hallway she'd come out of and then into the second room along the hall. It was a small cozy office, mostly filled with an L-shaped desk. A laptop sat on one side, connected to a desktop monitor on the other. Three frames situated around the desk showed three different children of varying ages.

Bailey took a seat and wasted no time getting to the point. "The cause of death was easy to determine. Cassie Leigh's COD was asphyxiation, or more simply put, strangled."

Rebecca took the offered seat across from her. "I figured as much. Any great big fingerprints or pieces of DNA found?" Rebecca lifted a hopeful eyebrow.

"We actually did find a small piece of skin under one of her fingernails, so cross your fingers it gives us something to work with." Bailey typed something into her laptop, clicked a few times, and then spun the desktop monitor around so Rebecca could see it. A picture of Cassie's neck filled the screen. Bailey pointed while summarizing her findings. "Now, these results are all just preliminary, and I still have a few tests I haven't been able to run. As for right now, I've only done an external visual inspection of the body as well as x-rays. As for what we have right now, you can see the definite shape of two fingers and then a partial third. But that's just the shape. And the softened edges lead me to believe the assailant was wearing gloves. Now, if you look here," she pointed to an area just above the most noticeable finger shape, "you can see a very small crescent-shaped bruise. See it?"

Rebecca did, and she thought she knew what it meant. But before she could say anything, Bailey went on.

"I'm pretty certain this means the killer used both hands, and this crescent shape is the thumb of his other hand—the left—coming in to get a stronger grip."

Bailey clicked again, and the picture on the monitor changed. Now, Rebecca was looking at the side of Cassie's neck. There was bruising there too, but not nearly as pronounced as what she'd seen along the girl's windpipe.

"And here, you can see where the hand wrapped around her neck. It's clearly visible on both sides. In other words…"

"Strangulation." Rebecca nodded, glad to look away from the rather close-up pictures of the dead girl's neck. "Did her blood show anything interesting? Specifically, alcohol or drugs."

"Zilch. No alcohol, no drugs of any kind that showed up in our tests so far. Now, those are just the rapid results. We won't get the end-all and be-all until much later. The lab is always busy, but we do try to hurry these things along. The vast majority of the time, the rapids are accurate."

"Any signs that she was sexually assaulted?"

"It doesn't appear so. She'd had sex. Or something close to vaginal intercourse. Swelling, some fluids I found with the black light. No signs of tears, no bruises, no semen, and no obvious indications of anything violent. But I did take samples to send to the lab as well."

"The boyfriend claims to be a virgin. Says they both are…were."

"You believe him?"

Rebecca didn't have to consider her answer for long. "I think I do. For him, at least."

The M.E. huffed, and a *sorry* smile split her lips. "A lot easier when it's the boyfriend or husband for the murder. Better sharpen your shovel."

Rebecca nodded again, because there was nothing else to do. In fact, she couldn't think of any other questions to ask. It wasn't like she could ask if Dillon was right, and the girl was still a virgin. Despite myths that went back ages, you couldn't tell that from a physical exam most of the time. "Has there been anything at all out of the ordinary from your observations and tests?"

Bailey shook her head and frowned. "Sorry, but there's nothing. There was the smallest bit of dirty water in her lungs, but being that she was discovered in the marshes, that makes sense. I took samples of that, of course. Aside from that...sorry."

"That will help. We can compare it to the samples I took from the marsh and see if they match. Well, thanks again." Rebecca got to her feet, doing her best not to automatically assume this was a wasted visit. Putting a face to a name was always a good idea. "Would you please call the sheriff's office when those final blood results come back?"

"Absolutely." Her tone indicated that a reminder wasn't needed.

Bailey escorted Rebecca out of the office and back down the hall. There was a strange silence between them for a moment, which Bailey ended in a quiet voice that wasn't quite a whisper.

"It's great that you're helping Sheriff Wallace. I heard he's sort of understaffed. And if that man keeps going at the rate he's currently working, he won't have many years to enjoy retirement."

Rebecca appreciated the M.E.'s concern. "You know him well?"

Bailey waggled a hand back and forth in a so-so gesture.

"We're not buddies or anything, but our paths cross more than enough for me to have developed a large amount of respect for him." They'd come to the end of the hall, to the door that led back to the lot. "I'd consider it a personal favor if you'd keep an eye on him while you're helping out. He's one of the really good ones, you know?"

Rebecca hoped so, but knowing the sheriff was ignoring an issue as large as the Yacht Club made her wonder.

"I'll do my best. Again, thanks for meeting with me."

Rebecca headed back outside with the images of Cassie Leigh's neck still in her head. In the marshes, she'd wondered if the killer had worn gloves. The M.E.'s confirmation suggested the unsub had planned the murder. Had he followed Cassie? Was he someone Cassie knew? A stranger who'd taken advantage of a girl alone in the night?

No.

Her gut told her that it hadn't been a chance encounter. *It's a small world, after all.*

She mulled this information over as she drove back to the island. Crossing the bridge, the afternoon sun gleamed brightly along the ocean. But the thoughts in Rebecca's mind were clouded with darkness.

16

When Rebecca arrived back at the station just after six that evening, she was surprised to see Viviane still on the clock.

"Staying late tonight?"

"Gotta stay 'til I get relieved, and Melody's running late. Besides, someone has to keep Greg company." Viviane buzzed her in, and Rebecca glanced around the bullpen.

Greg Abner sat at his little desk in the back. He greeted Rebecca with a brief nod as she passed through the gate and headed toward Wallace's office. She lifted her hand in return.

The sheriff's door was open, so she offered a courtesy knock on the frame before entering. He was concentrating on his laptop, squinting at the screen in a way that made her think he had poor eyesight or hated doing anything with a computer. He looked up when she knocked, and he genuinely seemed pleased that she had returned.

"You get anything useful from Bailey?"

"Just enough to rule out drinking or drugs, from the rapid tests at least. She also said there was no evidence of a sexual assault, though Cassie had been sexually active."

"Was she able to confirm strangulation?"

Rebecca stuck her tongue out and scrunched up her face. "Yes. Vividly."

Wallace chuckled, leaning back in his seat. "Yeah, that's Bailey for you. Meanwhile, I reached out to the Leigh family as well as Dillon Miller to see if anyone knew the passcode to get into Cassie's phone. No luck."

"Yeah. Personal securities often come back to bite us in the ass. Have we gotten her computer in yet?"

"Her dad brought it in and dropped it off. It's already been sent out to the techs. Her mom did have a password for that but said Cassie rarely used it for more than schoolwork."

Rebecca nodded. Why be tied to a desk when you could relax on your bed and still do the same things? It did give her an idea, though. She dug her phone out of her pocket and pulled up Instagram. One of the main go-tos for teens these days. To Rebecca, it was simply another tool for assholes to beg for attention. "Any idea if Cassie Leigh is on any social media sites?"

"No clue."

Rebecca typed Cassie's name into the search field and got four results. Two were clearly not the Cassie Leigh who had recently been murdered on Shadow Island. The two other accounts had been set to private.

"Nothing." Luckily there were other ways to see if she had an account. Not everyone used their real names.

Wallace leaned forward, intrigued. Rebecca was relieved how quickly the sheriff was on board. "What about Facebook?"

"Younger people don't use Facebook anymore. It's more like an older person thing."

"I have Facebook." He sounded a little upset by this news.

Rebecca let that speak for itself.

"Let's start with Instagram and then we'll work down the

list of social media sites that are hot for teens right now. Let's see if Dillon Miller has an Insta account." She typed his name in and got an entire screen's worth of results. But the second one down was the Dillon Miller she wanted. His tanned and smiling face peered directly into the camera. And beside him was the familiar face of Cassie Leigh.

"Bingo."

"Want to tell me what you're doing?"

As she scrolled through Dillon's pictures, she explained as best she could. "It could be a dead end, but I've seen it work before. Based on what I'm seeing, she either doesn't have an account, or it's set to private. Being a pretty seventeen-year-old who lives on a beach, I think it's a safe bet that she has one. We look through the accounts of people that were close to her and see if she's tagged in any pictures. Starting with her boyfriend. Of course, it won't be as good as looking at her account because we won't have access to direct messages, but it will give us a picture of her life."

"I've got a list of her friends' names. I got it when we still thought she was missing. Have you ever had to do that before?" Wallace flipped through the papers on his desk, then started writing a new list on a notepad.

"A few times. It works about seventy-five percent of the time. For anyone under twenty-five or so, it's a great place to start when other leads are slow to turn anything up. On Instagram, Snapchat, and TikTok in particular, you'd be surprised by the number of details you can get by just looking at the backgrounds and locations of pictures or videos."

She stepped around behind his desk so he could also see the posts on Dillon's account. Most of them were random... quotes from athletes, selfies with odd filters, and pictures of heavy metal bands. But roughly every fourth or fifth picture showed Dillon with friends, and most notably, with Cassie.

One picture showed them kissing, with their lips puckered and exaggerated like fish. Another showed Cassie laughing her head off about something, and yet another showed her gazing seductively into the camera. Rebecca also viewed a picture where Dillon was with a group of four boys, kicking a soccer ball around. She recognized one of them as Isaac Smith from earlier in the day.

She scanned back up to the pictures involving Cassie and reviewed the comments. Each one had about twenty or so, meaning Dillon didn't have many Instagram followers, but the ones he did have were fairly loyal. She supposed this might be an effect of living on an island.

"Would you mind writing a few usernames down for me?"

Wallace turned to a clean page. "Not at all."

"And match them up with any names you know too." She scrolled through the first batch of comments on the picture of Cassie laughing and then of the one of her and Dillon kissing. Three girls had commented on both posts. One of the girls even tagged Cassie in her comment of *"Too stinking cute @CasLeigh00!"*

Rebecca read the names of the three girls, and Wallace jotted them down. When Rebecca read the name Amber King, Wallace grunted. "I know her father pretty well. As far as I know, they're a stand-up family."

Rebecca checked the comment thread for the picture of Cassie staring intently at the camera. This picture had gotten more comments—many from other guys who talked about how lucky Dillon was. The same three girls, including Amber King, had also commented.

To know this girl was dead and Rebecca had seen pictures of her cold, bruised neck just a few hours ago made her sad for what might have been. Who could this girl have turned into if she had a chance to grow and mature? Would she and

Dillon have made it work? Could she have been the first female president of the United States? Or an Air Force pilot? Cured cancer? An FBI agent with murdered parents and a disgraced career? That was always the most depressing part of a murder investigation. The loss of future potential.

"So now," Rebecca explained, "we go to these girls' pages to see how many pictures Cassie is in. We'll see how recent the pictures are, where they were hanging out, who was with them, and so on."

The process took twenty minutes, Rebecca eventually sitting on the edge of the desk as they went through it all. As it turned out, two of the three girls posted a lot. Sometimes as many as three pictures a day. One of the girls, Serenity McCreedy, appeared to be trying her best to become Instagram famous. She had nearly four thousand followers and posted lots of semi-provocative pictures of herself on the beach, in pools, and on boats. Rebecca had no idea how many pictures were on the girl's account but scrolling down several times only took her back three weeks.

Rebecca sighed and shook her head. "This might take a while, but I've got the names, and that's a start. I'll dig through the posts on these accounts to see what I can find. Also…would you be okay if I took records for the past few years home with me?"

Wallace turned in his chair to peer up at her. "Pertaining to what crimes?"

Playing it cool, she kept her tone light. He didn't need to know she was actually more curious about this urban legend of the Yacht Club than he wanted her to be. "Just the more serious ones. Not little misdemeanors. I want to see if there's any patterns or people I should be keeping an eye on. People don't usually jump straight to murder. They escalate from less violent crimes. Whoever we're looking for might already have a record."

He seemed to buy her excuse. "Help yourself. Only, not the originals. Talk to Viviane. I'm pretty sure we have copies of them all. Maybe even digital. She can give you codes or passwords or whatever to give you access to the database from home."

"Or whatever? That sounds very technical." Rebecca gave him a wry grin.

Wallace chuckled and went back to poking at his computer again. "The techs have been teaching me some lingo. Instagram and digital files...it's too much for this old fart. Here I was thinking Facebook was still cool."

He chuckled, but Rebecca watched his eyes go soft with desperation, an expression that briefly made its way across the rest of his face. He was an aging sheriff who was having a hard time keeping up with not only the demands of his job but the rapidly evolving tools and approaches involved with law enforcement.

She felt a little sorry for him and recalled Bailey Flynn's final comment back at the hospital. *"He's one of the really good ones, you know?"*

Getting up from his desk and taking the list of three names, she offered a smile, hoping to lift his spirits. "I'll do some digging tonight. This is where I shine. I know that sounds conceited, but it's true."

"With a case like this one, I'll take a little conceit." His expression turned serious. "See you tomorrow, West?"

It was a dismissal and question all rolled into one. "Yes. Bright and early."

With the names and Instagram pictures to look through, Rebecca headed back to the front of the building to request the digital records from Viviane.

Or whatever.

17

The few boxes that were still scattered here and there were mostly empty, so Rebecca didn't feel the least bit guilty when she neglected them in favor of a ham and cheese sandwich and *Big Bad Bigfoot Hunters* on TV. Halfway through her sandwich, she reminded herself that a trip to the grocery store needed to be in her near future.

The Bigfoot show was really on as background noise. After showering when she got home, she slid into a pair of jogging shorts and a t-shirt and made her now repetitive, pitiful meal. She wasted no time pulling out her laptop and logging into the Shadow Island SD records database. The connection was a little slow, but the succinct way the database was organized made her job much easier. It also helped that the island boasted a very low rate of crime.

A quick review indicated the bulk of entries were things like public disturbances, public intoxication, drunk driving, and other things you'd almost expect in a beach community. The majority of *those* entries came during the summer months, likely the result of vacationers looking to cut loose.

In other words, it appeared the locals were mostly well-mannered and peaceful. It seemed to be just about every policeman's dream. While the low crime rate was certainly a positive, it also meant when a seventeen-year-old girl was murdered in such a place, it was even more devastating—not only to the town but also to the police force. And when your police force was currently understaffed and stretched thin, what else could you do?

Hell, she would have done the same thing. The timing had been perfect on his end. Not that she believed herself to be some great prize—but when an infamous FBI agent essentially fell in your lap when extra resources were badly needed, it couldn't be ignored.

She did make note of the three drug-related arrests he'd made—ones she assumed had come to nothing after being passed through the courts. She looked for follow-up reports, but there was nothing. And after the third arrest from two years ago, she saw no similar reports or files.

Either the Yacht Club had been smarter or were just staying away from the island. That, or things *were* still going on, and Wallace turned a blind eye. If that were the case, Rebecca didn't agree with the call. Letting crooks get away with small crimes only emboldened them until they did something bigger.

Like murder.

The third option, of course, was that the stories of this alleged Yacht Club were just stories. Perhaps a small-town legend was simply that, a legend. Going after the Yacht Club would be like chasing ghosts. Or Bigfoot.

She was skimming through records for the current year when a knock sounded on the front door. Strange. The only person who had come to visit her so far had been Sheriff Wallace.

Was he back with a report of another missing girl? She sure hoped not.

Of course, Rebecca supposed that word had gotten out, and a few others knew where she lived by now, but the only person she had told personally was Kelly Hunt, the lady who'd been walking her dog on the beach Saturday afternoon.

Rebecca shut the lid of her laptop and walked to the door, opening it just a few inches. She was surprised to find Viviane Darby on the other side. Viviane gave a small smile, the sort that looked a bit guilty. Rebecca opened the door wider and tilted her head, curious.

"Hi, Viviane."

"Hey, Rebecca. I hope this is okay. I figured you could maybe use some company after the last few days. I know you're new in town and how hard that can be and…" She trailed off, and her eyes grew wide and had a spark of mischief. She held up two plastic grocery bags, offering another smile that showcased perfect teeth. "I have beer, chips, and salsa."

Excited by the possibility of snacks, Rebecca opened the door wider. "Then, by all means, please come inside."

Viviane did, and Rebecca winced at the mess still cluttering the floor. "I really haven't done much with the place yet. Actually, I guess this is about all I'll do to it since I'm only here for a few months."

Viviane waved her off, the sleeve of her filmy blouse rippling in the air. "No, this is great. Less clutter, more open space. It's a nice house."

Without being asked to do so, Viviane sat down on the couch where Rebecca had been sitting. She reached into one of the bags, yanked out two beers, and popped the tops on both. She handed one to Rebecca, and as she did, her eyes went to the TV. A brief flash of embarrassment rippled through Rebecca as two men in camouflage attempted to create some sort of sasquatch call.

"God, sorry about that." Rebecca cut the show off as quickly as she could get to the remote while Viviane didn't bother to hide her laugh.

"What? No! Don't be." The laugh turned into a snort. "I find those shows fascinating."

Rebecca studied the woman's face. "I don't know you well enough to know if you're being serious or mocking me."

Viviane held up a hand in a semblance of a Scout's oath. "Fully serious. I don't know that I believe there are sasquatches and yetis and all that, though. I do, however, have a slight obsession with UFOs."

For a moment, Rebecca briefly considered telling her about her own story, but then Viviane started sipping from her beer, and Rebecca did the same. When Viviane tore open the bag of tortilla chips and twisted off the metal lid to the squat container of salsa, Rebecca nearly snatched it all from her hands.

"You mind if I check out the view from the back porch?"

"Sure. Let's sit out there, actually. I've been going through records and files for a while now. I could use the fresh air."

Rebecca scooped up the food before leading the way out. Chips and salsa weren't much, but they were better than the same ole ham sandwich again.

As Viviane cooed over the outdoor furniture, Rebecca smiled. She decided she liked Viviane's level of abruptness. They'd known one another for just over a day and hadn't spoken more than a dozen sentences to one another, and she'd already invited herself over, admitted she believed in flying saucers, and was sort of acting like she lived there.

"I have to tell you," Viviane said as they settled into the chairs, "Sheriff Wallace is excited you're helping. He thought you were going to say no."

Rebecca closed her eyes and savored the garlicy hot mix of the salsa. "I'm glad the sheriff feels that way. I sort of got the impression during my time at the precinct that not everyone does."

Raised eyebrows met her statement. "Who? Me? Hell no! I'm excited too."

"Not you. I was referring to Deputy Locke."

Rebecca positioned a little wooden table between them to set the chips and salsa on.

Viviane set the remaining six pack at their feet and chuckled at the mention of Locke as she looked out to the ocean. "Well, Locke has never been the most cheerful man on the force. And he doesn't handle change well."

"Good to know. Because based on what I've experienced, I assumed he just didn't like to see a woman in a position of authority."

Viviane's shrug was all innocence until she rolled her eyes. It made Rebecca wonder how she managed to keep the skillful sweep of blue eyeshadow from smudging. "Yeah, there might be some of that in there too."

Cracking the mystery that was Viviane might take all summer, but Rebecca guessed it would be a fun pastime. Based on the brief exchange about Locke, Rebecca presumed Viviane shot straight from the hip and avoided filler bullshit whenever possible. She might be the perfect person to give her the skinny on the topic no one wanted to talk about.

"Did Wallace tell you the Yacht Club came up today?"

"He didn't." Viviane frowned and sighed, swallowing all of it down with more beer. "I bet he wasn't a fan of that, was he?"

That was putting it lightly.

"No. I thought he was going to politely tell me he'd changed his mind about wanting my help. But then, when he cooled down, he just dismissed it. He said it's sort of the boogeyman of the island."

"No one likes to talk about it because no one can control

it, if that makes sense." Viviane chewed on her lower lip, and wonders of wonders, none of the pink lipstick came off. What were these jedi skills? "We're just a pissant little town on an island. Any complaints we make that go to the mainland don't really mean much. And Wallace has never been good at dealing with that. It's almost like it hurts his pride."

"But the club is a real thing?"

Viviane threw up her hands, causing the layers of bracelets to clink together. "I can't prove it's a real thing, but I believe in UFOs, remember, so don't take my word as gospel." She dunked another chip. "But everyone can see a bunch of big boats that pass by us, partying loudly, nearly every weekend. It doesn't take a lot of imagination to figure out what's happening on them either. But so long as it doesn't hit our shores, there's not much we can do about them."

That was an awful lot of "buts" for something Viviane seemed to believe in. "So, let's say the Yacht Club *does* have something to do with Cassie's murder. Do you think it's a hopeless case?"

Viviane thought about the question for a long while. "I don't know. We've never had a murder linked to them before. If it is, do you think the Yacht Club *is* part of it?" Viviane was leaning over in her chair as if she was about to hear some juicy gossip.

"I don't know." Rebecca swallowed the rest of her thoughts with another sip of beer and some chips. Those thoughts, though, would not be so easily dismissed. She held onto them as motivation.

I don't know if the Yacht Club is involved, but I'll find out when I catch the killer.

※

IT WAS ODD, but Rebecca thought that brushing her teeth in a bathroom she was not overly familiar with was somehow the most solidifying moment of her day—a moment when she realized she'd really come to live here for a few months.

Even when traveling for pleasure back when she'd been with the Bureau, she'd always felt that doing the simple routine over an unfamiliar sink was the most polarizing moment of being away from home. Not sleeping in a strange bed, not the peculiar colors and textures of motel carpets, but the glaring lights and too-white design of the bathrooms.

The overly sanitized white of most hotels wasn't in the Sand Dollar Shores bathroom, though the mirror showing a displaced version of herself sure was. She stared sullenly at herself as she brushed her teeth, trying to piece together the narrative that had placed her in her current situation.

Just as the chaotic timeline wound through her head, the light over the sink began to flicker. It was nothing dramatic, and the light ended up holding steady after about five seconds, but the discoloration tossed her mind back several months...a sharp reminder of the muted colors of a Washington, D.C. parking garage.

Sitting in her car, waiting for another one to arrive, all hell breaking loose once it did. She had not yet reached the point where she could think of that night and view it as if watching herself in a television program—though she hoped that would come soon. No, it all came in disjointed bursts.

The explosive sound of gunfire. Headlights bobbing as a car raced toward her, the screams of a man being crushed, the shattering car windows, and men howling in pain. The knowledge they were on the brink of death. Her gun arm failing when she needed it.

Her heart started thundering as her adrenaline spiked. She'd walked into that trap with open eyes and a willingness to do whatever it took to wrap up the case that was never a real case. And in the end, though she'd technically been victorious, she knew she'd lost something that night. More than just her ability to sleep in peace. She'd brought the men who had plotted against her father to justice despite the FBI telling her to back down.

Maybe that's why I am thinking about it now. Because I know there's something bigger going on here, but the man in charge says I'm seeing conspiracies where there's none.

What were Shadow's secrets? She needed to know.

She pushed it all away as the froth of toothpaste grew and spit swirled down the drain. But even as she walked into her bedroom and stripped out of her clothes and into her pajamas, she could still hear the phantom gunshots like faraway thunder on an invisible storm.

"Stop it. Focus on the case in front of you."

As if to cement her muttered words into action, Rebecca sat on the bed with only the bedside lamp illuminating the room and started doing another deep dive into the social media of the three girls: Amber King, Serenity McCreedy, and Nevaeh Johnson.

Within five minutes or so, she was able to ascertain that Nevaeh wouldn't be much help. While her account was fairly active, it was mostly just pictures of her siblings, the ocean, and a few snaps of food. She only popped up in group-oriented pictures when she was tagged by other people. A friend of Cassie's, but not a close one.

Amber King was another story, though. There were plenty of pictures on her account, averaging nearly two a day for the past year or so. Many of them were of friends, all of whom were pretty, tanned to a golden brown, and seemed to have no problem flaunting their bodies.

One thing Rebecca noticed about Amber's account was there were a few pictures that seemed to have been taken on expensive boats. In four of them, Rebecca could see the occasional blurred figure in the background that, to her, looked like an older man. They were never a focal point of the picture but seemed to be a fixture in the background.

Sure, it could have just been her family members—her father, or uncles, or older brothers—but the way she was dressed and pouting at the camera made that hard to believe.

Rebecca had saved Serenity McCreedy for last because the first glance at her account earlier had given her the impression the girl took Instagram a little too seriously. She was gorgeous without any doubt, and she had a bust size most lingerie models would pay big bucks for. Lots of her Instagram snaps showed her lounging on the beach, stretched out in a chair or by a pool, or gazing thoughtfully out to the sea.

Rebecca figured there were enough pictures on Serenity's account to keep her scrolling nearly the entire night. So, she made a decision to only look through the last two years— which was still a hell of a commitment. She figured any earlier than fifteen, and hopefully, Serenity wouldn't have been posting such provocative pictures.

It turned out, though, she didn't need to look that long. Within twenty minutes, Rebecca came across something that caught her eye. The picture showed Serenity on a boat with a few other girls. Like a few of Amber King's photos, there were out-of-focus men in the back. She could almost see the face of one, but his head was turned away. The caption read: *Best of friends, best of times, best of EVERYTHING! #YachtClub #summervibes*

In any other town where Rebecca had not heard a phrase like "Yacht Club" used with such hushed secrecy, she might have thought nothing of the hashtag. But as it stood, she'd heard too much and was starting to form a very specific idea of what the so-called club might entail.

She clicked on the hashtag, knowing it was a long shot,

and got pretty much what she expected. There were pictures from boating enthusiasts all around the world, from sailboats to yachts. There were a few people simply partying on various sized vessels, most of them older. She backed out of the search and refocused her efforts on Serenity's profile again. After scrolling for another half an hour, she found four more posts she'd hash-tagged with *Yacht Club*.

As Rebecca dug further, Serenity McCreedy seemed like a decent lead. She had to remind herself, though, this was not a case where she was trying to get to the bottom of the inner workings of some rapey party run by rich older douchebags. No, she was trying to find out who killed Cassie Leigh.

But the deeper she dove into it, the case seemed to suggest the two might be linked much tighter than she'd assumed. If both of her friends were involved in the club, then Cassie had to at least know about it. What would a naïve good girl, as everyone had said she was, do if she learned about something illegal happening where her friends were hanging out? So far, there was no known motive for her death, after all.

It was nearly one in the morning when Rebecca finally turned out her lamp. She thought images of Serenity McCreedy or Cassie Leigh would be flickering through her mind, but she was wrong. She was still thinking of that parking garage, still hearing the gunshots...and they followed her down into a restless sleep.

18

Worry started to settle in, eerily similar to bee stings, all in my gut. It had seemed so easy at first—too easy. A dead girl found in the marshes was going to be news, sure. But in this town, on this island, I figured that, with no hard evidence, her death would be linked with the Yacht Club, and that would be that.

The cops would ask a few questions, then sweep everything under the rug, as usual. Because Lord knew that no one on this island wanted to dig too deep into the Yacht Club. What I'd done wasn't exactly kosher, but those guys were the next level. Younger girls and worse crimes...for years.

But something had shifted. Something was different.

Sheriff Wallace was pushing to get this case solved. I'd never had anything against the man, but no one around the island respected him as an authoritative figure. He was an old man with a badge and a gun, who led the holiday parade once a year. I couldn't help but wonder if this new woman on the force might have something to do with his dedication to this case.

Whatever had caused it, it had me spooked. I didn't

usually worry, so this was new to me. *Is this paranoia, or just me overthinking things?* I couldn't seem to shake the feeling that perhaps I wasn't as thorough as I'd originally thought.

Maybe there were footprints left behind. Or maybe some scrap of paper or fabric or god knew what else might tie me to her death. I knew my house was clean. Nothing there to be found. I'd gotten damn good at hiding things there and cleaning up. But that was where I had full lighting and knew the setting.

That was all I could think about. I waited until midnight, walking alone in the dark. I'd brought a spotlight so I could search for anything I might have left. Not that I could use it without being seen.

By whom?

That was the crazy part.

In my gut, it felt like everyone was watching.

People in houses and cars, or even the cargo ships or freight liners out on the ocean seemed to have their eyes on me. It was a stupid thought, I knew, but I couldn't shake the feeling that my every move was being watched.

I know what you did.

I shuddered. The text had me spooked.

"Stupid." My own voice scared me even worse. Raspy and weak.

When did this happen? When did I become such a nervous wreck? Taking someone else's life should have made me stronger, a little less prone to being scared over every little thing. But in my case, the exact opposite seemed to be true. Since that day, I had been second-guessing everything. Would a guilty man say this? Would an innocent man do that?

I ducked under the crime scene tape. The tall grass of the marshes sat listlessly in the moonlight, and the sound they made when I stepped through them reminded me of someone leafing through newspaper pages. As I got closer to where I killed her, my legs wobbled a bit, and my fingers curled into loose fists.

Someone had been there recently. There were indentations in the tall grass, divots that appeared to be circling the area where Cassie and I experienced our last moments together. Had Wallace and his lady consultant come back after all the forensic people went away? Had they returned to searched for any traces of me? The thought sent chills down my spine.

What if they'd already found something that proved it had been my fingers around Cassie's neck, and they were waiting for the right moment to come knock on my door and haul me off?

The thought lodged in my head before I could stop it, and I was equally terrified and furious all at once. The anger was interesting because it was directed at myself, at Cassie, and at Wallace. If we wanted to talk semantics, it was really all Cassie's fault. I'd had no real choice that night. What the hell had she expected me to do? How was I supposed to react? She was the one who had messed everything up.

A breeze kicked up, coming off the ocean. The salty wind was soothing while the grass of the marshes leaned toward me, almost as if trying to wrap me up.

I took out my cell phone, deciding on the smaller light instead of the one that would point out my intrusion where no innocent man should be. Still, I ducked down low, so low that my head would be hidden by the tall marsh grass. I clicked the flashlight on, keeping it close to the ground in the hopes that no one looking out of their windows would see the glow and wonder about it.

Even as I scanned the area, I knew it was a lost cause. It was too dark, and the soft, mucky ground would make any sort of search a waste of time. The soft mud had been churned up, stirred around, and was full of tiny bugs that reflected the light back at me. Sparks danced on the water with miniscule waves as the skimmers and mosquitos danced about looking for prey, scattering the light and obscuring everything.

Even after just one evening, I couldn't even make out the footprints in any of the areas where the grass showed so many people had been walking. Hopefully, Wallace and his new sidekick had the same issues. I turned the flashlight off on my phone and stood upright, reassured that my secret was safe. No sooner had I started back toward firmer ground than another thought jumped into my head. A thought I sure as hell wished I'd had about half an hour ago.

You idiot. What if you made things worse by coming out here? What if you left something this time? Hair, fabric, maybe a nice solid footprint in the muck?

The nerves got so bad that I started to shake. I took my time leaving, sliding my feet in the muck and walking on the grass clumps when I could. Anything I could think of doing to hide my tracks or at least obscure them. I was trembling as I left the marshes and kept it up as I walked along the edge of the beach.

The long walk home had never seemed so lonely or with so many eyes watching than it did that night.

I know what you did.

What excuse could I give if someone saw me out here? Midnight stroll on the beach? Sure. Why not? It had worked before.

When I arrived at my own house, the fear abated slightly but was still there. Even when I went through the back door —which I'd disarmed upon leaving the house—and passed unnoticed into the kitchen, it was still there.

I'd accepted what I did. I killed a beautiful young woman.

I took a life. Deep down in my soul, this knowledge hurt. But really, she hadn't given me a choice.

This was what echoed in my head as I took my boots off and tossed them in the back of the coat closet. I'd have to deal with the muck later, but I didn't have the time to do it now. Silently, I walked through the kitchen and living room, heading straight to the stairs.

I took each one carefully, avoiding the boards I knew would creak. I headed straight for the bathroom, closed the door, and turned the lights on. A quick once-over showed no mud or dirt on my arms or in my hair. I wiped myself off, just in case. A shower was out of the question as that would be too loud.

Stripping down, I placed my clothes in the laundry basket. I rummaged through it a bit, placing tonight's somewhere in the middle to keep them hidden. Just in case.

When I slid into bed wearing only my boxers, my mind was still back out in the marshes going over every step I had taken, there and back.

Did I leave any traces? Would anyone check in the morning and notice someone had been there? Had the neighbors seen me?

The same worries I had tried to appease by going out tonight continued to chant in my head as I pretended to sleep.

I know what you did.

19

Alden Wallace woke with a sigh and rolled over to face the bedside table. Even before his eyes fell on the blurry numbers of the digital clock, he knew it would be somewhere between two o'clock and two-thirty in the morning. When his eyes settled in and adjusted, he read the numbers: 2:21.

Told ya, his bladder seemed to say.

This had been going on for the last five years or so. Without fail, every single morning, he'd have to wake up to take a piss. As far as he knew, it was just one of the few minor signs that he was officially old. That was fine with him.

As a man in moderately good health—some high blood pressure and his doctor mentioned he needed to exercise more—he was fine if an early morning leak was the worst of his problems. People much younger had been taken for things much worse.

He crept out of his bedroom and down the short hall to the bathroom. He did his best not to think as he took a leak because he knew if he got his mind going, he'd never get back to sleep. It was difficult to do most nights, though. Being the sheriff of a small town wasn't too taxing of a job on most days, but there were days occasionally that kicked his mind into gear the instant his eyes opened, no matter what time it was.

This had started before the nightly pee. It had been an issue almost immediately after his wife died. He'd wake up to that strange empty space on the other side of the bed and torment himself with memories of his life with her. Even worse were the nights when he'd get stuck wondering about the things that had not yet happened.

He had planned to take her to Spain because she'd always wanted to go to Barcelona. He'd fully intended to do it too. But of course, life had other ideas.

Tonight, unsurprisingly, his thoughts turned to the Cassie Leigh case. Being half-asleep and stumbling back to bed, it was easier to admit this case had rocked him more than the handful of other serious crimes he'd been involved with since taking the role of sheriff. He wasn't sure if it was because she was so young or because he was admittedly a bit understaffed at the station at the moment. Whatever the reason, it had rattled him—and he was damned glad Rebecca West had come along when she had.

He was glad to have her help, and he could already get a pretty good read on the sort of law enforcement official she was. She was determined, almost to the point of being stubborn. But what surprised him and made him enjoy working with her was the fact she did not take herself too seriously. She asked questions when she didn't know the answer rather than wasting time to find it on her own. She was also not robotic and monotone in her conversation. And most importantly, she didn't look down on him, the lowly small-town sheriff, just because she had eight years of experience with the FBI.

He did have to admit, though, that it was her time with the FBI that had him concerned. While he was quite sure not everyone in town knew about her presence, and certainly not about her involvement in this case, it wouldn't be much longer before word had spread through the island.

Nothing spread faster in a small town than gossip. Wallace believed she had done the right thing back in D.C., but she may have gone a bit too far. Working out a series of events that had resulted in a deadly shoot-out in a parking garage was the sort of event to make its way into dinner conversation. It was yet another example of that determined streak he had noticed in her.

Justice would be served, no matter who it took down...or how.

And with that thought, he knew he was not going to be able to get back to sleep.

That kind of blind justice was both thrilling and terrifying. Not that it mattered. She would be off the force soon enough. Once the Leigh case was closed, that would be it.

Ah, but what if she stayed?

It wasn't the first time the question had crossed his mind, but it seemed a lot more concrete as the digital numbers on his clock ticked closer to three in the morning. The idea of Rebecca staying on the island seemed ridiculous, but at the same time, he assumed there was *something* about the place that had lured her back following a traumatic course of events. It was a tantalizing thought, for sure.

He couldn't help but wonder what the inclusion of someone like Rebecca West would do for his little department. Of course, it would look good in terms of public perception just because there would be a female on the force for the first time in its history. But Alden was more interested in the skills she brought to the table—her keen instincts, political savvy, and her Bureau experience. Maybe it was time things changed around here. Consequences be damned.

He couldn't help but wonder what she'd say if he offered her a job. How long it would be before the other officers on the force would start to complain about Rebecca. The only person he was really worried about was Locke.

Locke had a set of values that, even to Wallace, seemed a little outdated. He was a good officer and friend, but he seemed to be about a decade behind everyone else in the office in terms of tolerance and manners.

As for Hoyt Frost, he wasn't too sure. Hoyt was one of those guys who liked everyone he met...eventually. In fact, he was similar to Rebecca in that he could be a little too determined at times—a trait that often evolved into stubbornness for his friend.

Hopefully, this Cassie Leigh case would be wrapped before Hoyt came back to work. He and Rebecca may very well hit it off, but Alden would much prefer the case be solved before Frost returned.

Let's just wrap up this Cassie case first.

20

Rebecca arrived at the precinct early, a little after seven. The only other person who had reported to work for the morning shift was Viviane Darby, but when Rebecca arrived, she was on the phone.

From what Rebecca could gather, Viviane was speaking to a woman trying to file a complaint against a neighbor because their dog seemed to enjoy urinating into her bougainvillea. Rebecca waved a quick hello as she made her way back to Wallace's office. As per usual, the door was opened, even though the sheriff was not yet in.

Instead of sitting around waiting, she spent the next several minutes getting ready for the day. She helped herself to a cup of coffee from the old-school percolator in the small breakroom and started making a list of the things she wanted to get done. Normally, she wasn't a list-maker, but without a list or solid plan to go by, working with Sheriff Wallace might become a bit difficult.

While she wouldn't go so far as to say he was being lack-adaisical about this case, he did seem to meander from point to point and topic to topic as if on a whim. As she typed up a list on her phone, she was surprised to find she rather enjoyed it. It made her think, even if only briefly, of her father.

Dad had always made lists for just about anything he could manage: music to take on family road trips, movies he wanted to see over the summer, chores that needed to be done around the house, vacation destinations for the family to choose from, and on and on.

As she typed the last few entries on the list, she heard Wallace come in. Viviane was apparently off the phone by then because she could hear them talking. Viviane lowered her voice to a whisper because only the hiss of words made it to Rebecca's ears, not the words themselves. Rebecca assumed it was Viviane letting the sheriff know Rebecca was already in for the day.

When Wallace appeared in the doorway, he smiled widely. He looked tired, as if he had not slept well, but the smile suited him. "You look like you could manage a desk… maybe even an office like this."

She laughed. "Oh, I had my fair share of desk-riding in the Bureau. It doesn't really suit my personality."

Wallace took a seat behind his desk. The old chair creaked as he reclined back in it a bit. He seemed to not mind that she'd more or less made herself at home. "You're in early. You got something to go on?"

"Not particularly. But I do have a list of things I want to investigate today."

He nodded, still smiling. "You don't strike me as the sort to make lists and keep them."

"That's a good gauge of character. I'm *not* that sort. But I'm also not the sort to sit still, so the result is sometimes a weird tilt toward organization and order." She went back to the work on her phone but not so much as to dismiss Wallace.

"How long is the list?" He leaned over to examine it more closely.

"Seven items deep."

"What are the most pressing two items?"

She skimmed the list and found it was an easy decision. "Last night, I did a deep dive on the social media accounts of those girls we dug up yesterday. I'd like to interview them. One of them used a hashtag to call out the Yacht Club."

He grunted at that, and she wasn't sure if it was because she'd brought up the club again or because he didn't know what a hashtag was. Maybe she should have said "pound" sign. "I can get on that and get those numbers for you. What else?"

"Have we found Cassie's car yet?"

Wallace sighed. "No. Locke is on that today. I might even ask Greg to drive around and look for it."

This was a good plan but was likely to bite her in the butt later. It was such a menial task that Locke would probably take it poorly that he was assigned to do that while she was off doing other things. Maybe there was a way to make it sound more important.

Before she had a chance to suggest that, Viviane showed up holding a small square box. Even with the top closed, the scent of doughnuts made Rebecca's mouth water. All other thoughts slid out of her mind as her stomach reminded her she hadn't eaten since that bag of tortilla chips last night.

Viviane smiled, pretending not to notice the growling, and placed the box on the edge of Wallace's desk. "Morning delivery."

"Thanks." Wallace popped the top open to reveal what may have been the fluffiest doughnuts Rebecca had ever seen. He offered the box to her, and she took what she hoped was jelly filled.

"There's something else that's been sticking out to me."

Rebecca spoke around the fluffy pastry with just a hint of raspberry filling. "We know Cassie was strangled, and her clothes were in disarray. We still don't know where she was before then."

Wallace chewed on a plain glazed donut, nodding. "And if she was running, that brings up the question of *what* she was running from. Or who she was running from."

"Exactly. It's her clothes that's throwing me off. No bra or panties, and her dress completely unbuttoned. Have you considered she was running to someone instead? Was she maybe going there to meet with someone for a hookup? And if so, did she run into someone she wasn't expecting? Or the person she was expecting and things turned bad?"

"It's a good avenue to look down, that's for sure. The state of her dress could certainly indicate she was up to something. And if she was meeting someone out there along those marshes, it was pretty clear it was meant to be in secret. I'm assuming she was cheating on Dillon Miller and was keeping it quiet."

Rebecca wasn't pleased with how easily the sheriff had written the boy off. After all, they didn't have a precise timeline of when Cassie was in the marsh versus when Dillon left his friends. There was no one who had seen him after he supposedly headed home. If he had even gotten home when he said he had. Cassie could have been sneaking off to meet with Dillon after he'd left his friends. His messages to her were all made from his phone, so he could have been anywhere at the time. Which reminded her...

"Have we gotten a warrant for Dillon's phone yet?"

The sheriff shook his head. "Not yet."

"If that's the case, I'm hoping some of these girls I'd like to interview can prove helpful." One thing she was sure of, if Cassie had a lover, whether it was Dillon or not, the first people she would tell would be her girlfriends. And if there was no one, then they would be the ones most likely to know what she could have been doing that night.

Wallace reached to the corner of his desk and grabbed a thin stack of sticky notes where he'd written the names down the day before. "I'll start making those calls right now. I'd let you handle it, but it *is* a small town, and people are liable to freak out if someone from outside the department calls."

Even though Rebecca was technically on the department, she understood what he meant and even agreed with the idea. When asking for cooperation, it was best coming from someone they already knew and trusted. "I completely understand."

"Well, then...have a seat. Let's see what we can get done."

Rebecca sat in one of the chairs in front of Wallace's desk as she finished what did turn out to be a jelly donut—and a very good one, at that. She was interested to see what channels Wallace would use to get the numbers of these three girls. She was rather surprised to find that, for the most part, it wasn't too different from what she would have done at the Bureau.

He started clicking around in the station database, leaning in so close to the screen that Rebecca started to wonder just how bad his eyesight was. "I'm pretty sure Serenity got a speeding ticket a few months back. Deputy Hudson was the one to give her the ticket. He said he had a mind to give her a second ticket for all the flirting she was doing to get out of it."

After a while, he nodded and jotted something down on the same piece of paper. He continued trying the database, and after another few minutes, got another hit. "Nothing on Amber King, but there *is* this complaint her mother filed last year about kids blasting their music too late at night, going up and down their street. So, we have her number on file." He jotted it down as well.

Rebecca crossed her fingers. "And Nevaeh Johnson?"

"I've got nothing. Well...nothing on the database." He picked up his phone and placed a call. Within a few seconds, he was talking with the sort of bright and cheery demeanor that told her a familiar friend was likely on the other line. "Hey there, Greg. I didn't wake you, did I?"

Rebecca assumed he was talking to Greg Abner. She wondered if Wallace used him as a walking Rolodex of sorts —the type of older man who knew just about everything there was to know about everyone else in town.

"Good to hear," Wallace went on. "Look, I was wondering if you or anyone you might know would have Tom Johnson's number. I need to get in touch with his daughter on this Cassie Leigh case." He paused a moment, then chuckled. "No, he's not in the white pages. I already looked. He must not have a landline, like so many other people now. Yeah. Yeah, it is a shame."

Rebecca watched as Wallace nodded, making *uh-huh* noises on occasion. After about thirty seconds, he gave a boisterous, "Talk to you later, Greg," and ended the call. He smiled at Rebecca. "He'll have it for us in a minute. In the meantime, I think we should go ahead and call these first two, Serenity and Amber. I'll put it on speaker so you can hear it all."

Rebecca nodded, eyeing the box of donuts and wondering if she wanted another one. She resisted the urge as Wallace made the first call. She sat forward with bated breath as he once again spoke sunshine into the phone.

"Hey there, Mrs. King. It's Sherriff Wallace. I know it's a little early, but I need to speak with your daughter, if possible."

"I'm sorry, but she's not in right now." The woman's voice

was sharp through the speaker. "Can I ask what this is in regards to?"

"Sorry to say, I need to ask her some questions about Cassie Leigh. Could you have her call me when she gets in? Being underage, you may want to be part of the call too. In fact, if you can call her cell and tell her I need to speak with her right away, that would be great."

"Yes, of course, I can do that. Should I have her come here, to the house?"

"Yes, if that's okay."

"Of course." The woman's voice softened. "She's devastated by the loss, so I'm sure she'd be more than happy to speak with you."

Wallace nodded and gave Rebecca a little wink from across the desk as he ended the call. He didn't fight the urge Rebecca had beaten down and reached into the box of donuts for a second one. He held it a few inches from his mouth. "West, what are your thoughts on donuts without coffee?"

It seemed like an out-of-the-blue question, but then again, she was starting to understand that Wallace was an out-of-the-blue fellow. "I'm not for it."

"Same here. Come on. I'll take you out for the best cup of coffee on the island while we wait to hear back from Amber King."

Rebecca felt there were more productive ways to spend that time, but she also wanted to respect Wallace's wishes. She followed him out of the station, hoping the day would somehow turn out to be much more fruitful than the morning had been.

21

When Rebecca and Wallace arrived at Bean Tree Coffeehouse, Rebecca experienced one of those moments when it felt as if the universe was aligning perfectly just for her. She'd experienced it before when certain aspects of a case just seemed to fall right at her feet.

Was that happening now?

Rebecca, who wasn't quite sure if she believed in the universe owing anyone a damn thing, liked to think that coincidences just happened sometimes—and often to those who needed their convenience.

Moments after she and Wallace had stepped in line at the counter, Wallace nudged her with a sharp elbow. "See the girl sitting behind us and to the right? The one who's all alone and looking at her phone?"

Rebecca had conducted a discreet stretch and spotted the girl in question. Wearing a long-sleeved t-shirt and khaki shorts, the girl was deeply tanned and wore her brown hair in a cute ponytail. "Yeah. What about her?"

"That's Nevaeh Johnson."

Which was the moment Rebecca was flooded by the *universe is aligning for me* feeling.

Rebecca blinked. "Are you serious?"

"I am."

Rebecca caught him smirking, and once caught, he chuckled and shrugged. "A teen out this early on summer break, they're either here or at the beach. This is easier to canvass, but they really do have the best coffee."

She grinned. Maybe this encounter was less about the universe at work and more about a clever sheriff being sneaky.

It didn't matter. She'd take the opportunity to speak to the girl either way.

When the woman ahead of them took her time making her decision on her drink of choice, Wallace gave Rebecca a frustrated grimace and stepped out of line. Rebecca followed, knowing that the opportunity was indeed too good to pass up. Of course, none of the questions here could be used in any legal sense, but maybe a casual conversation would lead them to conduct a more formal interview in a controlled environment.

Wallace wasted no time. "You're Nevaeh Johnson, right?"

The girl's eyes went wide as she nodded with a hesitancy Rebecca couldn't blame her for experiencing. "Yes, sir."

"Nevaeh, this is Rebecca West. She's a former special agent with the FBI who is helping to figure out who murdered Cassie." Rebecca noticed that Wallace made a point not to seem too authoritative. He used that same calm and reassuring tone she was coming to like so much. "I was hoping you'd give us just a few minutes to speak with you. Maybe just ask a few questions."

"Oh. Um...yeah. Sure." Nevaeh frowned and started to lightly thumb the plastic lid on her coffee cup, obviously nervous in spite of Wallace's gentle approach. "FBI? This must be pretty serious." She blushed a bright pink. "I mean, I know murder is serious and all, but…" She clamped a hand over her mouth, tears shimmering in her eyes.

Rebecca offered a gentle smile. "We know what you meant, so no worries."

Wallace took a seat on the other side of the table. There were four chairs, so Rebecca took the one next to him.

"You're right…it *is* serious." Wallace tapped his knuckles on the table. "There have been no hard clues yet, and I'm hoping Deputy West can help wrap this before it stretches on. Nevaeh, would you happen to know where Serenity McCreedy and Amber King might be?"

Nevaeh glanced at her smartwatch. "Amber is actually supposed to be meeting me here. But I think Serenity had one of her modeling interviews."

This tweaked Rebecca's curiosity. "Modeling interviews?"

"Yeah. Serenity has been invited to two different modeling agencies and some sort of school. She's being flown to New York in like three weeks for one of them."

Seemed the girl's Instagram habit had paid off.

Just then, the door opened, and another teenager walked in. Rebecca knew without even asking or getting confirmation that this was Amber King. She'd spotted the girl in a few of Serenity's Instagram pictures.

Nevaeh turned and greeted the young woman with a hesitant smile and a shrug. The shrug seemed to say, *Sorry… didn't know the cops would be here.*

Wallace's smile was welcoming as he gestured to the seat beside Nevaeh. "Ms. King, have a seat, please. We were just asking Nevaeh some questions about Cassie."

"Oh." With wide blue eyes, Amber glanced at her smartwatch. "Well, I have to be quick, because Dad told me I needed to hurry home. I was just coming by to grab a coffee and tell Nevaeh I couldn't stay."

Wallace nodded with a grandfatherly dose of sympathy. "Any reason you two were meeting up?"

The girls shared a glance, but there was nothing guilty in it. More reassuring and comforting than anything else. "We haven't had a chance to really talk ever since Cassie was...found."

Nevaeh sniffed, and Rebecca studied the perfectly done makeup, and how little it hid the red eyes. Looking closely, she could see the puffy bags both girls were sporting. The clear skin and smiles were all a façade to hide the pain they were both in and trying not to show.

"We decided we were going to try to be normal today. Ever since it happened, we've been getting hounded by people asking about Cassie or wanting to talk about Cassie, wanting to know what we know about Cassie." Nevaeh dabbed at the corners of her eyes with her fingers. "We just wanted a break. To go back to how it had been before all of this happened. But that's obviously not going to work."

Rebecca empathized with the young women. She knew exactly how they felt. That longing to go back to how it had been before their worlds had changed for the worse. She also knew there was no going back, no matter how much they tried or how hard they pretended. There was only one way to get past it, and that was time. Not even justice could make things right again.

With a long sigh, Amber finally took a seat next to her friend and eyed Wallace and Rebecca with a timid sort of fear. "I'd rather help you guys find out who did this. My parents are terrified something else is going to happen. They've been beyond helicoptering at this point."

Again, Wallace wasted no time but also somehow managed to not come off as pushy. "We need to find out a bit more about Cassie's personal life." He held up both hands. "Now, I don't expect you to just offer up big, juicy secrets that aren't relevant. But we do need to know about anything you might feel could have contributed to what happened to her. Do you understand?"

Rebecca leaned forward. "Even if you're not sure the information will be useful, please go ahead and share it. You never know what tidbit will create a connection that'll help solve a case."

Both girls nodded, and after several seconds went by, Nevaeh started to talk. She didn't seem too sure of herself, a trait girls who were usually spoken down to by their parents often possessed. "That's just the thing. Cassie wasn't really the kind to keep secrets. Sure, she wasn't perfect or anything, but I don't even know if she *had* secrets to keep."

"Well, let's start with Dillon Miller." Rebecca waited until she had the girls' full attention. "He was her boyfriend, right?"

Both girls nodded, though Rebecca was pretty sure there was the smallest bit of doubt in Amber.

"And from what we can tell, they were happy. Is that right?"

"For sure." Nevaeh smoothed a hand down her long ponytail. "And I guess you have to wonder if it was Dillon, but I'm pretty sure it wasn't."

"Same here." Amber picked at her bright green fingernail polish. "Dillon is a really good dude. I mean, he has a temper, but I think that's true of just about any boy."

Rebecca wasn't about to let that comment slide. "What do you mean by temper?"

"He was protective, you know?" Amber shrugged. "He'd get really crabby when guys looked at Cassie the wrong way. He was also really competitive. Even at board games and things like that, he'd sort of lose it a bit. I don't know that I ever saw him lose his temper around Cassie, though. Or, if he did, it was never *at* her."

Rebecca and Wallace shared a look, and the sheriff passed her a small notepad he'd pulled from his pocket. She took both the pad of paper and his small nod as permission to more or less take over, so she did.

"Were Cassie and Dillon having sex?"

Everyone at the table's mouths fell open at the abruptness of the question. Rebecca let it hang in the air for a while. Girls talked, and Rebecca knew this group of friends wouldn't be an exception.

"Well, I don't...I mean. I think they were doing stuff. But—"

Amber held up a hand, annoyance flashing across her pretty features. "Look...none of us have gone all the way, okay? Or...look, we're not sluts, okay? And yeah, it's like, Dillon's cute and all, but Cassie wasn't dumb."

"Right." Rebecca changed the subject with a mental eye roll. "Girls, I know Serenity is pretty big on Instagram. Nevaeh, you already mentioned how those talent agencies are after her. But one thing I noticed while looking through her Instagram account was that she hash-tagged the phrase *Yacht Club* a few times. Now, I've only been in town a few days, but this club has popped up before. Do either of you know if Serenity is actively involved in it?"

Both girls looked alarmed. But Amber leaned forward almost right away. "She isn't like a member, but she does get invited to parties with them sometimes."

Finally, something solid on the local legend. "Did Cassie ever get invited to these parties?"

"I don't know." Amber looked to Nevaeh to see if she had a different answer, but she didn't. "I'd be surprised if she didn't, though."

"Why's that?"

Again, the girls shared a look. Nevaeh got a bit stone-faced, as if she no longer wanted to talk. Amber, though, seemed almost anxious to spill the beans—as if she'd been looking for a reason to discuss it for quite some time.

Her voice was barely above a whisper. "Because I've been invited before. And if I've been invited, I know damn well Cassie had been."

"And who invited you?" Rebecca noticed Wallace was now sitting sternly forward. She knew she was asking questions that went deeper than anyone typically asked about the Yacht Club. He seemed just as interested as she was in what the answer might be, but he also looked irritated. She wondered how much longer he was going to let her press in on this.

"I don't know his name, but I'd seen him around the island a few times. Maybe in his early thirties. A really good-looking guy."

"And he just asked if you wanted to go to a Yacht Club party?"

"Not quite." Amber raised a shoulder. "I was working at Dewey's as a waitress, and on his way out, he slipped me his phone number and a fifty-dollar bill as a tip. He said there was a way I could make an easy five hundred dollars if I wanted. He said I just needed to come to a party with him. When I told him no, he asked me, 'Don't you know about the Yacht Club?' And I just shook my head and walked away. My parents would kill me if they ever found out I went to one of those."

Rebecca scribbled the information in the notepad. "How long ago was this?"

Amber frowned at the wall for a few moments before shrugging. "Three months ago, maybe."

"Can you tell me what goes on during these parties?"

Nevaeh stuck her finger in her mouth, pretend gagging. "It's gross. Older guys drooling over girls, giving them booze and drugs, spending money on them, and hoping to get lucky. I think most of the time, it's really just like a strip club. Nothing really happens, you know. But sometimes...I mean, based on rumors I've heard, I'm sure there's more going on. Everyone says so."

So, she didn't actually know. Rebecca had expected as much and knew the questions she needed to ask but also knew it might be tricky with teenage girls. Gossip was one thing, but gossiping about something potentially serious was a completely different story. But if Serenity had been to one of the parties, her friends would surely know.

"You're sure Serenity isn't more closely associated with the club?"

Nevaeh wrapped her arms around herself, physically distancing herself from the question while Amber leaned forward. "I really don't think so, but I'm pretty sure her boyfriend is."

Nevaeh's eyes widened, and she shot Amber a look that practically screamed at her to shut up. But Amber had started, and she turned her face away from Nevaeh, refusing to be stopped. Apparently, the dam had been released, and much more was going to come out.

"She doesn't let everyone know it, but she's unofficially dating this thirty-two-year-old guy who lives in Norfolk. He's like a banker or an accountant or something."

"And how old is Serenity?"

"Seventeen." It was Nevaeh who answered this time, and she sounded sick.

"Is she with him a lot?" Rebecca asked, already aware that any sexual relationship between the two could be considered a crime.

"Well, Serenity drives to Norfolk at least one night each week, and he'll sometimes come pick her up on the weekends."

Wallace had apparently heard too much and couldn't stay quiet any longer. "Do her parents know?"

Amber looked appalled. "God, no. And, like, this is confidential, right? We can't be the town tattletales."

"Everything you tell me stays between us." Rebecca placed her hand over her heart. "That's a promise. But based on what you girls know about this guy, does he treat her well? Any abuse of any kind?"

Amber stifled a laugh. "Um, no way. He's always buying her things and sending these sappy texts."

As if a man in his thirties having a sexual relationship with a minor wasn't already abuse. But of course, these girls wouldn't see it that way. And likely wouldn't until they were older. Keeping the disgust out of her tone, she continued the interview. "Would you happen to know his name?"

Both girls went quiet, and it was Nevaeh who gave Rebecca an uncertain, almost guilty glance. "I don't want Serenity to get into any trouble."

"I don't see why she would. At this point, this may not even be a real lead. If anything, I just want to eliminate the Yacht Club from this investigation."

"I've only ever heard his first name." Nevaeh shot a questioning look at her friend, furrowing her brows as she tried to remember. "It's Chris something."

"Same here. I don't know that she's ever said his last name around us."

"Do you think you could—"

Rebecca's phone interrupted her question. She almost ignored it so she could finish speaking with the girls, but with this case having so many threads weaving all over the place, she thought it might be risky to miss a call. She checked the caller display and noted a local area code.

Shit.

"One second, ladies." Rebecca stood and moved to an empty corner of the building. "This is...this is Rebecca." She'd almost answered with, *this is Agent West.* It was funny how just a few days of investigative work had her feeling like an agent again.

"Hi, Ms. West. This is Bailey Flynn, the medical examiner."

Rebecca's pulse thrummed with hope that the M.E. might give them their first big break. "Hi, Dr. Flynn. Is everything okay?"

"Well, I've made a discovery over here that may change the trajectory of your case."

Never one for drawn out theatrics or dramatics, Rebecca gripped her phone tighter. "And that is?"

"It seems Cassie Leigh was approximately twelve weeks pregnant at the time of her death."

Pregnant.

Cold lightning skipped through Rebecca's body. More blood in the soil.

If this was true, it changed the entire face of the case. And everyone who thought they knew Cassie was wrong. "You're certain?" She lowered her voice, already knowing the answer.

There was a slight pause on the other side of the line, and Rebecca hoped she hadn't insulted the woman. "One hundred percent. As sad as it sounds, the evidence is solid."

Or maybe the woman was working to keep her voice professional. Evidence? How big was a twelve-week-old fetus? She really didn't want to know. The thought of that being stored in an evidence locker on a microscope slide? A petri dish? Rebecca tried to push those thoughts from her mind as the smell of breakfast pastries turned her stomach.

"Okay. Thank you, Dr. Flynn."

She ended the call and ignored the girls completely as she got herself back under control again. Cassie had been adding skeletons to the closet. And if her friends were to be believed, she was very good at keeping secrets. What else were they going to find out about this young woman before the case was over?

If working Rebecca's own parents' murder had taught her anything, it was that no one truly knew anyone else. Everyone kept pieces of themselves hidden from the world. It took a lot of digging and asking different people to find out what the whole truth was, if that was even possible. As she headed back to the table, Wallace was frowning. He had apparently seen her surprise at the news.

"What is it?"

"It can wait."

The worry line between Wallace's eyes deepened, but he nodded. "All right."

Cassie had probably known she was expecting. Twelve weeks. Around the same time Amber was invited to the party.

Rebecca cleared her throat and schooled her features back into a gentle smile. "Amber, can you tell me more about the guy who invited you? Do you still have his number? And do you know of anyone else Cassie might have been involved with?"

Amber was already shaking her head. "Dillon was everything to Cassie. She would doodle her name but with his last name on her notebooks. If she wasn't at home, she was at his house. A few times I'd call her, and she'd be waiting at his house for him to show up when he was out with his friends. She was devoted. As for the guy, I tossed his number that night at work. Sorry." She brightened, sitting straighter. "But I do remember what he looked like, if that's any help."

The sheriff brightened too. "Do you think you could come down to the station and help us make up a sketch of him?"

Looking slightly ill, Amber nodded. "Do you think he had something to do with Cassie getting killed?"

"I'm not sure, but it's better to have too much information instead of not enough." Rebecca tried to smile reassuringly at the girls. She wasn't as good as Wallace at making herself seem harmless with his good ole boy grandpa smiles. "It doesn't have to be right now."

Amber rolled her eyes. "My parents are going to freak out so hard. They're never going to let me have another summer job."

Sheriff Wallace patted her on the back. "I'll tell your dad you may have seen a person of interest in this case. We don't need to tell him about the offer or the number. Or if you'd rather, you don't have to tell him at all. It's up to you, legally speaking."

Rebecca glanced at the sheriff, wondering if that was technically true. She wasn't an expert on the fine details of the law in this state.

Amber, however, didn't seem bothered at all. "That could work. Yeah. But I have to run now. Before he sends the cops to come get me and..." She dropped her head in her hand. "Sorry."

Nevaeh bit back a giggle. "Foot in mouth syndrome at work."

Rebecca couldn't manage a laugh with the autopsy results weighing so heavy on her mind, but she did give an amused smile as she stood. "We wouldn't want that. Cops can be so annoying."

And she was about to go prove that by breaking a young man's heart. Either by proving he was lying or by proving his girlfriend had been lying to him.

Rebecca wasn't sure which was worse.

22

"You okay with having Amber come to the sheriff's department for the sketch without her parents?" Rebecca blew on the steaming latte she managed to snag before leaving the coffee shop.

Wallace shrugged, taking a sip from his own cup of bitter black. "Around here, anyone can give statements, including working up a sketch, at any age. We usually like to have a parent around when they're little, just to keep them focused and not get scared."

Rebecca understood the law, and she also understood that many jurisdictions avoided speaking to juveniles without their parents like the plague. It would take her a while to learn how close Wallace walked that line.

Not that she needed "a while." She would be back to being a beach bum five minutes after this case was solved.

"That makes good sense to me." And it did. "Laws like that are necessary since a kid couldn't turn their parents in for abuse or neglect with them hovering nearby."

Wallace rubbed his knuckles on the star covering his heart. "I don't like to make a habit of it, but sometimes, it's the minors that are involved, and we have to work fast. Like right now."

He opened the door and climbed into the driver's seat, turning the air conditioner on high as she got in. "So, how about you tell me what that phone call was about and why it made you want to cut the chat short when we were just getting somewhere."

It occurred to Rebecca that the sheriff had followed her lead without hesitation, and she felt a bit of pride about that. As a former agent, she was used to the locals going along with whatever she did, but here, she wasn't FBI. She was just a lowly newbie deputy, and he was the tried-and-true sheriff who had hired her without compunction despite the sordid end to her federal career.

"That phone call made me realize that Cassie's friends might not have the information we actually needed to solve her murder."

Wallace glanced over at her, keeping his eyes off the road for a little longer than Rebecca found comfortable. "Why's that?"

Rebecca waited until he'd stopped at an intersection to break the news. "Cassie was twelve weeks pregnant when she died."

She almost felt the ripple of shock that went through the sheriff, but he did an admirable job of keeping it off his face. "No shit?"

Rebecca wished that she had been joking with the older man. She detested that they were dealing with the leading cause of death in pregnant women...homicide.

It made her sick to her stomach.

"Guess you're right about Cassie's friends. The only guy they know about is the boyfriend. We need to go speak with Dillon Miller again." Wallace's knuckles were white from where he gripped the steering wheel. "We can speculate about other people all we want, but Dillon is the only one we know who was intimate with Cassie in any way. I don't think it's too out of the ordinary for a teenage boy to lie to authority figures about his sex life."

On the drive to the Miller's house, Rebecca did her best to reframe the basics of the case with this new filter in place. If Cassie was pregnant when she was killed, it changed almost everything about the investigation. And if Cassie told her baby's father, that instantly made the would-be dad a prime suspect. The main question, of course, was...who was the father?

When they arrived at the Miller residence, Dillon was outside shooting a basketball at a hoop set up at the edge of their driveway. He was making free throws in a halfhearted way, not really putting much effort or energy into it.

When Wallace pulled into the driveway, Dillon rebounded his most recent shot and watched as they parked. Though the young man appeared pale and sad, there didn't appear to be any worry on his face.

She almost felt bad for him—a seventeen-year-old kid who could very well be on the verge of having his world flipped upside down. Or a seventeen-year-old monster who was about to learn that they knew he was a killer.

Which would it be?

Wallace took the lead as they got out of the Explorer. He extended his hands, wordlessly asking Dillon to pass the ball to him. Dillon did, and Rebecca watched as Wallace hit an effortless three-pointer.

Impressive.

"Are your folks home, son?"

Dillon nodded at the sheriff, his face growing paler. "Yeah, Dad's inside working."

"I see." Wallace rested his hands on his hips, and Rebecca thought the movement was to center himself for what was to come. "Well, we have some news for you that we'll probably need to share with him after we speak with you. But I want to show you the respect you deserve by letting you know first. Between the three of us, I really should ask your dad for permission to speak with you, but I'm going to choose to ignore that for now. Okay?"

The ball fell from Dillon's hands. "Okay." The young man's breathing increased as anxiety caught him in its grips. Within seconds, he was the very definition of freaked out.

Was Wallace employing this tactic on purpose? After all, he didn't actually need to talk with his dad first, as he'd just explained to her. Was he trying to upset Dillon before they even spoke with him, bringing the kid's defenses down a bit?

Wallace scooped up the ball, holding it against his hip as he faced the young man. "Dillon, we received a call from the medical examiner today. The results of Cassie's autopsy revealed she was pregnant."

Dillon did nothing, said nothing, and for a long few moments, Rebecca was afraid the poor boy had forgotten how to breathe.

Rebecca watched him closely, searching for any micro expression that might provide the truth. That Dillon had known of the pregnancy. That he had murdered Cassie Leigh because of it.

Nothing.

Dillon finally inhaled a breath and glanced around as if he were expecting the crew of *Punk'D* to appear at any moment. He blinked just once. "Pregnant?"

Rebecca kept her gaze on the boy while the sheriff answered. "Yes. About twelve weeks."

Dillon opened his mouth to speak, but no words came out. His jaw slammed shut, and he swallowed so hard Rebecca could see it. She really hoped he wasn't about to throw up.

Stepping closer, she held her hand out in case he was about to topple over. Her kind gesture was negated by the fact that she was watching his expression, his eyes, the pulsating throb in his thin neck as his heart rate kicked into overdrive. Definitely an adrenaline rush, but was it from heartbreak or fear?

"Did you know?"

Dillon startled at her voice and shook his head violently, his hands coming up like a shield. "No. I told you before...we never did it."

Rebecca felt for the kid, but she also knew he could have been the person who squeezed the life from a beautiful young woman. She needed to press. Needed to make him snap. "Not a single time?"

"No. We did..." He scrubbed his face so hard with his hands Rebecca thought he might rip his skin off. "I mean, we did other stuff. But not that. We were both adamant about that. The risks were too great."

"You're certain? Not even the tip? Not even for a moment?"

Dillon Miller glared at Rebecca with the sort of anger that transformed him into a full-grown man. "Yes, I'm certain! I'm not an idiot." He pounded the sides of his head with his fists, and neither Rebecca nor Wallace tried to stop him. "I know how sex works. There's more than one way to get off risk-free. Nothing we did could have..." The rest of Dillon's words seemed to get stuck in his throat.

There it is.

The reality of what he'd almost said settled over Dillon, and all the rage seemed to drain from his body. Both Rebecca and Wallace stood, respectfully silent, watching as this young man's world turned upside down.

Dillon clasped his hands behind his head, his elbows

coming together to shield his face. "That means…that means she…" He dropped to his knees.

The kid was either telling the truth, or he was as skilled an actor as Rebecca had ever met.

She wouldn't put money on either.

Wallace cleared his throat and placed a hand on the young man's shoulder. "Dillon, you understand how this development could make you look more suspicious, right?"

"How?" Dillon threw up his hands and pushed to his feet. "If we weren't having sex and she died pregnant, it's pretty clear what was going on, right? What she was doing…did." Another fit of temper flashed over the boy's face as he shot a nasty glare at Wallace.

"Son," Wallace took a step closer to Dillon, "I know you're upset and—"

"Upset?" Dillon scoffed, spittle flying from his mouth. He reached into the collar of his shirt and ripped something off. Rebecca wasn't able to see the necklace closely, but it was obviously a keepsake from his girlfriend from the way he glared at it with pure disgust. Instead of throwing it like she half-expected him to, he stuffed it into his pocket. "It doesn't matter now."

Wallace glanced over at Rebecca. "We good here, West?" She nodded, and Wallace gestured toward the house, tossing the basketball into the grass. "I think we need to get your father involved, okay?"

Shoulders slumped, Dillon walked to his house and opened the front door to let them in. As he closed the door behind them, he took his phone out of his pocket and unlocked it. He handed it to Rebecca and seemed to search her face for something. Compassion, maybe? Pity?

"There's something on there I never told anyone about." His voice had gone soft again, and a single tear trickled down his face.

Rebecca took the phone from him, scanning the device for what he could be talking about. All the usual apps were there, but nothing stood out.

"One second, West." Wallace hooked a thumb over his shoulder. "I'll go get his father and fill him in."

Rebecca agreed, but it seemed Dillon was anxious to get out whatever he'd been holding in, because as soon as Wallace disappeared from the room, he turned to her.

"A few months back, this guy invited Cassie to a Yacht Club party. He did it very discreetly, and she told me about it...but no one else." He sounded nervous but, in a strange way, hopeful. Rebecca had seen this occur with a few interrogations back at the Bureau. When a secret came out after being kept for a while, the secret-keeper usually seemed to be overcome with a sense of relief from freeing their conscience of the burden.

"What happened?"

Dillon wiped his face on his shoulder. "She has this friend Serenity who sometimes goes to those parties, but Cassie didn't even tell her. I think she was afraid Serenity would feel like Cassie was stepping on her toes or something." He sank into a nearby chair. "Cassie and I fought about it because I didn't want her to go...but she went anyway."

The stirrings of a lead shot a jolt of anticipation through Rebecca. A lead not only in answer to Cassie's case but one that might unknit this disgusting Yacht Club too. "Do you know this guy's name?"

"No. She never told me. I think she was afraid I'd tell her parents or something."

Rebecca kept her voice as low as his. Clearly, Dillon didn't want his father to hear about any of this. Or was it the sheriff the young man was hiding this secret from? "Did she tell you what the party was like afterward?"

"Not really." Dillon dropped his face into his hands. "I just asked if she'd screwed anyone, and she swore she hadn't." He glanced up at her. "Probably bullshit, right?"

The question didn't need an answer, so Rebecca side-stepped it. "What did she say the party was like?"

"She said it was a lot of fun. She said Serenity showed up, and they got along really well. Had some drinks, partied, and that was it. A few days after that, though, she said she felt weird about it. She felt sort of dirty because of the age difference between the girls who had been invited and most of the guys. She got a text from someone from the party, asking her to come to another one, but she said no."

Rebecca held her breath. "And you don't have any names?"

"No. But...he texted me too."

Another jolt of anticipation shot through her, but Rebecca kept her voice low. "When?"

"About a week after Cassie stopped answering his texts." Dillon took the phone back and opened the messages. "Right here."

Dillon handed the phone back to her. There was a message opened, but no name attached, just the number of whoever had contacted him. It was an actual text message, not a messenger app like most kids used these days.

"How did he get your number?"

"I have no idea." Dillon's nostrils flared. "But now that I know what she was doing behind my back, it makes sense why the Yacht Club would want her to come hang out with them again. She did more with them than she ever did with me. If this is the guy that..." He scrubbed his face with his hands again. "You can test his DNA, right?"

Rebecca nodded. "Yes, if we can find him."

The boy's face collapsed into a mask of grief and pain. "And from...from Cassie? That will prove once and for all that I wasn't lying. I didn't get Cassie p-pregnant." His voice cracked and tears shimmered in his eyes. "I couldn't have. You can take my DNA to prove it as well."

The pain in those words tugged at her heart, and she reached out to place a comforting hand on his arm, but he shook his head, stepping back and slumping into a chair instead.

This kid was willing to offer up his DNA as proof. He was either telling the truth and had nothing to do with this or was so full of himself that he thought he could get away with cold-blooded murder. Dillon didn't look that stupid or arrogant.

Too bad she didn't have a swab to take him up on his offer right now. Of course, she would need permission from one of his parents for that. Rebecca scrolled through the messages, noticing that the incoming number was unlisted. It was a brief conversation, but the undertones said more than enough.

Unknown: *This is Dillon, right?*

Dillon: *Yeah, who's this?*

Unknown: *A friend of Cassie's. She came to my party a few weeks ago but is ghosting me.*

Dillon: *Good for her. Fuck off.*

Unknown: *Trying to be brave? I'll level with you. Your gf is too hot for her own good. I want her back at my parties. Think you can convince her?*

Dillon: *Think YOU can convince ME not to take this to the police? This is the Yacht Club, right? Those parties?*

Unknown: *I can pay you. You get her to come to another party or two and I'll give you a cut. Maybe 15%?*

Dillon: *Reporting you. Don't text me or Cassie again.*

Rebecca read each word closely, a bit surprised by the brazenness of the sender. Then again, if they'd been getting away with this sort of thing for years, it was sort of expected, she supposed. That's what happened when you didn't stop a criminal. They kept getting bolder. And more violent. Growing like a weed that needed to be ripped out of the earth before it killed innocent people in their own kitchens.

Rebecca pushed that thought—and the painful visual memory of her parents' deaths that came with it—aside and focused on the task at hand. She wondered if a basic trace would find that the sender had been using a burner phone.

From behind Rebecca, Owen Miller approached, each step a loud clomp on the tile. "What is it, Dillon?" He sounded alarmed but not angry. "Were you keeping something from us?"

Rebecca looked back to Wallace and raised her eyebrow inquisitively, hoping he understood what she was asking: *You told him about the pregnancy?*

Reading her mind, Wallace nodded just once.

Dillon bounced up from his chair, taking a step back. "Dad...I swear, we never had sex."

"I believe you." The elder Miller gestured at the device still in Rebecca's hand. "But...what's on the phone?"

"Mr. Miller," Rebecca swiped the screen back to the beginning of the messages, "Dillon was contacted by someone who was entirely too interested in Cassie. With your permission, I need to ask your son a favor."

Owen chewed his bottom lip for a moment and seemed to calm down. He shoved both hands through his hair before nodding slowly. "That's fine. If you think it will help, and if Dillon wants to."

"Yeah, I want to." Dillon lifted his chin. "What do you need?"

Rebecca didn't know if her idea would work, but it couldn't hurt to try.

"I want you to text him back. Let's see if our mystery man has anything to say."

23

Though they waited with the young man for over two hours, Dillon didn't get a return text, and Rebecca assumed one of several things could possibly be true…

The Yacht Club recruiter was the killer. Or he'd heard about the murder and was staying away from the texts to distance himself. Or he was removing himself from anything to do with Cassie because Dillon had threatened to report him.

Whatever the reason, Rebecca knew they could not waste the day sitting around the Miller home, waiting for a text that might never even come. So, leaving instructions with Dillon and Owen to contact them if the man texted back, Rebecca and Wallace left to head back to the precinct.

Wallace scratched his chin. "This is getting uglier and uglier, isn't it?"

Holding back a scoff and an eye roll so vicious it would have given her a concussion, Rebecca simply nodded. "And it's going to get uglier if you keep treating this Yacht Club nonsense with kid's gloves. I'm not so sure how much you know about my history, but things left in the dark tend to come back and bite you in the ass."

Wallace might be a good guy, but he was still a guy. He would never understand the depth and breadth of the problem. Men killing their pregnant partners was far from uncommon. Women were more likely to be killed by their partners than nearly anyone else.

This was ugly, but it was also just another day in America. Cassie was just another statistic in a tidal wave of other cases just like hers. Except on this one, this time, Rebecca could do something about it. And maybe stop other young women from falling into the same trap of trusting the men they were sleeping with.

Wallace said nothing, just kept his gaze on the road as he drove back into town. "Okay. What do you need?"

"I need help getting any reports you have related to the Yacht Club in any way."

"That's fair. However, I need you to admit the Yacht Club might be nothing more than a dead-end distraction. So far, we only have evidence that Cassie went to a single party months ago." He finally glanced over at her. "I need you to focus on this girl's murder and not a local myth."

Fat chance of that.

Rebecca's jaw tightened. "I bet there were a few Germans in the thirties who thought Hitler was a myth, Sheriff Wallace. And I bet if someone would properly dig deeper into this shit, there would be a lot more truth uncovered."

Wallace didn't respond and stayed quiet the rest of the way back to the precinct. Rebecca wanted to ask him once again how he could be the sheriff of an island town and just let an organization like the Yacht Club exist but resisted.

For now.

She understood the dangers of pissing off the wrong people, as she had experienced more than her fair share of that while working to avenge her father. She also understood how awkward it might be for a small-town sheriff to get caught up in legal matters that stretched to wealthy individuals in much larger towns. Surely, it had to be a mess.

But if even half of what they'd heard—and what Rebecca was starting to assume—about the club was remotely true, it seemed like a travesty to just allow it to happen. Her instincts made her question if Wallace was telling her all he knew.

When they got back to the precinct, Wallace pointed over to a desk in the central area. There were a few cards waiting on the desk, contained in Hallmark envelopes. There was also a stuffed stork. She assumed this was Sergeant Hudson's desk, due back from his paternity leave in a few days.

"Take Hudson's seat, and I'll bring you all I have on the Yacht Club."

Rebecca did as he asked, noticing that Viviane was the only other person in the building. Apparently, Locke was on patrol, and Greg Abner was not on duty today. If he ever was. She honestly wasn't quite sure how his schedule worked.

Viviane spun around in her chair to face her. "I'm about to make a lunch order to Mi Caretta, the Mexican place down the road. You want anything?"

Rebecca almost said no, but the idea of a taco was too much to turn down. "A few soft tacos would be great. Extra hot sauce."

Viviane gave an enthusiastic thumbs-up and turned back around to scoop up the phone. Wallace returned, carrying several thin folders in his hand. The speed in which he'd retrieved the files struck her as odd. It made her wonder if he had them sitting aside, separated from the rest of the records.

Interesting.

Maybe she was being a little too hard on him about his turning a blind eye to the Yacht Club if he had the files already placed in a separate spot. It was almost as if he'd been expecting it all to come back and severely bite him in the ass one day.

"That's everything I have from the last five years. That was when I started to think that there might actually be something to these stories. As you can see, the files aren't very thick because each instance left us with pretty much no evidence, no reports, not much of anything." He placed the folders on Hudson's desk and gave an exasperated sigh. "When you get through it all, I think you may see why I stopped wasting my time digging into the club. And you will too. Too little to go on, and no good convictions."

Though she still felt polarized about his seemingly flippant approach to the club, she also understood that she didn't know the full story. As she pulled the first folder to her, Wallace wandered back to his office. He didn't shut the door, and she was beginning to understand that he was all about open communication and transparency in the workplace.

Rebecca began to dive into the little bit of information she'd been given. Because there wasn't much to go on, she took her time with each report. There were only six folders, and from what she could tell, four of them amounted to little more than complaints being made by the public.

The most recent, from a little less than a year ago, detailed how the "bobbing lights a good distance away from the shore were creating too much noise. Loud music, extremely loud shouting of a celebratory kind, and fireworks."

Even Rebecca doubted this was the Yacht Club, though Wallace had included it with their files. A somewhat secret organization wasn't going to go around blasting loud music and shooting off fireworks. That would be *asking* for attention, and attention wasn't something the club seemed to be interested in. Unless hiding in plain sight was part of their plan.

Or they were too arrogant to care who spotted them.

She searched the other three basic complaints and found them to be a bit more serious in nature. There were two that reported very nice-looking boats pulling up to docks on the eastern edge of the island. The people who had made the complaints reported that older men had been approaching younger women in a very sexualized way.

One of the reports even called out one of the girls by name—a girl who, at the time, had only been fourteen years old. According to the report, a search had been made for the boat in question, but it had never been found. In fact, a few boats had been specifically named, but because there was no hard evidence and no crimes being committed at the time of the reports or searches, nothing had been done.

The other two files were reports of actual arrests. The first was for a fifty-three-year-old man who had been arrested on counts of attempted sex with a minor, as well as public intoxication. He spent four days in jail before his fifteen-thousand-dollar bail was paid, and he was released. The report was from three years ago, and there had been no update made to it since.

The final file was the most interesting of all, and Rebecca thought it gave a clear picture of the underlying nature of the Yacht Club. Two summers ago, a forty-one-year-old man named Hank Bulger was arrested on Shadow Island. According to the report, he'd been arrested by Deputy Locke.

Apparently, a long trail of evidence pointed directly to Bulger as a key player who was bringing drugs to the island. Also listed in the report were several other crimes he was suspected of: possession of an illegal firearm, sex with a minor, attempting to solicit sexual favors for money, and public intoxication.

Scanning the information, Rebecca couldn't see where any jail time was mentioned. In fact, on that section of the report, the only thing she found was: *All charges dropped—RE: Henry (Hank) Bulger.*

The name rang a slight bell, but it wasn't a very loud one. She pulled out her phone and opened Google, typing the name in. Bulger sounded familiar because she'd heard it in the news a few times. Edward Bulger was a senator out of Norfolk, usually a little heavy-handed on the right side of the political aisle.

Rebecca absorbed all of this for a moment. She tidied the pile of files, and as calmly as she could, walked to Wallace's office. She propped herself up in the doorframe and crossed her arms.

"Please tell me the reason you haven't really chased after the Yacht Club is because you're afraid the son of a senator is involved."

"That is *not* the reason." He gave her a disappointed look before crossing his own arms. "Well, it might be about ten percent of the reason. I'll admit that."

Rebecca threw up her hands and let them flop to the side. "So, it's only ten percent fucked up. Not bad, considering. Maybe they'll only give you ten percent of your pension after you're tarred and feathered." She shook her head, not breaking eye contact.

The sheriff's eyes narrowed. "Here's the thing, West. And you aren't going to like it, but it's the hard truth of a small town like Shadow Island. If an angry senator with a good deal of influence starts bitching, that makes the news. And for a town that relies on tourism as a huge part of getting by, that's not a good thing."

He was right…she didn't like it.

"But—"

Wallace held up a hand. "In the case of Hank Bulger, we

did indeed settle things in an off-the-books sort of way. A plea deal on lesser charges that resulted in a warning. I should point out we've never had another problem with Hank on this island. As a matter of fact, it seems his daddy shipped him away because of his little display here." Wallace gave her a smug little nod of his head.

As if getting in trouble with Daddy was a good enough punishment for a forty-one-year-old man with serious criminal charges. Sadly, it looked like politics in policing wasn't limited to D.C. or the Bureau.

Rebecca sighed. "So, it's politics?"

"No, more like image upkeep." He leaned forward a bit and gave her a look that was far too close to a father giving his daughter some difficult facts of life. "On the other hand, you're just going to have to take my word that if something came along that was hard, irrefutable evidence that the Yacht Club is one hundred percent, without a doubt doing the things people gossip about, we would absolutely get involved."

"How often does the Yacht Club show its pathetic face around here?"

Wallace lifted a shoulder. "I'd say there are at least two times a year when this damned club is discussed among myself and a few guys with the State police. We know the corruption's there, and we keep our eyes and ears open for it, but the people we're talking about have pockets deeper than the entire island."

Rebecca understood, but her sense of justice balked at it. "Any chance I could speak with Hank Bulger?"

The snort that she got in return said it all. "Doubtful. Last I heard, he was living in Louisiana. Which would rule him out in regards to the murder of Cassie Leigh. And don't forget...*that* is the case you're working on. Not trying to capsize the Yacht Club."

Rebecca didn't waver, and she didn't like the way he was speaking to her, but she knew it would be foolish to argue. For the first time, she felt the barbs of resentment. She hadn't needed to take this on—hadn't needed to agree to help. The only reason she was doing it was because the idea of someone getting away with the murder of a teenage girl pissed her off. And now that they knew Cassie had been pregnant, there was nothing else but this case.

She searched for a diplomatic way to keep the conversation going, to maybe come up with some ideas on how to get an insider's view of the Yacht Club. But before she could put anything together, her phone rang. Because the last phone call had offered up the huge news of Cassie's pregnancy, Rebecca wasted no time in taking the call.

"This is Rebecca West."

"Hey, it's Dillon. Dillon Miller."

Excitement sizzled through her veins. "Hey, Dillon. Is everything okay?"

That got the sheriff's attention. He leaned forward on his desk, but his hand reached for his hat, readying to leave.

"Yeah. But the guy…he texted me back. I would have called sooner, but we've been texting back and forth for the last five minutes."

"One second, Dillon. I'm going to put you on speaker so Sherriff Wallace can listen."

She switched the phone to speaker and set it down on Wallace's desk.

"Okay, Dillon, go on. You've been texting with this man, yes? Do you happen to know if he's aware that Cassie is dead?"

"It didn't seem that way to me. I told him I think I had C-Cassie convinced…that she was down to go to another party." Rebecca heard the doubt and heartbreak in the boy's voice.

She didn't have time to console him, though. "How did he respond?"

"He said there would be a nice chunk of cash in it for me if I could make sure Cassie shows up tonight."

Tonight? Hell yeah.

She dragged a notepad across Wallace's desk. "Shows up where, exactly?"

"Near the lighthouse."

Wallace looked alarmed as he leaned even closer to Rebecca's phone. "And you agreed to this?"

"Yes, sir. He's showing up at twelve-thirty tonight." Dillon swallowed so hard Rebecca heard the gulp over the phone. "I thought that might be helpful."

"It is, Dillon." From the worried expression still crinkling Wallace's face, Rebecca didn't need to be a psychic to know they weren't in agreement. "That was very brave."

The boy swallowed hard again. "I don't have to go, do I?"

"No, Dillon. Of course not. Sheriff Wallace and I will take it from here. Just let us know if he contacts you again. Or if anyone else does about Cassie."

Rebecca ended the call and pocketed her phone before studying Wallace's face, trying to gauge his reaction. "You don't look happy."

"It's a great opportunity for sure." He dropped his chin into his palm. "Even if the Yacht Club has absolutely nothing to do with Cassie's death, we have proof that an older man is planning to pick up a seventeen-year-old girl late at night. But still…it feels dangerous."

Rebecca only nodded. She thought of the last time she'd planned a meeting for so late at night. Her mind again conjured images of that parking garage, recalling how that night had ended. It did feel dangerous, but, like the night at the parking garage, she hoped it might help bring this entire ordeal to a close.

24

That evening, Alden Wallace made a point to show up at Hoyt Frost's house when he hoped dinner would already be over. He had nothing against Angie's cooking—she was a damn fine cook, actually—but he felt like a third wheel whenever he ate with them. Not only that, but if he was being honest with himself, it made him miss his own wife something fierce.

Luckily this time, Alden caught them just after the clean-up but accepted the beer his friend handed him. Hoyt walked past his favorite seat on the back porch and down to the little dock on the backside of the property.

The dock sat in a strange little bay-like body of water that seeped off the ocean and into what was a river in some places and swampy land in a few others—places like the edge of Hoyt's yard. They sat on the dock with beers in hand, looking out over the weeds to the creeping body of the ocean about eighty yards farther out. The sun was just starting to set, casting little orange and white crystals of light along the water.

"Rebecca West is going to get me killed." Alden was sure

there were better ways to start the conversation, but if there was one thing he valued above all else about his friendship with Hoyt, it was that he knew he could be honest and not be judged for it.

Hoyt chuckled, the sound almost like sandpaper coming from his gruff throat. "I always figured a woman would be the end of you one way or another. Care to explain?"

"She's zoned in on the Yacht Club. The moment it came up in the Cassie Leigh case, she fixated on it."

"Do you think it could have *anything* to do with Cassie's murder?"

Alden could practically feel Hoyt's gaze on the side of his face but wouldn't meet his friend's eye. "There's no strong evidence, but there *is* evidence that she was involved with the club at...at least once." He sighed and lowered his voice before adding the next bit. "It doesn't help that the M.E. told us the autopsy revealed Cassie was pregnant when she died. Twelve weeks along."

Hoyt cursed under his breath. "It wasn't that Miller kid who did it?"

"He swears up and down it wasn't. Says he's a virgin." Alden took a long sip of his beer. "Not like he'd admit to it. Kid's not dumb. Even tried to explain how what he did with her couldn't have gotten her pregnant."

Hoyt snorted. "As if accidents don't happen all the time."

Alden lifted his bottle in a silent *amen*. "Course, that don't mean it wasn't him that killed her either, whether the baby turns out to be his or not. DNA will be able to tell us for sure if he was. He's got to know that too. Jealous boyfriend with a cheating girlfriend isn't a great alibi. Then there's her trip to the Yacht Club...about twelve weeks ago."

Watching Hoyt think it all out made Alden aware of just how much he'd missed his friend. When he returned in a week, maybe things might feel back to normal. Maybe, he supposed, that was one of the unseen negatives of having such a small police force; when someone was gone for more than a few days, the vibe of the place and the force itself just felt off.

He knew asking Rebecca to help with the case had been necessary, but that didn't mean he had to like it. Nothing against West, but she wasn't the same as having Hoyt at his back.

When his friend finally spoke again, it wasn't with the sort of comment Alden had been expecting.

"You know, this Yacht Club nonsense was always going to blow up in our faces. It's like that bomb you know is hidden somewhere, just tick-tick-ticking, but you ignore the sound of it, you know? Maybe it's a good thing you brought West on. Maybe it's going to take an outsider to blow the shit out of it."

Alden wasn't so certain. A town that relied on tourism to feed the bellies of the locals had to be careful about who they pissed off.

"You understand how bad that could be for the community, right?"

"I do. But if even half the vile shit that is rumored to go on at those parties is true, it needs to be brought to the light. What sort of community are we if we know it's out there and just let it keep going?"

It was a thought that had crossed Alden's mind several times before. But hell, most of that shit couldn't be true. It was just wild speculation. He sipped his beer, already knowing he wouldn't finish it. He was technically off the clock, but the twelve-thirty meeting loomed large in his mind.

Hell, he might as well say it. "We're meeting with a guy from the club after midnight."

Hoyt did a double take. "Who?"

"Me and West." He filled in Hoyt with all the details concerning Dillon Miller and the mystery texter.

When he was done, Hoyt chuckled, but the sound held very little humor. "You were right. That woman might very well get you killed."

That didn't help settle Alden's mind at all. "You think going tonight is a mistake?"

"Not at all." Hoyt paused to take a long swallow of his beer. When he lowered the bottle, his demeanor seemed to have changed a bit. "If anything, I'm upset I can't help. From the very first time I heard about it, I wanted to be part of breaking up that elitist bullshit."

Alden went to work on the bottle's label, peeling it from the corner. "You mean the Bulgers?"

Hoyt scoffed. "Among other things. I'm sure the Bulgers aren't *nearly* the end of it."

"That's what I'm afraid of. What if we get into this and someone bigger than Hank Bulger is caught? What if we get tied up with someone who has no interest in keeping things quiet? What if it gets too big?" Alden's hand began to tremble, so he sat the bottle down before Hoyt noticed. "What if someone of note gets pissed and takes things public? With the way the public views law enforcement right now, we—"

"To hell with that." Hoyt slapped his thigh. "I say bust it up if you can. It's a hell of a way to work things, don't you think?"

"What do you mean?"

"I mean how, no matter the outcome, the blame and shame tends to fall on the side where people are trying to uphold the law. Especially when someone with money is on the other side. Makes me wonder if this job means anything at all sometimes. Plus, what the hell. My boys are both moved out. You're circling the grave. What's the worst that could happen?"

Circling the grave was true.

Alden had heard his friend get on a soapbox about political things before, but this was a bit more passionate. For the first time, he was glad Hoyt wasn't at the station while Rebecca West was there. Together, they'd make a huge mess out of what was already becoming a powder keg.

Hoyt finished off his beer. "How does West feel about it?"

"Like I said, she's sort of fixated on the Yacht Club, so she's all in."

"Good." Hoyt chuckled. "Can't wait to meet her."

They fell into silence as dusk settled in around them. The oranges sparkling from the sea seemed to turn red as blood as the sun sank. Alden tried his best not to see that as an omen for how the night might unfold.

25

Rebecca's dinner consisted of a peanut butter and jelly sandwich, barbeque potato chips, and a soda. The view from her patio made up for the lackluster dinner, though. The beach was relatively empty as the sun set.

A family of four walked past, and then a lone man on a jog. She smiled at it all. Despite her anxiousness about the upcoming late-night meeting, she thought this might be the most peaceful she'd felt since arriving on Shadow Island.

She'd made photocopies of the Yacht Club files and had read them at least five times since returning home. She'd also done a bit of research on the Bulger family but had found nothing out of the ordinary.

While Edward Bulger was known to work closely with people in the Senate who had some public demons, there was nothing damming about Bulger himself. His son, Hank, on the other hand, was a different story. He'd been popping up in headlines since his eighteenth birthday. There were a few car crashes, rumors of mingling with prostitutes, and a brief gambling problem that was linked to an assistant coach in the NBA.

Gazing out to the ocean as she finished her meager dinner, she did her best to remind herself that a rocky past did not instantly make Hank Bulger a suspect in this case. It had been two years, and his name hadn't come up in regards to the Cassie Leigh case until she'd started digging through the Yacht Club files.

As she stared out to the sea, a figure jogged by with a dog. The dog appeared to be on the younger side, skirting along the edge of the water and sniffing frantically at everything. Sitting up straighter, Rebecca realized she knew the owner. She'd met him yesterday while having lunch with Wallace. It was Ryker Sawyer, her old friend. A local.

Before she could stop herself, she stood and walked down to the bottom step from her deck. Feeling a little silly in doing so, she lifted her hand and waved.

"Ryker…hey!"

He stopped, and when he spotted her, he didn't seem to realize who she was at first. When recognition hit, he responded with a "Hey!" of his own. He seemed a little hesitant when he redirected his dog and started up the beach toward her backyard.

He nodded at the cottage behind her. "So, this is where you're staying?"

"Yep."

"The same place you stayed when you were a kid." His smile widened, and she wondered just how fresh his memories of their childhood summers might be.

"How about you? Are you in the same house?"

"No. Though, I *am* only about two miles away from the house I grew up in." The smile turned into a playful grin. "And yes, I realize there is something very sad about that."

"Not at all." She gestured to her deck. "I'm just finishing up dinner. Do you and your friend want to come up?"

The friend seemed to be a chocolate lab, maybe not quite

a year old. He sniffed at Rebecca's feet and then looked up to her as if to ask why she wasn't petting him yet. She obliged and scratched between his ears.

"This is Humphrey. He's usually a good boy and has no problem saying hello to absolute strangers."

"Well, he's well met." Rebecca gave his ears a tousle. "Come on up, both of you."

They marched up the stairs and sat down in the Adirondacks. Humphrey started sniffing around, licking up the crumbs of Rebecca's chips.

Ryker stared out at the ocean and smiled warmly. "This is a pretty great view. It's a quiet stretch of beach. Probably stay quiet even when the tourists really start to roll in."

"That's good to know it wasn't my childhood memory being wrong about that."

He grinned wide enough that his dimples appeared. "Are you on a summer sabbatical or something?"

"Or something. But then I got a request to help Sheriff Wallace with a case, and it became...well, it became something very different."

Ryker leaned forward, resting his elbows on his thighs, studying her closely. "I don't know if I'm allowed to ask this or not, but is it the Cassie Leigh case?"

Rebecca didn't feel right confirming it, but she nodded anyway. There were no secrets in a small town like this. "Yeah."

"I figured. There usually aren't many crimes on Shadow that require outside help. This one seems to have everyone shaken up, though."

Having a young woman murdered in your town should shake people up. All too often, anymore, it simply didn't. Rebecca was glad this town wasn't like that. "Did you know Cassie?"

"Not personally, but I know her father pretty well. It's the sort of place where you recognize everyone, you know?"

Rebecca nodded, at war with herself. Her brain was insisting she steer the conversation in the direction of the establishment that had been bothering her all day. But should she?

It was odd. A very strange sort of nostalgia settled in her chest at seeing Ryker Sawyer again, and the frayed memories of her childhood wanted to be pulled out and analyzed. She wanted to discuss their lives after their pre-teen years, where they'd once played together on the beach. But her mind was elsewhere, and she knew there was no point in trying to pretend it wasn't.

"So," guilt lengthened the word, "I need to be honest with you."

He lifted an eyebrow. "I'd hope so."

"If I asked questions about what you'd been doing over the past twenty years or so, or how the island's changed since we last hung out as kids, I'd only be half-listening. I do think it would be very cool to reconnect, but right now, my mind is mired in this case."

"Oh...okay." The dimples disappeared as he picked up Humphrey's leash. "Do you need us to go?"

"No, not at all." She waved for him to stay seated. "Sorry, I invited you up, but what I'm now realizing is it may have been for selfish reasons."

"How's that?" His white smile was a sharp contrast to his deeply tanned skin, though, this time, it seemed a bit forced.

Had he always been so charming, or was it something she'd totally missed when they'd been ten, eleven, and twelve years old? Or was his charm something Ryker had simply picked up later in life?

Stop thinking about his cute dimples and ask your damn question.

"Can I ask you some questions about a few people? About the case…"

"Sure." He stroked Humphrey's head. "If you think it'll help."

Rebecca turned her attention to the adorable puppy. It was a tactic she had learned long ago, not to appear to be looking at someone when asking awkward questions, all while simultaneously watching every twitch or eye shift. Otherwise, her expressive face always gave her away. It sucked she had to use it against Ryker, but it would be worth it if she got some answers.

"Looking into some different angles for this case, an organization called the Yacht Club came up. It seems to be common knowledge among a lot of people on the island, but something no one ever really talks about. Do you know much about it?"

Ryker actually appeared relieved, blowing out a breath and rolling his eyes a bit. "I know that it's an excuse for a lot of rich folks to have parties on their boats. We're talking weekend-long parties that involve catered lunches and hundred-dollar bottles of wine. Those are the only *facts* I know about it." He stroked the lab's ears.

"And the rumors?"

Humphrey's ears pricked, and the dog scampered as far as his leash would let him go. Ryker glanced around the beach as if checking for eavesdroppers. "Probably the same rumors you've heard. Underage girls. Drugs. Maybe forced prostitution. Maybe drug cartels from South America. But let me stress…I have no proof of this. It's all just hearsay."

"Would you happen to know if Hank Bulger was involved with the Yacht Club?" She watched his face as she said the senator's son's name, but Ryker didn't react. This wasn't a well-kept secret, it seemed.

"Depends on who you ask. Some people say he was basically running the thing when he got into a bit of trouble here a few years ago. Others say his rich father is a member of the club, and Hank just sort of tagged along."

Rebecca took it all in, matching it up to what she'd read online. She knew rumors always had to have a starting point, and that point was usually based on truth, no matter how stretched that truth might become with later retellings.

"I wonder if you can confirm or deny another rumor I heard today. I don't yet know if it's directly related to the case, but there seems to be a link. Do you happen to know the McCreedy family? Particularly their daughter, Serenity."

"Yes. That's a name that pretty much everyone knows around here."

"Any reason?"

The smile that had played at his lips during their conversation fell away. "Serenity McCreedy is a walking sexual allegation suit waiting to happen, if you want my opinion. She dresses like the whole world needs her skin showing to survive. Parents don't intervene on it much, so it sort of goes under the rug."

That was a stark difference from her other two friends but seemed to be something she had in common with Cassie, if the red dress was an indication. "No parents...do you know if there are problems at home?"

He shifted in the chair. "Not that I know of. Jill McCreedy, Serenity's mother, died in a boating accident several years ago. Her father remarried and is usually away on business. The stepmom is more interested in being a friend than a parent. That sort of thing."

"Any truth to her boyfriend?" She purposefully posed the question vaguely, but his frown told her that he knew exactly what she was talking about.

"The middle-aged banker creep from Norfolk? Not sure, though I have heard the rumors about them. Same as everyone else. Never met the man myself." He paused and gave her a perplexed look. "Please don't take this the wrong way, but does police work usually seem so close to gossip?"

She couldn't help but laugh. "More often than you'd think. I'm so sorry. I'm just trying to wrap my head around it all, and it seems like the island officials are a little wary of going after the Yacht Club."

"Are you thinking it may have had something to do with Cassie's death?"

"I don't know. And for the sake of professionalism—as if I haven't already ruined it—I should probably not say anything else."

He nodded but looked away, clearly no longer comfortable in her presence. "I get that. And at the risk of seeming like a jerk, I think Humphrey and I will go now. Your mind is clearly consumed by the case, and I don't feel right digging up dirt on my neighbors and talking about rumors." His expression softened. "Nothing against you. If anything, it's making me uneasy because I'm getting far too curious."

He got to his feet and patted his leg. The good dog that he was, Humphrey obeyed the signal, albeit a bit reluctantly, as the dog didn't appear to be done sniffing every inch of the area.

Rebecca stood as well, guilt mixing with embarrassment. "You don't need to go. This is on me. I should never have put you in this position."

"No, really. It's okay." He shrugged as he and Humphrey started back down the stairs. Ryker turned and met her gaze. "Maybe reach out again when the case is over."

She tucked a strand of hair that had escaped her ponytail behind her ear. "Do you mean that, or are you just being polite?"

His dimples flashed again. "I'm not that polite...so..."

Rebecca watched the pair head back to the beach as they

shrank away in the distance and then remained even longer to watch the evening grow dimmer and dimmer as the sun gave up the day. Night would be there soon, and with it, a late-night meeting that was already starting to feel a little too familiar.

Her mind went back to the bobbing lights and gunshots. She pushed the thought away but not before a chill ran up her spine. Rebecca wondered for the briefest of moments if she was out of her depth on this case, but the moment soon passed.

She hoped it wasn't a premonition.

26

It was a pretty view, all reds and pinks with streaks of purple where it wasn't blocked by other buildings. Serenity McCreedy stood in front of the sliding glass door, watching the water as the sun slowly settled into the sea.

The view wasn't as good as the one at home where she could stare out at the ocean and hear the waves, but it was decent. Well, it was decent if she could ignore the constant noise coming from Granby Street, where all the bars were.

The high-rise apartment complex Chris lived in was considered luxury by Norfolk standards. It had a doorman you had to sign in with as well as a pool and hot tubs. Even though the parking lot flooded at high tide and the water view was just a pitiful little waterway and not the ocean.

There was a better view on the rooftop, but that was where the pool was, and it was always crowded at this time of night.

Right now, Serenity needed space to think, and if she were being honest with herself, she was afraid of Shadow Island. She was safe here, and Chris was taking good care of her. He'd even run out to score them something for the night.

With him gone, she finally had a bit of time to herself. She needed that.

A tear slid down her cheek.

Her best friend was dead, and the cops were useless, just as she knew they'd be. They had no idea who had killed her, and they sure as hell didn't know anything about Cassie. She was sure they were off somewhere chasing their own tails like the pathetic pigs they were.

Sure, Serenity had avoided them by spending the last few days off the island, but they hadn't even called her. She was Cassie's best friend, and they couldn't even bother to call her to ask a single question?

Not like I'd tell them anything, anyway. Knowledge is power.

Serenity snorted in derision. As the sun sank, her reflection in the glass became more noticeable. Her naturally sun-streaked blonde hair was still a mess from her earlier exploits in bed. It looked good on her. Made her look sexy and mature. Except right now, she also looked tired. The last few days had been hard, so she had buried herself in experiences that made her feel good.

She straightened, adjusting her silk robe, making sure it laid smooth over the curves of her breasts. It was Chris's favorite part of her, so she made sure it was always displayed nicely. Her makeup was perfect, her lipstick a flawless, classic matte. As always, she made sure she looked her best when she wasn't at home.

Leaning against the sofa, she ran a finger down the cheap fake leather. Okay, so maybe the "luxury apartment" wasn't really all that luxurious, but at least here the only man she had to get made-up for was Chris. He treated her well enough, even if he didn't blow as much money on her as she would like. At least he didn't pass her around like some of the other daddies had.

She couldn't complain, though. It was easy enough work for the money she was getting. She still went to the parties, still made good money there, but that was only dancing and flirting. Chris went with her to every event and made sure she went home with him each night, no matter how messed up she might get on the boats once he was done showing her off to his friends.

That was one of the reasons she'd been so happy to see Cassie at parties. Serenity had taken her under her wing and showed her the ropes like no one had done for her. Told her how to get the best money in the easiest ways. It had been lonely when Cassie'd stopped coming.

Instead of feeling rejected, Serenity had tracked her friend down and forced Cassie to tell her what was wrong. Her friend's response had been shocking...

Cassie's period had been eight days late.

To be honest, the last thing Serenity had expected was sharing a pregnancy scare with her friend. The very next day, Serenity had driven Cassie to a mainland pharmacy where they prayed no one would recognize them and purchased several tests.

Serenity remembered being just as nervous as Cassie as they waited for the lines on the stick to share Cassie's fate.

Positive.

Serenity had held Cassie as she'd cried, then had been the one to reassure her that everything would be all right. That all Cassie had to do was tell the daddy, and she'd be taken care of for life...or at least the next eighteen years.

But it hadn't been all right.

A quiet, guilty part of Serenity hadn't stopped screaming since she'd learned of Cassie's fate. What if it had been her advice that had gotten Cassie killed?

That couldn't be true. She knew it couldn't be true.

Please don't let it be true.

Cassie's man was a regular guy, not a gross party drunk. A genuine, caring man they'd both known since they were kids. The perfect guy for Cassie. And everything had been going perfectly. And then…

Positive.

Had he killed her because of it?

No! Something else had to have happened. Serenity knew there was no way a tiny baby could have led to her friend's death.

Right?

She didn't know anymore.

Serenity pulled out her phone and stared at that last message… *I know what you did.*

She had taken sadistic glee in making Cassie's baby daddy twist in the wind, telling him that she knew his and Cassie's secret. But she'd sent the text before she'd known Cassie was dead.

And now? Now she needed to get away. Away from him. Away from the island. Away from the entire state of Virginia.

But how?

Although her Instagram account was picking up traction, she wasn't making nearly enough money to run away to New York or California. She'd need enough money for the expensive rent as well as cash for the high dollar portfolio photographs she'd been told she needed if she ever hoped to break into the modeling business.

Her friends thought that agents were begging her to sign to join their modeling agency, but that wasn't exactly true. It could be, Serenity knew. If only she could get away from Virginia and the old men and memories that nearly caused her heart to freeze in her chest.

But where could she get the money?

And was she brave enough to escape?

A bolt of inspiration struck her, bringing a real smile to her face for the first time in days.

Knowledge wasn't just power. It could also be money. And money meant freedom.

Since Cassie wouldn't get paid by her baby daddy, maybe Serenity could.

Taking a deep breath, Serenity pulled her phone from her pocket.

She had another text to send.

I TOLD my wife I was going out for a bit of night fishing. She didn't argue or even ask any questions. She knew it was something I liked to do whenever work was getting stressful or if it had been a long week.

While work had indeed been stressful, it wasn't even close to the primary reason I was currently sitting in my little aluminum boat. In fact, fishing was the furthest thing from my mind. My rod and reel sat between my feet, untouched. No, tonight I needed dark ocean around me, that seemingly endless expanse.

I needed to be lost.

Honestly, I thought I might do something crazy if I didn't get out of the house. I was suffocating in there as a very plain and simple truth dawned on me. Yes, killing Cassie was tearing away at my conscience and my heart, but there was something much rawer than that lurking beneath the surface of it all.

I missed her.

While I'd always enjoyed her company, the gnawing ache of her absence wore on me. When we were together, and she was really into it, I felt like a teenager again. But I had never expected to *miss* her like this. I knew I'd made a mistake, and if I could take it back, I would.

When she showed me the positive pregnancy test, all happy and smiling and filled with all the ways we'd live happily ever after, I'd reacted in the only way I could. The more I thought about it, I still couldn't see any scenario that would have worked out for me...hell, that would have worked out for *either of us*.

This was the hand I ended up with. I'd been dealt different cards, made some bad decisions, and there I was. I hadn't been safe enough before, but I was going to play it safe from now on.

My phone buzzed, the notification sound telling me it was a text. I froze as the new message from an unknown number popped up on the screen.

Are you ready to pay for what you did?

"No." Emotion hit me like a brick, and I started to cry for the first time since I'd chased her into the marsh. The paranoia, the hiding, and processing the fact that I actually killed a sweet young girl I cared for, all built up over the last few days.

The pressure was growing in my head, in my heart. In my soul and spirit. But I couldn't let one mistake ruin my life.

Besides, what good would I do the world locked up in prison? What kind of man would I be if I let Cassie's death mean nothing? Alive and free, I could make up for my transgressions by becoming a better human being. I'd donate more to charity, maybe even become a Big Brother to a child in need.

Yes! That was it.

I'd turn my life around. Be a better husband and father. A better everything.

"That's what I'll do." My voice sounded stronger than it had in days. "I'll honor Cassie by being a better man."

My happiness drained away as the damn phone buzzed again.

With deep dread, I forced myself to read the words that appeared on the screen.

Baby killer.

Resisting the urge to throw my phone as far as I could manage, I inhaled a deep breath a pocketed the device.

It was a lie.

I wasn't a baby killer. I wasn't even a Cassie killer anymore.

Someone else had done those things…not me.

Picking up my fishing rod, I checked the bait before rearing back and making my first cast of the evening. It was going to be fine. Better than ever.

I was a new man now. A *good* man.

Nothing was going to ruin my future.

Nothing or nobody.

27

As far as plans went, Rebecca supposed it could be improved upon. But with a police force that was already stretched thin and an estranged FBI agent in their back pocket, it wasn't the worst plan she'd ever been a part of.

Sitting in front of the old cottage the lighthouse over-shadowed, Rebecca turned the air conditioner vent of her truck until it blew directly in her face. The cottage looked like a haunted relic of the past in the shimmering light cast by the lighthouse. Though it was dark, she knew Wallace and Locke were inside the small home that now served as a local historical point, waiting for the arrival of whoever had been texting Dillon Miller.

Anticipation thrummed through her veins as she watched the clock tick from 12:22 to 12:23. The plan was for her to get out at precisely 12:25 and walk down to the beach because the chances of someone recognizing Wallace or Locke were too high. Hopefully, by the time their suspect realized Cassie wasn't there, maybe the appearance of another female—albeit a bit older and more mature—might throw them off just long enough to ensnare them.

Gritting her teeth, Rebecca sat in the dark until the clock ticked "go time." Time to take a predator off the street. Maybe more than one.

As she closed the Tacoma's door, her gaze was drawn to the sea. They had no hard confirmation their visitor was coming via boat, but it just made sense to Rebecca. The man did, after all, belong to a club consisting of boats.

Passing by the cottage, she peered over and through the window on the right side and spotted both Wallace and Locke standing against the far wall. She was pretty sure the sheriff gave her a quick nod as she passed.

The lighthouse loomed to her right, and Rebecca wished the building provided more light to the immediate area instead of just beaming its lantern out at the sea. Past the tall structure, a small dune waited for her, the only real barrier separating the structures from the beach and the crashing waves farther out.

She only had to stand on the beach for roughly thirty seconds before she spotted a small white light bobbing around on the water to her left. It came from the direction of the mainland, cutting in at a hard angle to approach her little strip of beach. The low sound of the engine was faint but grew louder by the moment.

In order to appear as small as possible, Rebecca sat on the sand with her arms wrapped around her knees, hoping to disarm her suspect. In doing so, she also made sure the light-weight pullover she was wearing properly covered her holstered sidearm.

It took about two minutes for the boat to get close enough for her to see any real detail. It was black and gray, making it ideal for late-night runs like this one. Only one person was visible at first—the driver—but two more came into view as the boat neared the shore. It came forward without any hesitation, its light focusing on Rebecca as it headed for the sand. Music pounded from its speakers.

The driver maneuvered among the waves with great experience, allowing one of the men to hop over the side. The water came up to his knees, and he walked toward the shore with cocky confidence. With a lone female sitting on the beach, he probably assumed everything was going as planned.

When the driver cut the lights, probably not wanting to draw attention, the low light from the moon and lighthouse made it hard to judge, but Rebecca doubted this man was any older than twenty-five. His dark hair swooped over his forehead, obscuring his right eye. A wifebeater barely showcased his intricate tattoos. Rebecca rose as he moved closer, wanting to be in a less vulnerable position.

He stopped only a few feet away, and Rebecca backed up a step, careful to manage their physical space if he decided to lunge.

"Well, now, what've we got here." He chuckled. "No offense, lady, you're mighty fine but not our usual type. Where's Cassie?" He appeared to be genuinely curious.

Rebecca eyed the boat, still rising and falling gently on the tide. Neither man onboard showed any signs of hopping off to join their friend. In the dark, it was hard to know if this was a good thing or bad.

Rebecca grinned at Tattoo-dude, trying to flirt but knowing she was failing miserably. "I'm Cassie's...advocate."

Tattoo-dude took a step closer, reducing their distance, and though everything inside Rebecca screamed at her to back up, she let him get within touching range. "That's cute, blondie, but advocate or not, I'm afraid it won't matter. You're not who I was expecting. Did Dillon-boy send you?"

"Dillon who?" The lie came easily.

Tattoo-dude seemed to be smarter than he looked. "That's cute. You know who I'm talking about, so how about we stop this word play, and you tell me why you're here."

Rebecca licked her lips, both in an attempt to appear seductive and because her mouth had gone as dry as bone. "I'm here to party with the Yacht Club."

Though Rebecca couldn't see him sizing her up, she could practically feel his gaze taking in every inch of her. "You can still come out and party with us." He motioned to his friends. "I can promise you a real good time."

Rebecca laughed, genuinely amused. "Really? I'm over thirty, you know? That's much too old for you and your friends from what I hear."

He reached out and tugged at a strand of her hair, and Rebecca very nearly kicked him in the balls. "We're not as picky about our women as the gentlemen are."

She batted her eyelashes. "What gentlemen are you talking about?"

Tattoo-dude wrapped the strand around his finger. "Some old dudes who aren't nearly as fun as we are."

Though Rebecca's nerves screamed for her to fight him, she held her ground. She needed more information first. "Who are you talking about?"

The music coming from the boat stopped, and a man's husky voice boomed over the speaker. *"Hunter One. This is—"*

One of the crewmen took the call off intercom and lifted the microphone to his mouth.

Shit.

She'd came very close to hearing two of the Yacht Club's call signs.

Hunter One? The very name caused goose bumps to raise on Rebecca's arms. These guys were the ones who hunted down the girls to take back to the predators. She just had to prove it.

Tattoo-dude had turned to check on his crewmates, clearly as interested to hear what the caller wanted as Rebecca was. While he was distracted, she took a step backward, only wincing a little as her hair caught between his fingers before slipping away.

Tattoo-dude lifted his hands to his mouth, creating a megaphone of sorts. "Who's calling?" As his shirt lifted from the movement, Rebecca spotted a bellyband and the black grip of what appeared to be a Glock.

Shit!

The boat rocked as one of the men ran to the side. "Cassie Leigh's dead. Get back here now!"

Stunned, Tattoo-dude's mouth fell open, and it took him a few seconds to react. It was one second longer than Rebecca needed.

Quick as a cat, Rebecca took the man's arm while simultaneously planting a leg behind his. The moment his feet left the sand, she turned hard to her side, forcing his fall into a crude hip toss that landed him face first on the beach, his dominant hand behind his back.

"Police! We need to talk."

She didn't have enough evidence to arrest him or his crewmen, but she was determined not to let them leave before they had a nice little chat.

"Hey!" The shout came from the boat.

She pinned Tattoo-dude down with a knee to his spine and glanced up just in time to spot one of the men reaching to his waist.

Holy shit!

"Police! Don't do it!" She prayed that Locke and Wallace had heard her shouts and were sprinting her way.

The boat had drifted until it was close to twenty yards from the shore, so she couldn't see every movement, but the glow from the lighthouse showed her enough. The man who wasn't behind the wheel held a gun in his hand.

"Drop your weapon!" It was Locke's voice, and the sound was like music to her ears.

Rebecca glanced back long enough to spot both him and Wallace coming down the little dune, guns drawn. Her little calvary. The sight of them running in the sand almost made her smile.

Almost.

Wallace flashed his badge. "Sheriff Wallace. Turn off the engine and—"

Bam!

The gunshot was so unexpected that Rebecca didn't trust her ears at first. Had one of the morons on the boat *really* fired at law enforcement officers? Could they be that stupid? She got her answer when Locke returned fire from directly behind her.

Adrenaline and instincts tangled together, sending Rebecca even lower to the ground. Her knee was still on the tattooed man's back as she crouched, reaching for her weapon.

Her suspect had other ideas, though, and started bucking, trying to escape.

"Don't move!" Planting one hand on his head, she pushed his face into the sand while yanking his arm higher up his back, pinning it there with her thigh.

Sweat dropped into her eyes, threatening to blind her as she worked to get his other arm behind his back so she could cuff him and help her fellow officers in the battle. If the asshole hadn't been armed, she would have just let him go, but she wasn't that fortunate.

The man on the boat fired again and sand exploded two feet from where she knelt. She ducked as more shots rang out, and Tattoo-dude started yelling for his mother. Had he been hit? Rebecca couldn't tell, but the fear for his life had distracted him enough that she got his other arm behind his back.

Just as she clicked the first cuff around her suspect's wrist, a sharp cry of pain came from somewhere to her left. Rebecca couldn't tell who it was, and she cursed the fact that the little sheriff's department hadn't owned any Kevlar vests.

Bam! Bam!

The driver of the boat's head snapped back, and he dropped into the hull like a rock. The boat's passenger was nowhere to be seen. Rebecca didn't know if he'd already been hit or if he was crouched down, waiting to take another shot.

Silence descended on the small slice of beach with only the sounds of Rebecca's heavy breaths and Tattoo-dude's soft cries. She clicked the second cuff around the man's wrist and was finally able to pull her weapon.

Pulse hammering in her ears, she waited for the boat's passenger to appear, shocked by how quickly the entire scene had escalated.

"I think I got them both."

It was Locke, which meant...

"Wallace." His name was barely a whisper on her lips.

Rolling her suspect just enough to yank his weapon from the bellyband, Rebecca pushed to her feet. "Call for an ambulance and don't take your eyes off that boat."

Locke nodded, one arm still raised and locked in shooting position while he triggered the radio at his side. "Shots fire. Officer down." His voice was thick with grief. "We need an ambulance now."

Please, God...no. Please not Wallace too.

Rebecca found the sheriff within seconds, a dark shape on the sand.

Grief clawed its way from her heart and through her

throat as she ran over and sank to her knees. He wasn't moving. "Sheriff? Can you hear me?"

She wasn't sure where to touch him since he seemed to be bleeding from every pore. Pressing her fingertips to his neck, she held her breath and waited.

Nothing.

Then the faintest of pulses against her skin.

Leaning close so he could hear her, she brushed his hair back from his clammy forehead. "Hang in there, Wallace. Help's coming."

The sheriff's eyelashes flickered, and it seemed to take forever before he was able to open his eyes, his gaze settling on her face.

"Ssss…"

Rebecca leaned even closer. "Hush. Don't try to talk. We'll talk when you're better."

His mouth worked again, the stubborn old man refusing to be quiet. "Sss…stop them. You…you're the on…only one who…c-can."

Taking his hand in hers, she blinked back the tears that threatened to flow like a river as she made an impossible promise. "I will."

28

The Shadow Island Sheriff's Department was practically empty, but electricity seemed to sizzle in the air. Adrenaline and worry cascaded through Rebecca in a dizzying cocktail.

Wallace was alive, but barely.

Locke had accompanied his friend to a mainland hospital while Rebecca had stayed until the boys from State arrived and took over the scene. She'd been forced to relieve Locke of his weapon, bagging it for the necessary investigation that followed officer involved shootings.

The bastards.

Rage simmered in Rebecca's veins as the evening replayed in her mind.

Only one of the men in the boat was dead. The other was also heading into a surgery suite.

Fuck him. Fuck them all.

By the time forensics had arrived, false dawn had already started in the east, turning the sky a dark purple as the stars began to fade. Once Rebecca had handed over the scene, she'd driven back to the station with Tattoo-dude locked in the back of Wallace's Explorer. It had taken everything inside her not to pull the vehicle over and pistol whip the bastard until he was crying for his mommy again.

Driving on the dark streets had really hammered home just how thin this little sheriff's department was stretched. And now...

"Any update on Wallace yet?"

Rebecca jumped as Viviane came rushing into the little bullpen. Apparently, she'd been called in by the night shift woman, Mandy or Melody, or whatever her name was. The pajamas and flip-flops she wore were a sure giveaway.

"No." Rebecca cleared her throat, swallowing the emotion that wanted to strangle her. "Last I heard, he's still in surgery. Locke's with him and is supposed to let me know when he gets out."

Greg Abner was the next to come in. After shooting Rebecca a pissy look, he'd gone straight to his desk where he cradled a cup of coffee in his hands, eyes closed like he was praying for the sheriff. He probably was.

"You okay, hun?"

Rebecca couldn't meet the dark chocolate of Viviane's eyes. She knew she'd burst into tears if she did, so she began shuffling papers. "Yeah."

She wasn't, of course.

In fact, she was mentally beating herself up in every way possible. After all, it had been her bright idea to stage the meet-up, and maybe if she hadn't made such a show of over-powering her tattooed friend currently sitting in the interrogation room, things might not have escalated so quickly. Or if she'd been able to pull her gun instead of wrestling with the *Hunter One* asshole.

If. If. If.

Stop it!

Rebecca had been there before, questioning her every

motive and move. She knew it did nothing but cause unnecessary heartache and doubt, so she shoved it down. Now that Greg Abner was here, she could finally go talk to the tattooed scumbag.

"I already filed the paperwork for Locke to be on admin leave. It just needs a signature. You're the incident commander, so we'll do your paperwork later." Viviane spoke softly. "I can't believe he had to shoot a man." Anger flooded her face as her lips tightened. "But if he was the man who hurt Alden, then I'm glad he did it!"

It took Rebecca a moment to remember who Alden was because she never thought of him by his first name. Alden Wallace. The kindly sheriff she'd grown fond of over the past few days.

The same man fighting for his life.

Because of her.

And now, the only other full-time deputy on the island was on admin duty. That left everything up to her. Taking over at the scene had been second nature. She was incident commander. Now that she was back at the station, it seemed she'd have to take charge here too.

A glance over at Abner showed he'd already realized all of this and was waiting on her to decide what to do first.

The first thing she did was to sign the form Viviane had written up. "Where's...." She trailed off as she remembered that she still didn't remember the other woman's name.

"Melody." Viviane gave her a gentle smile. "She'll be right back. She had to make a call in the back office for privacy."

With all of that taken care of, Rebecca turned to Abner. At her nod, he stood and followed her. On legs that felt like water, she walked down the hallway, and when she came to the interrogation room, she didn't bother taking a moment to cool down outside the door. This was one of the times her inability to hide her emotions would work well for her.

Angry cop in the middle of the night was just what was needed.

She walked in and leaned against the wall, glaring at the man sitting behind the small metal table. He looked irritated more than scared, but Rebecca supposed she could change that pretty quickly.

Abner went straight to the video camera, turned it on, and leaned against the wall. Rebecca still wasn't certain of his actual role or rank, but he was her backup now. And her witness.

Once the red light came on, she got right to the point, providing the date, time, and other specifics before glaring at the man across from her. "What's your name?"

He'd been silent on the ride over, and she expected his vocal cords to still be unmoving, so she was surprised when he answered right away. "Jay Griles."

"What's your address?"

He hesitated and seemed to study her for a moment. A flicker of alarm flared in his eyes, and she wondered how truly angry she appeared. "Nags Head."

Perfect.

"So, you crossed state lines to commit a felony. Nice. Was it you who's been texting Dillon Miller?"

Rebecca knew she wasn't asking the right questions in the right order, but she was too pissed and tired and emotionally distraught to fall back on her training. She just wanted answers.

Griles hesitated again, and the shift in his eyes told her that he was considering telling her a lie. Her words had certainly shaken him. She gave him the time, though her patience was wearing thin.

"No."

"Have you ever met Dillon Miller?"

"No."

He was answering the questions fast, and Rebecca intended to keep asking them in a rapid fashion as well. She'd used this approach before, as it was easy to trip up a guilty party verbally like this.

"What about his girlfriend, Cassie Leigh?"

Another pause, another shift in his eyes. Before he could speak again, Rebecca approached the table and leaned across it. His hands were still cuffed and clasped in his lap, but even if they weren't, she didn't think he'd try to strike her. She'd already proven how much faster and stronger she was out on the beach.

"You don't want to make this worse for yourself than it is right now." She kept her voice calm, her expression neutral. "One of your friends shot and very seriously injured Sheriff Wallace. If he doesn't make it, you and your injured friend are screwed. Even if it was your buddy with the hole in his head that killed him, you and your third man are in a world of trouble. Honest answers are going to help you more than you realize. So...I ask you again. Did you ever meet Cassie Leigh?"

He swallowed hard. "Yes."

"At one of the Yacht Club parties?"

Griles nodded.

"For the record, Mr. Griles nodded in the affirmative." She glanced at the camera again, checking that the red light was on. "And someone in the club was trying to recruit her, right? To keep her coming back to the parties?"

"Yes."

"I need their names."

Griles shook his head like a dog shaking water from its ears. "I can't do that."

Rebecca knew that pushing the subject could derail his ease in answering the rest of her questions, so she let it go. For now. She'd come back to it later.

"Why were the three of you sent out tonight? Give me your instructions, and then tell me everything you can about Cassie Leigh's involvement with the Yacht Club."

With every question, the reality of the situation seemed to settle in. Griles fidgeted in his seat and scanned the room as his leg jumped like a piston under the table. But, as she'd expected and planned, he seemed a little relieved she'd moved on from wanting names. It allowed him to talk with a bit more confidence, feeling that he was out of the muck of pointing fingers. Still, the nerves were there, practically sizzling through his skin.

"I was sent to pick up the girl, Cassie, and take her to the party. If she wasn't there, or if the Miller kid was pulling some bullshit, I was supposed to rough him up a little bit. He was trying to be a tough guy before, so we didn't know if he'd actually changed his mind. Or if she had. He coulda been trying to pull something." Griles used his shoulder to wipe the sweat from his face before catching her eye again. "Is Cassie really dead?"

Rebecca puzzled over the question, curious why neither the man in front of her nor whichever member of the Yacht Club had wanted Cassie's company knew of her death. Was that because these men weren't from the island and the news hadn't reached them yet? Did they not follow the girls' social media accounts? What had been the communication breakdown?

Or was Griles lying?

She'd have to think about that some more.

"Yes. She was strangled to death and left in the marsh to rot. Forgive me if I don't buy your attempt at surprise."

Griles actually flinched. "What? No!" His handcuffs clinked together as he raised his hands in protest. "I had nothing to do with that. I wouldn't."

Rebecca kept her face carefully blank. "So, you just *hunt*

down underaged girls and feed them to the predators who pay you, huh? And if you're so innocent, why did you and your pals have loaded guns? Seems you intended to do more than rough Dillon Miller up." Rebecca cocked an eyebrow.

"I have a carry permit, so there's nothing illegal about that." He lifted his chin. "It's for self-protection."

Rebecca made a show of scoffing, going so far as to smack the table to emphasize her mirth. "Self-protection, huh? From one-hundred-pound teenagers?" She wiped fake tears from her eyes. "That's funny."

His nostrils flared. "It's true."

Rebecca turned serious again. "Did you have sex with Cassie Leigh?"

"No!"

"Tell me your exact relationship with Cassie Leigh."

He threw up his hands, the chains clanking on the table. "There is no relationship. I just met her at a party." He frowned. "No…two parties. The first one, she was sort of nervous. She had a few drinks, but that was it. But she let loose at the second one. She seemed to have a good time."

Interesting.

"To your knowledge, did she have any sort of physical relations with anyone at the party?"

"Not that I know of. She did give a pretty memorable dance in a bikini, though. But after that, some of the men at the party got handsy, and she flipped out." Griles shrugged, like it was a normal day occurrence. "She sat at the back of the boat and sulked the rest of the time. Someone called another boat to come get her and took her back to shore."

"Is it common for girls to freak out at these parties?"

"No." The leg under the table slowed its jittering. "Most of them actually seem to enjoy it. The partying, hanging out with men that don't mind spending money on them. I know people in authority don't want to hear it, but the vast majority of these girls enjoy the whole experience." He had the audacity to smirk. "Well, at least the ones who don't get sent to the kid's table in back to wait to be dropped off with their mommies."

Kid's table? For the girls who wanted respect? Rebecca locked her hands behind her back to keep from punching him. She needed answers, not revenge.

"There's a lot of rumors about the Yacht Club. I've only been on the island less than a week, and I've heard the name numerous times. Drugs. Men paying young girls for sex. Rape, abuse…"

Griles released a long breath. "I don't know nothing about those rumors." By the way his shoulders relaxed, Rebecca could tell this was a more comfortable subject. "I've never seen anything like that. I drive happy guests to the boat. They all get onboard on their own. Only complaint I ever had was their nice shoes getting wet."

"But is there any truth to the rumors?"

Griles spread his hands as far as the cuffs would allow. "I don't know what goes on behind closed doors. I just know I've never raped a girl. The girls are *willing*, you know, and there's no money exchanged. They come to these things and—"

Rebecca wasn't buying that after the threats he'd thrown at her earlier. She rounded the table and came a hair from grabbing him by his shirt and slamming him against the wall. Fully aware of the camera rolling, she managed to hold back. Barely.

"They come to these things because you're exploiting them. Taking advantage." Rebecca's voice was low and dangerous as she hissed the words an inch from his face.

Griles reeled back as far as he could. "I don't get to go to these parties. I-I just drive the boat."

"And tonight, you came after a young woman, or you

were going to beat up her boyfriend because he dared to question the whole thing. Because he lost a girlfriend who'd been lured in by you!"

"I didn't do—"

"Tell me something." She paused, making sure he was paying attention. "Does every girl you take to that boat come back?"

Her random question froze him in place. Then she watched as horror seeped into his eyes. That was answer enough. Not all the girls who left with him came back. "Do you ever take them into international waters?"

"Look! I'm just the help. I didn't do anything illegal."

Rage became a living thing inside Rebecca, and she grabbed the man by the straps of his wifebeater shirt. "Your idiot friends opened fire on law enforcement officers tonight! You understand what that means, right?"

Griles tried to pull away, but he had nowhere to go. Rebecca knew she was crossing a line but found it hard to give a damn.

Greg Abner cleared his throat, and the sound forced some sense back into Rebecca's brain. Very slowly, she released their suspect's shirt and backed up a step.

She held up a finger, delighting when Griles flinched. "You crossed state lines to transport a minor for the purpose of sex, a felony." She held up a second finger. "During the commission of that felony, your accomplices opened fire on three identified officers of the law." A third finger went up. "You, personally, assaulted me. Shall I go on?"

The weight of her words settled on the young man's shoulders. *Good.* "Look, I don't even know—"

Rebecca slammed her fist into the table, startling the men. "You don't know?! What, huh? I don't give a shit what you don't know—"

Rebecca stepped back, clenching her hands into fists. She

caught fleeting images of the parking garage, those gunshots echoing in the enclosed space, feeling like her life was on the line. That emotion was rampaging through her right now, and she feared if she didn't get control of herself or remove herself from this room, she was going to lose control.

"You'd better hope you fucking remember enough that the D.A. offers you a deal. Otherwise, it's iron bars and bean curds for the next twenty-five years." She settled herself, letting the silence spread as thickly as the fear spreading across Griles's face.

Just when she thought he might actually shit his pants, she chose a new direction of questioning. "How many girls have you taken out to those boats?"

And this time, the bastard began to tell the truth.

•

Hoyt Frost was tired and afraid, but in a strange way, he hadn't felt this alive in a long time. He'd gotten from Locke that Sherriff Wallace had been shot and was currently in the hospital. As soon as he'd heard that, he'd started to get dressed.

He still wasn't completely filled in on what exactly happened. Viviane Darby had mentioned something about the beach and the Yacht Club, and while there had been chatter all over the police band radio, it all seemed clumped together and panicked.

Hoyt learned long ago to not take hearsay from the radio as gospel. He much preferred to wait until he heard it from someone's mouth, face-to-face, once things were reasonably calm. However, one of the things he had also managed to gather was that Rebecca West was at the precinct with a member of the group who had shot Alden.

The thought of Alden anywhere close to death spooked him. Sheriff Wallace was the sort of man he'd just assumed would live forever, despite a few brushes with illness and the weariness of age here and there. He should be creeping up to the century mark in a retirement community and bitching about Bingo. Picturing him bleeding out in the back of an ambulance just made no sense.

Yet, there was another side of him thrilled that the Yacht Club was finally being pulled into the light. He only wished it hadn't taken Rebecca West's stubborn will and a life-threatening gunshot wound to Alden for it to happen.

In fact, that was one of the reasons Hoyt was currently speeding his truck toward the station. After Viviane explained the situation, she'd ended his call with, "You might want to get down to the station. Rebecca is losing her shit."

How, exactly, she was losing her shit had not been explained, and Hoyt wanted to make sure he got to her before any real damage could be done.

While his mind was on Alden, duty told him he needed to be at the precinct. He wasn't about to pull Hudson from his last few days of paternity leave, and he doubted there was much of anything Greg Abner would be able to do to help.

He was pushing his old GMC along so quickly that the front right wheel struck the curb along the sidewalk as he turned into the parking lot. Maybe there was a good reason his doctor had told him not to drive for six weeks. Making turns had been a real bitch.

He didn't bother going around to the side lot where the patrol cars and deputies parked. He pulled up right in front, killed the engine, and got out, moving as fast as he had in quite a long time.

When he got inside, Hoyt found Viviane sitting in her usual spot, though not in her usual attire. Pajamas? Really? He intended to give her a little hell about her wardrobe but was interrupted when he heard the muffled, raised voice of a woman coming from the back of the building. It wasn't a voice he recognized, so it had to be the new deputy. The one who was losing her shit.

"How long has she been back there?"

Viviane shrugged, her eyes wide. "Well, she took a break for coffee and a pee break, then back in for round two about ten minutes ago. A better question is...are you feeling well enough to be here?"

Hoyt gave a nervous smirk. He didn't want the already spooked woman to see just how unraveled all of this had him feeling. "At least I remembered to put my pants on."

He hurried to the back, where a panicked man was now speaking. His voice was low, and Hoyt couldn't quite make out what he was saying. When he reached the interrogation room, he found himself reaching out to knock. Knocking out of courtesy was a habit, but he wasn't going to show such measures right now. He opened the door and stepped inside, taking a moment to get a good look at the scene.

A woman he assumed to be Rebecca West stood several feet away from a twenty-something man who looked somewhere between frightened and confused. Hoyt didn't recognize the suspect, but it was evident from his expression he was not accustomed to being on the losing end of anything. He looked like just about any kid who had gotten away with hundreds of lies or petty thefts, not sure how to act when he was finally busted.

Both the man and the woman turned to him. Hoyt noticed the woman flexing her hands in and out of fists.

The man's eyes took on a pleading gaze. "Thank god! She's lost her mind, man. I don't know who the hell she thinks she—"

"Shut up." Ignoring the man in cuffs, Hoyt asked the question he already knew the answer to. "You're Rebecca West?"

"Yes." She raised her chin, anger burning in her eyes. "And you are?"

"Deputy Hoyt Frost. I'd like to have a word with you out in the hallway."

She scowled back to the man before nodding to Greg, who Hoyt was relieved to see had been standing there silently all along, and headed for the door. Hoyt let her pass and followed her out to the end of the hallway.

"Alden told me he hired you. You're former FBI, right?"

She crossed her arms over her chest and leaned back against a wall, her eyes boring into him. "Yes."

"Then you surely know that if you assault this guy in any way, he'll walk."

Rebecca rolled her eyes. "Yes, I'm aware of that. This isn't my first interrogation. Which is why I only touched his shirt. Nothing says I can't push him into ratting out the Yacht Club's actions."

Hoyt stared into her eyes. Had this new-to-town temporary cop gotten answers about a club the department had been struggling with for years?

"What's your plan?"

Rebecca rubbed her face. "My plan is to get him to flip on the big fish."

Hoyt nodded. "Sit it out a bit, then. Let me have a word with him."

He expected her to argue, not wanting to hand over the man she'd captured and questioned. That and the fact that he wasn't technically back from medical leave. But she nodded as she held his gaze.

"Yeah, that's fine."

He wanted to ask more questions, but he left her alone for the moment, turning back to the interrogation room. When he stepped inside, the man sitting behind the table seemed a bit more composed but gave Hoyt a distrusting glance as he closed the door behind him. Greg was still leaning against the wall, not saying a word, but doing a very good job of looking menacing.

Hoyt began asking questions before his butt was in a chair. "What's your name?"

"Jay Griles." The man straightened, his handcuffs clinking on the table.

"Mr. Griles, you understand you're in quite a bit of trouble here, right?"

Griles said nothing but looked to his hands and nodded solemnly.

"I need you to actually say it for the recorded record."

Griles sighed and narrowed his eyes. "Yes."

"Did you pull the trigger that took out the sheriff?"

"No. No, I was on the beach with that crazy bitch that was just in here!"

"Well, I wasn't. Tell me what happened." Hoyt rested his wrists on the table, clasping his hands together and giving his best open and patient look.

Though Hoyt had no way of knowing what Griles had told Rebecca, when he was finished, Hoyt glanced over to Greg to get confirmation. The deputy nodded.

"Mr. Griles, when we fingerprint that boat, whose fingerprints are we going to find?"

"Mine, for sure. I mean, I was on the boat."

"And to your knowledge, who pulled the trigger on the gun that shot Sheriff Wallace?"

"I honestly don't know. I didn't see all of it with that bitch holding my face in the sand, but it wasn't me, I swear!"

Hoyt understood he'd already shown his level of ignorance in the matter by asking if Griles had pulled the trigger. To cover up this error, he laid a subtle trap. "I understand things got out of hand with Deputy West. Now, is there anything you told her that you'd like to alter or amend?"

Griles thought about it for a moment and finally shook his head. "No. I just...man, I just want to get out of here."

"I'm sure you do." This was the man who had, at the very

least, worked with one of the people responsible for Hoyt's friend's current plight. Even if he hadn't pulled the trigger on Alden, he'd been in the company of someone who had. Hoyt was quite sure Griles was looking at felony charges. "Hold tight, Mr. Griles."

Without another word, he exited the interrogation room again. He found Rebecca pouring a cup of coffee. Viviane and Melody sat together at the reception desk.

"Melody, we need to get some paperwork going. Looks like we're going to have Mr. Jay Griles as a guest in our holding cell. As for you, Ms. West...I need you to tell me everything you can about what happened on that beach and why one of my oldest friends is in the hospital."

30

Eyes burning with exhaustion, Rebecca stared at the computer screen, willing some new piece of information to find its way into her brain. She dropped her face into her hands.

"Come on. Give me something, dammit."

Hoyt Frost hadn't managed to get any more information out of Griles than she had before he left, but it would have been irresponsible and in bad taste for Rebecca to simply retreat back home to get some sleep. Besides, she still had a teenage girl's murder to solve.

After writing her report and adding her notes on what she'd learned from Griles into the system, she searched the databases for any files on the man. The only thing she found was that he'd been questioned regarding a drug bust four years ago but had never been viewed as a suspect. The two on the boat were still unidentified, so she had zero to go on with them.

The M.E. hadn't even started the autopsy, and the other was at the hospital getting stitched up. Neither one of their faces showed up as known accomplices of Jay Griles.

As her search came to an end, she scanned the records she'd already viewed—records involving the Yacht Club. She searched for any link to Griles or Nags Head but found none. Not surprising, considering how little information there really was on the organization.

That, at least, was no longer a rumor. The Yacht Club was real. There was a hierarchy, and she'd already caught one of the minnows. And he'd been hired, along with the other two, by someone in charge.

Who? She was determined to find that out.

She reclined in the seat at Deputy Hudson's desk and replayed the conversation she'd had with Griles. Based on what he'd told her, as well as her gut reaction to his story and denial, she was starting to feel quite sure the Yacht Club had nothing to do with Cassie's murder. If that was the case, it meant Wallace's original hunch that the club had nothing to do with the girl's death had been spot on. And it also confirmed that the shoot-out that took the sheriff down had been ill-advised and unnecessary.

But he'd gone along with it.

Maybe because Wallace had trusted her insights, or maybe because he, too, was desperate for answers. Regardless, Rebecca felt beyond guilty, and she sat with that culpability heavy on her shoulders.

From where she'd taken up position in Deputy Hudson's chair, she had line of sight on the entire bullpen. Greg Abner was still at his station in the back, reading something on a battered Kindle. Clearly, this was a man who was used to the late nights and random bouts of inactivity.

Frost had left some time ago while she dealt with the paperwork. Not that it mattered, he couldn't really do anything to help that process along.

Not wanting to bother Abner, Rebecca went to the front desk and found Viviane Darby's small station employee directory. Finding Deputy Locke's cell number, she placed a call, well aware that she was likely the last person he wanted to speak with right now.

When it rang four times without an answer, Rebecca expected to be kicked to voicemail. But Locke surprised her, answering before the fifth ring. "This is Locke."

"Hey, it's Rebecca. Any news on the sheriff?"

"He's still in surgery." Locke's voice was stern, heavy with blame that he clearly wanted to place. "One of the surgeons came out. Said in bullshit medical speak that it's not looking promising."

The news hit Rebecca like a punch. All she could say in response was, "I see."

"Did you get anything out of the guy from the beach?"

She was surprised he bothered asking, having assumed he'd want to be done with her as soon as possible. "A little. Enough to feel a bit more confident that the Yacht Club probably had nothing to do with Cassie's murder. The guy we apprehended is Jay Griles, and he's heading to a holding cell. That name ring any bells for you? I don't have the names of the other two yet."

"No." The answer came without much thought. "Look, I'm wiped out. I'm going to sit in the waiting room until there's news. I'll call when there's another update."

He disconnected the call, leaving Rebecca in silence. She thought of Wallace explaining to her why he tended to stay away from Yacht Club issues that didn't directly impact life and peace on Shadow Island. Yet...he hadn't rebelled against her plan to meet with Dillon Miller's contact.

Wallace had trusted her, and now, it seemed like he might very well die as a result. The guilt was a heavy knife cutting right into her. Without even thinking about it, she walked back to Greg's desk and jotted her cell number on a scrap of paper.

"I'm heading to the hospital. If anything comes up or there are any updates at all, call this number, and I'll be back as soon as possible."

"You sure about that?" There was a hint of respect in his voice. Apparently, he'd expected her to not give much of a damn about the well-being of Sheriff Wallace.

"Deputy Abner, I'm not really sure of anything right now."

She left that comment hanging in the air as she hurried to the door.

When she arrived at the hospital, Rebecca discovered Wallace was still in surgery. That wasn't good news, she knew as she grabbed a cup of coffee and headed to the third floor waiting area.

When she entered, she didn't see Locke, but Hoyt Frost was there, sipping coffee from a plastic cup and scrolling on his phone. When he glanced up to find her standing there, he looked surprised.

"Did you just get here?"

"Yes." She cupped both hands around her own warm cup. "I talked to Locke about half an hour ago. I thought he'd be here too."

Frost's gaze flickered away. "When I got here, he filled me in and then decided to head back to the island. A friend of his took him back." He shrugged. "But that's Locke. He's never been one to just sit idly by when there's work to be done."

She frowned. "He's on administrative leave, so there isn't much he can do right now until the officer involved shooter bullshit is taken care of."

Frost lifted a shoulder. "He'll find something to pass the time."

Silence sat between them like a living thing until Rebecca

was compelled to ask the question burning in her mind. "He blames me, doesn't he?"

Frost's lips twitched. "I think he blames the situation. Not *just* you."

Rebecca didn't believe him. After all, Locke hadn't even bothered calling to let her know he was heading back to the island. She also felt sure that he never had any intention of calling her with updates on Wallace. And why should he?

She wasn't part of the team. Not really.

"Any updates?"

"A nurse came in five minutes ago. He's still in surgery, still hanging in there. His liver was shredded by one of the shots, and another one missed his heart by less than an inch. I asked about the likelihood that he'll survive it all, and she didn't answer. Not with words, anyway."

Rebecca's stomach sank. "She gave you the *look*?"

His smiled dripped with sadness as he nodded. "I almost forgot you're FBI. You've probably seen those faces that tell you the answer when people don't want to talk."

"Yeah. I've *given* quite a few of them too." She sat in the chair next to him and took a deep, shuddering breath. "Frost, I know you and Wallace are good friends. Just the way he spoke about you, that was all I needed to know. I'm sorry about this. If you get right down to the core of it, it's my fault."

Frost put his phone away. "I won't lie to you, West. When Locke told me what went down, I felt the same way. I blamed you instantly. But if that's where the case led you, I think it was a good move. It's not your fault. The fault lies with the idiots who pulled guns on a couple of cops."

Rebecca appreciated the comment, but it did little to assuage her guilt.

Frost sipped his coffee, grimacing a bit as it went down. "Want to know something pretty special about Wallace?"

She perked up at that. "Of course."

"As Locke was riding in with him, Wallace only said a handful of words because he was so out of it. Despite how hurt he was, Wallace managed to tell Locke to let Dillon Miller know that what went down wasn't *his* fault."

She nodded, admiring Wallace's character. And he was right. It wasn't Dillon's fault. It was hers. Another brick of guilt stacked on top of all the others she carried.

"Can I ask you something?"

Frost's question yanked her out of her self-pity. When she turned back toward him, he was looking directly at her. There was something about the way he met her gaze that reminded her of Wallace, and she could see why they were such good friends. "Sure."

"You barely knew him. Why'd you come here rather than stay on the island?"

Rebecca didn't even have to think about it. "I'm a cop. FBI, ATF, state, city, county, doesn't matter. We come together in times like this. But...other than that, I like and respect the sheriff. It just felt right to be here."

"Well, I'm here. I've known the man for a very long time, and at the risk of making him seem a little uncool, I'm just about the only thing resembling family he has." He made a shooing gesture with his hand. "You go. You do what needs to be done back on the island, and I'll stand guard here."

Rebecca glanced at her watch and read the time, blinking to make sure the numbers were right. She'd been working for over twenty-six hours straight.

"It's ten after eight. No way forensics has anything ready for us yet." She yawned so big her jaw popped. "I need to check on the shooter who's getting stitched up for his mugshots. Coastal Ridge is going to transport him when he's out. I don't know that there's much to be done."

"Well, I think Wallace gave Locke the next instructions.

Check in with Dillon Miller before the rumor mill reaches him. But, between you and me, I'd start with some sleep. Just a few hours. You're not a bad looking lady, West, but right now, you look like death warmed over."

She allowed a small smile. "I feel like death warmed over, actually, but here..." she waved a hand to indicate the hospital waiting room, "doesn't seem like the right place to complain." She managed to stifle a second yawn, but just barely. "I don't know. It seems wrong."

"I can see why you'd think that. But if you're worried about perception, what's going to be more fitting? You being here on the other side of the bridge after this shoot-out, or back on the island making sure more shit doesn't hit the fan with a clear head and enough energy that you don't fall down from exhaustion?"

He was right, and she knew it. When she got back to her feet, she wondered if her bones had been replaced with cement. The adrenaline from the gunfight, the interrogation of Jay Griles that followed, and the reams of paperwork had wiped her out.

"Call me when you hear something."

Frost only nodded, again sipping and grimacing from his hospital-grade coffee. It seemed like an appropriate send-off as Rebecca made her way out of the waiting room and back to the elevators. By the time she returned to the visitor parking lot and got to her truck, she was pretty sure she was sleepwalking.

Before entering her truck, though, she inhaled the ocean air, reveling in its coolness, surprised as always by how it could be both pungent and alluring at the same time.

The wind picked up, pushing her weary frame toward the driver's seat. Rebecca got the message. She wasn't needed here. Shadow needed her more.

31

Serenity McCreedy stared at her phone's screen, rereading the message for the dozenth time.

She knew Dillon Miller well enough. They'd known each other since kindergarten, but Serenity had distanced herself from him and most other boys like him as early as sixth grade. She was pretty sure she'd never spoken more than three or four sentences to him since middle school, even though he'd dated Cassie for a month shy of two years.

But now, Dillon had texted her. She'd almost told Chris about it but didn't want to stir that hornet's nest. From what she understood, there were already some guys from the Yacht Club who were nervous about Dillon Miller.

Apparently, Dillon had texted one of the guys who'd been trying to recruit Cassie. And now, based on what Chris had told her during the drive across the bridge to drop her off at home, there had been some sort of shoot-out. Someone was dead, and a guy Serenity sort of knew, Jay Griles, had been arrested.

If Chris knew Dillon had texted her, they might kill him.

And she might be in some trouble just because the idiot had her number.

Even though it was risky, Serenity had texted Dillon back the moment she got into her house, promising to meet up with him later, though she wouldn't commit to a time. Her father was gone, as usual. She was pretty sure he was in Dallas this week. Or maybe it was Miami. She really had no idea. It was impossible to keep up with his work schedule.

After returning Dillon's text, Serenity had known she wouldn't be able to go back to bed or even play on her phone. As tired as she was, she was also wired. She'd done a bit of coke just before Chris let her out of the car, and that was still firing in her system, keeping her mostly awake.

So here she was. She just hoped meeting Dillon wasn't a huge mistake.

As she walked across the beach, she spotted him in the distance. He was sitting in the same area Serenity had tanned with Cassie on multiple occasions. He'd picked the spot for that reason, she supposed—a way to tug at her heartstrings.

When she finally approached him, she didn't bother sitting down, but inspected him closely. Would he try to record their conversation? She didn't know.

Maybe she was paranoid, but she needed to be careful.

Dillon appeared wiped out, pale and sick. Serenity had always thought Cassie was out of Dillon's league, so she supposed losing her had wrecked him even more so. It certainly looked like that was the case. Not like he loved her nearly as much or as long as she had. Cassie had always been her best friend. They were practically sisters.

"Thanks for coming." The words sounded like sandpaper coming from his lips.

"You said it was urgent. What choice did I have? So...*is* it urgent?" The lack of sleep and drugs in her system were making her especially bitchy this morning. All she really wanted to do was lay down and forget about everything that had happened in the last week. But she had to keep up appearances until she managed to get away.

"Depends on how you look at it."

"I know you were texting someone in the Yacht Club who knew Cassie. And I know that resulted in a massive shoot-out last night."

Dillon seemed genuinely surprised. "What?"

His ignorance pissed her off almost as much as his stupid, sad face. "Someone was killed, Dillon. And Sheriff Wallace is in the hospital." Her words struck home, and she internally smirked as she watched his face crumble.

"Fuck."

"Fuck is right. What the hell were you thinking bringing the Yacht Club into this all? You know they don't play around."

Dillon returned his gaze to the ocean, apparently finding it hard to look directly at her. "Dad said if I had anything that linked Cassie to them, I had to tell. Look...the cops have been talking to me a lot the last few days. I found out yesterday Cassie was pregnant when she was killed."

Serenity frowned, pretending to be surprised. "Pregnant?"

The idiot was trying to nod his head while shaking it at the same time. "Yes. And before you ask, no...it wasn't me. We never even had sex, so I'm assuming it was one of those child-predator scumbags in the Yacht Club. *That's* why I did it."

Serenity couldn't stop the disgusted sigh that came out of her. They weren't child predators. Dillon didn't know what the hell he was talking about. He didn't even know the daddies, certainly not as well as she did. She'd been partying with them for years now.

"Dillon...I think you may want to get back to your house. If you really did set that meeting up last night and someone in the club is dead because of it..." She let the silence fill in for her. There was no need to tell a local what the Yacht Club might do to someone who fucked with them.

"I know." He tried to say something else, but a bout of weeping stopped him. He hung his head low and wiped at his eyes. "She was pregnant, Serenity. I thought she loved me, and she was..."

He trailed off, and Serenity was glad. Not only did she not want to step knee-deep in drama that would get her into hot water with the Yacht Club, but god, she hated to see a boy cry.

"Do you know who it was?" Dillon looked up at her with tear-filled eyes.

"No. I swear it." She didn't even feel guilty about the lie. Bored and even more tired now, she made a show of looking at her watch. "I need to get back home now. I have no idea when my dad might show up from his most recent trip, and I just got back home from a night out, so..."

He waved her away, as if he really could care less. The feeling was mutual. Serenity took a few steps backward before turning away from him, glad to have the wreck of a boy out of her sight. She waited several more minutes before turning around to see how much space she'd put between them.

When she was comfortably out of his sight, Serenity pulled out her phone and pulled up a number she had saved a while ago but had never assigned a name to. She pressed *Call* and placed the phone to her ear. It rang twice before he answered, his voice barely above a whisper. "Yeah?"

"Hey, it's me. I just spoke with him, and he has no idea. You're in the clear."

"You're absolutely certain?"

She smiled at how lame Cassie's baby daddy was. This was going to be too easy.

"Yes. He doesn't know. But you're not in the clear with me." She lowered her voice, almost spitting out the words. "And I think you know I have more than enough information on you. More than that, I have *proof.*"

"Don't do this." He sounded like he was on the verge of tears. So pathetic. "Please."

Serenity smiled as she continued down the morning-kissed beach. Though she liked the Yacht Club daddies, it really wasn't her scene anymore. She wanted out, and this might be her only means of escape. "Oh, I won't. I'll keep it to myself...for a price."

There was hardly any hesitation before he responded. "Name it."

32

Rebecca woke to the alarm on her cell phone. She silenced it, swinging her legs over the edge of the couch and looked out the living room window to the beautiful June morning.

It was nearly ten, and she'd managed to get a little less than an hour and a half of sleep. She checked her phone to see if she'd somehow missed a call or text from Frost or Greg Abner, but there was nothing.

Running through a brief morning routine, she showered, brushed her teeth, grabbed a bite to eat, and pulled on some clean clothes. It was nine-fifty when she walked out to her truck. As far as she knew, it might still be too early for a teenage boy to be awake on a summer weekday, but she didn't care. If Dillon wanted answers concerning the death of his girlfriend, he'd just have to adjust.

It was a serene moment, driving along the highway with the ocean just off to her left, the morning colors dancing off the water. The scene was undeniably beautiful, but knowing Sheriff Wallace was hanging somewhere between life and death made it almost painful.

She made her way to the Miller residence, going slightly over the speed limit. She thought of going by the precinct to check in but didn't see the point in risking a tense run-in with Locke, if he was sitting behind a desk. It was an encounter she knew was coming, but she figured she'd get the equally tense moment with Dillon Miller out of the way first.

She pulled into the driveway of the Miller residence less than thirty minutes after she'd opened her eyes. Like just about everything else on the island this morning, it looked bright and tranquil at the same time. As she made her way to the front door, she passed by the basketball hoop Dillon had been practicing on the last time she'd spoken to him—the same hoop where Wallace had made that impressive three-point shot. She turned her head as she continued on to the front entrance, where she knocked softly.

The door was answered almost right away by Mrs. Miller. She held a cup of coffee in her right hand and a comb in the other. Rebecca assumed she'd disrupted Mrs. Miller's morning routine.

"Deputy…West, right?"

"Yes, that's right. Mrs. Miller, is Dillon home?"

"Actually, no. He stepped out early this morning. Said he was going for a walk to clear his head." She frowned and looked beyond Rebecca, out to the yard. "Lord knows he needs it. I did think he'd be back by now, though."

"When did he step out?"

"A little before six-thirty. It's not like him to wake up that early, but he's understandably had some things on his mind."

Rebecca tried to gauge the mother's level of concern, but it was hard to read her. She appeared to still be tired and obviously in a hurry to get out the door. "Would you like for me to go looking for him?"

"No, no. He'll come back. He's fine."

"Oh, okay." Rebecca mentally crossed her fingers. "Well, while I'm here, I'm wondering if you'd allow me to have a look around Dillon's room."

If Mrs. Miller had been indifferent to Rebecca's presence before, it changed in that moment. A wildfire sprang up in her eyes—the protective grit of a mother. "And what for?"

"To be frank, his tip about the messages on his phone led to a substantial lead." She hated the underlying lie and also how much she was leaving out. But telling the woman that the tip had also led to the shooting of Sherriff Wallace certainly wasn't going to help. "And he didn't tell us about it until much later after the first time we spoke to him. While I don't see Dillon as a strong suspect, I do see him as someone who might keep secrets to preserve Cassie's memory."

And just like that, another lie had flown out of Rebecca's mouth. Dillon was still a strong suspect officially. The death after a pregnancy not caused by him had him at the top of her list again...she just hadn't allowed herself to fully accept it.

Mrs. Miller's face went from hard to soft and then back to something resembling pure contempt. "At some point, you have to leave my boy out of this."

"I agree. And I hope that time comes sooner rather than later. But for now—"

"Just go ahead." Mrs. Miller waved a frustrated hand. "I'd much rather you do it while he's not here than have him watch you go through his personal space."

Rebecca took the offer, no matter how disgruntled it was. She stepped inside as the mother opened the door wider. "Thank you."

"Sure." Mrs. Miller responded with pure sarcasm, her voice thick with anger. "Why not just take an entire circuit of the entire house while you're here?"

Why yes, I think I will. Thank you very much for the offer.

Rebecca managed to keep her own sarcasm at bay. "Are you the only one home?"

"Yes. Dillon's gone, and Owen left about fifteen minutes ago to run an early morning errand for work. I believe it was just dropping some packages off at the post office, so he should be back soon."

Rebecca was quite sure this was meant as a thinly veiled threat, a way of telling her that, if she was still searching Dillon's room when Owen got home, there might be a scene.

So be it.

Mrs. Miller led Rebecca through the living room and into the hallway at the back of the house. She said nothing at all when she stopped at the bathroom and stepped inside to resume her morning routine.

Rebecca overlooked the rudeness, and after a few steps, found what was unmistakably the room of a seventeen-year-old boy. The door was opened about halfway, revealing an unmade bed, a pair of flip-flops on the floor, and a television sitting on a low dresser. An Xbox and several games littered the top of the dresser as well.

Rebecca stepped inside, not quite sure what she was looking for. If Dillon had gone for a walk on the beach, he'd likely taken his phone with him. She spotted a MacBook sitting on the floor at the foot of the bed, but when she opened the lid, she wasn't at all surprised to find that it was locked with a fingerprint ID.

She took another careful scan of the room, but the only thing of note she could find were a few printed pictures of Dillon and Cassie, the sort a couple took in those little booths in the mall that came out on strips. She studied them for a moment and then recalled two things Mrs. Miller had told her.

First, she'd given a veiled threat that her husband would be home soon—not that Rebecca really cared. But she'd also given a very flippant sort of approval for her to check the entire house. Sure, it had been angry and sarcastic, but that would be enough to pass in court if she was accused of snooping around.

She moved out of Dillon's room, listening to the sounds of Mrs. Miller getting ready in the bathroom. Rebecca looked toward the end of the hall and saw three other rooms. One, also partially open, was a coat closet. Another, the door standing wide open, was the master bedroom. The third appeared to be Owen Miller's office.

It was a clean and tidy space, decorated minimally. A thin, long desk sat against the back wall. It was occupied with a laptop, a desktop monitor, and several folders. She tried to recall what Owen Miller did for a living, but his occupation didn't want to surface in her tired brain.

She hurried into the office and had a look around. With no drawers to search on the minimalist desk, she studied the papers on top. Everything appeared to be work-related, and again, she was faced with a locked laptop. Discouraged, she left the office and started back down the hallway, ready to give Mrs. Miller her thanks once more before making her way out.

Passing by a coat closet, though, she decided another couple minutes wouldn't matter. She peeked inside to find a few windbreakers and raincoats hung from a rod up top. On the floor, an umbrella was propped against the wall, and a few pairs of shoes were lined neatly at the back. She nearly shut the door, but at the last moment, she did a double take.

There were five pairs of shoes in the closet. Three of them clearly belonged to Mrs. Miller; a pink pair of Crocs and two pairs of very feminine-looking sandals. The others were a beat-up pair of flip-flops that were larger than the ones she'd seen in Dillon's room as well as a pair of well-worn low-cut boots—the sort that were built with the frame of sneakers but more closely resembled a work boot. They were the same size as the old flip-flops, and she assumed they belonged to Owen Miller.

But what had caught Rebecca's attention was how dirty the boots were in comparison to the other shoes, and how they'd been tossed into the back corner, not lined up as the others were.

She recognized the brand right away. They were common footwear for rougher work and labor. Heavy duty and comfortable, Rebecca's father had owned a pair despite rarely needing to use them. Kept them in the closet "just in case." She knelt to get a better look at the caked-on dirt, especially how it stained the top of the toe area. It was dark in color, almost black.

What was that?

Shining her phone's flashlight on the boots, Rebecca studied the tiny specs of blue and green.

Colonies of algae. The same family of algae that had been turned up by the storm the night Cassie was murdered?

It was exactly like the muck down in the marshes. She knew because she'd had plenty of time to inspect the gunk as she'd scrubbed it from her borrowed waders. In fact, she remembered that the muck hadn't gotten onto the toes of those until she had knelt down, putting all her weight there and sinking farther into the soft soil. Whoever wore these not only walked in the marsh, they very well could have knelt there.

Like you would have to do in order to choke the life out of a young pregnant woman?

Interesting.

Rebecca didn't even take time to consider what she was doing when she tapped the camera app on her phone and snapped several pictures from different angles. She didn't have an evidence bag on her, or even gloves. Otherwise, she would have taken a sample of the muck. If she did that now, she risked tainting the evidence.

If the boots even were evidence, she reminded herself, though her gut instinct was nodding its head. Plenty of people had similar work shoes in their houses, but without forensics, even the algae filled mud was circumstantial at best. She needed something to give to a judge in order to get a warrant. Hopefully, visual confirmation would be enough.

She didn't dare take the boots from their current location without a warrant, and it was a big risk leaving them where they were. Made from leather, she reasoned that, even if they were washed between now and when a judge signed the document, forensics would likely be able to pull them apart and find some traces. So long as the owner didn't notice she had disturbed them and got rid of them entirely.

Being careful to close the door without a sound, Rebecca lifted her voice so the woman down the hall could hear her. "Thanks again, Mrs. Miller. Sorry to have bothered you."

"Uh huh." The woman didn't even bother coming to see her out, which was perfectly fine with Rebecca.

As calmly as she could manage, Rebecca walked to the front door. When she got out onto the porch, she broke into a sprint. She needed to get back to the office so she could send the pictures to her computer…and the forensics lab.

Speeding away, Rebecca's mind turned back toward the marshes where Cassie Leigh had died. Though she didn't know the science behind it all, Rebecca knew that different areas of land possessed their own distinct mixture of soil, water, salt, and minerals, plus a whole bunch of stuff she probably couldn't even pronounce.

Along with the storm produced algae, with luck, the little sliver of marsh possessed its own special recipe of dirt soup. And if it did, the muck on the boots could be the missing link they needed to get a DNA swab.

From both Miller men.

33

Serenity McCreedy stared at the back of the old surf shop as anxiety crept into her stomach. Had she gotten too deep into this? Had she made a mistake by saying she'd help keep an ear to the ground to make sure the local pigs weren't getting too close to the Yacht Club daddies?

It was sure starting to feel that way—a feeling that was intensifying as she listened to the voice in her ear. It was the second Daddy she'd spoken to today, and it made her wonder if she was being used by just about everyone involved in the whole damn mess.

"And you're sure he'll come?" His question was more like a command.

"Yes." Serenity rolled her eyes, glad he couldn't see her reaction. "I told Mr. Miller that his secret would be safe with me if he had the money ready by noon."

"Good girl. Just as long as you *know* he'll bring it."

"He will." Realizing her voice held a slight tremor, she strengthened her tone. The daddies needed to know they could trust her. "I mean, he sounded out of his mind." She snapped her fingers, acting as if she'd just learned the news she was about to share. "Oh and get this…Dillon admitted to setting Jay and his guys up…said he told the cops about all of it and arranged that meeting out near the cottage last night. That's why the shoot-out happened. Dillon admitted it right to my face."

The growl was loud in her ear. "That little shit. Well, then, I guess he needs to be taught a lesson."

Serenity envisioned Dillon Miller in her head, torn to pieces in an "accident." Her heart went out to him…a bit. That, coupled with the still-growing nerves tearing through her, made her feel she had to try *something* to slow this all down. To end it completely if she could. Maybe she didn't like the guy as a friend, but he was still a friend of a friend, if nothing else.

"Yeah, but I'd wait a bit. Wait until I get this cash. The cops are really pushing hard now that Sheriff Wallace got shot. Let him stew in it a bit."

The daddy on the other end chuckled. "Damn, you do have a mean streak in you, huh?"

"Sometimes." She hated herself a bit as she said it. But as her actual dad always said, it was time for her to put her big girl panties on and deal with it.

"Maybe we just set the whole damn Miller house on fire. One little family causing us too many problems. How the hell did Dillon not know what was going on?"

Serenity covered her eyes with her hand, wishing she'd just kept her big mouth shut. But this particular daddy was powerful and had a way of convincing her to spill her guts.

It wasn't that she was afraid of him. Not exactly. But being on his good side was definitely preferable if a person wanted to live happily ever after.

Unlike Cassie.

Poor Cassie.

Serenity still couldn't believe she was gone.

After learning she was pregnant, Cassie had refused to tell Serenity who the father was, which had pissed her off more than a little. Just two days before she died, Cassie had finally shared the whole story...

"Owen's the father."

Serenity didn't even know the name. "Who?"

Cassie dropped her chin on her knees, gazing out on the ocean from where they sat on the sand. "Dillon's father."

Serenity gaped at her friend. She was both horrified and proud. Who knew little Cassie Leigh had it in her. "How long?"

Cassie blew out a breath. "About three months now."

It had been like pulling teeth to get the entire story out of her friend, but the nutshell version was that Cassie had felt like a stupid little girl after her freak out at the Yacht Club party. It wasn't rebellion, not really, but just a way for her to feel as if she was doing something grown-up to redeem herself. Not with Dillon, though. With someone who knew what they were doing.

"I'd seen how Owen looked at me, so I knew it would be easy to, you know..."

Serenity laughed. "Screw him?"

A wistful smile played on Cassie's lips. "Seduce him. Or even better...make him want to seduce me."

They had talked about how Owen could be both her sugar daddy and baby daddy, and how he would set Cassie up in an apartment or even divorce his wife and they'd elope to some wonderful tropical island.

Owen wasn't ridiculously rich, but he did own rental properties. They'd have a good life and maybe a couple more babies. Cassie had only come down off her cloud when Serenity reminded her that those babies would be Dillon's half siblings.

Cassie hadn't liked being reminded of that.

On Friday, Serenity and Cassie had role-played how she was going to break the news about the baby, and though Cassie had been nervous to tell Owen, she'd sworn that she wouldn't back down.

And then she was dead.

Even before Serenity had learned how Cassie had been killed, she'd known who'd done it right away.

She'd gotten his number and texted him, letting him know she was on to him. Letting him know she knew about the baby. Telling him that she'd keep his secret in exchange for half a million dollars.

Hush money that would allow her to run away from this island and start a new life. She could go to New York and get an apartment with one of those photographers who clearly couldn't get women their own age.

I could live like a queen up there.

"Yeah, right."

New York was nothing but a pipe dream, Serenity knew. She was in too deep with the Yacht Club. They'd never let her go. Well, not until her boobs began to sag at least.

Staying on the island wouldn't be that bad, would it?

They'd take care of her, she knew. They'd provide her with a life of luxury, and all she'd have to give them in exchange was herself. Not as much as Cassie, but still…

"Let me know when you get the cash."

Serenity blinked, having nearly forgotten she was still on the phone. "Yeah, of course."

After a few more dictates that only an asshole man could make, Serenity ended the call and again stared out at the empty parking lot behind the old, abandoned surf shop, wondering why Owen had wanted to meet here.

It was daytime, at least, so she wasn't afraid he'd do anything crazy. Nothing bad ever happened in the light.

Did it?

Sitting in her car, she grew more scared as she waited for Owen to arrive, and then got fed up with her fear.

"Screw that asshole. Cassie deserved better." She blew out a breath. "And so do I."

34

After tracking down Owen Miller's place of employment, Rebecca called the place, only to be told that, "Mr. Miller isn't available to take your call."

Rebecca had thrown around her law enforcement weight and finally learned that Miller hadn't been to work since Friday.

Interesting.

The man was lying to his wife. Bad sign.

Rebecca had a feeling she knew what else he'd been lying about.

She just needed to prove it.

Parking her truck in the same place Wallace had stopped the patrol SUV just a few days ago, she was filled with a rush of melancholy from walking the same path to the marshes. It was pretty and peaceful this morning. The police crime tape was gone and only the tops of the long grass stirred in the morning breeze. Their sound reminded Rebecca of a faint radio station on a stereo from another room.

She walked around the farthest edges of the tall grass, making sure not to cut too close to where Cassie had been killed. Even when she had to eventually angle herself in that direction, she was careful not to trample over the ground where the girl died. Besides, she only needed to see the mud near the area where Cassie had taken her last breath.

As she made her way over, taking her phone out to bring up the pictures of what she believed were Owen Miller's boots, she forced herself to take a closer look at both Miller men.

She started with the son. Maybe the young man had discovered Cassie had been sleeping with someone else, and in a jealous rage, he'd wrapped his hands around her throat and squeezed.

Then, after coming to his senses, maybe he'd told his father what he'd done, and Owen had come out to make sure his son had left no clues. That theory lined up, she supposed, but she hadn't found Dillon's shoes with muck all over them now, had she? And damn it all to hell, she believed the boy when he said he and Cassie hadn't been having sex.

There was another plausible scenario. Perhaps the person Cassie had been sleeping with was Owen Miller, and he had killed her to keep his name out of the public ear. Some of the pieces did line up, she supposed. Maybe Cassie and Owen had been having an intimate moment when she decided to tell him she was pregnant. He'd clearly not taken it very well, and she only had time to pull on her dress before she ran. Her death had been the result.

Rebecca was close enough to the location of Cassie's murder to compare the dirt. She knelt and held her phone as close to the ground as she could. She zoomed in and saw what she'd suspected. The varying colors of the dried muck on the shoe were lighter, but that was to be expected, as it had dried. Even the greens and blues of the algae colonies had dried to the same shade. In other words, it was an exact match. And she was quite sure the pictures that had been taken by forensics shortly after Cassie's death would serve as yet another bit of evidence.

Did it prove that Owen Miller had killed Cassie Leigh? No. But it did prove that he'd been in this exact area since the storm. It could be enough for a warrant.

Rebecca snapped a few pictures with her phone camera and hurried back to her truck, now more determined than ever to find the answer.

When she arrived back at the station, she was not at all surprised to see the only people present were Viviane and Greg Abner. Greg remained at his usual spot, and Rebecca couldn't help but wonder if the old man had moved at all since last night.

"Hi, Viviane, any updates on the sheriff?"

The smooth skin on Viviane's forehead creased into a frown. "Still in surgery as of five minutes ago."

Rebecca placed a hand on the woman's shoulder, trying to appear more confident than she felt. "That means he's strong."

Tears shimmered in Viviane's dark eyes as she squeezed Rebecca's hand. "I pray that's true."

Rebecca resisted the urge to take the woman in her arms and nodded instead. "Me too."

A stranger appeared in the doorway. He wore a deputy uniform, and considering he wasn't Locke, Abner, or Frost, Rebecca came to the brilliant conclusion that this must be Deputy Darian Hudson.

As much as she hated the idea of pulling a man away from his newborn, Rebecca sure was glad of the support.

She stuck out a hand and was surprised when the deputy took it. She was sure he'd already been told about the seaside battle and Rebecca's part in it. For his part, Hudson, though not likely to throw her a party, didn't appear to place any blame on her shoulders as they introduced themselves.

"Thank you for coming in."

He lifted a broad shoulder, and Rebecca was struck by how beautiful his pale brown eyes were, especially in contrast to his dark umber skin. "It's what cops do in times like these."

The deputy was right. When the shit hit the fan, they came together. And last night, shit had hit the fan at full speed.

She met his gaze. "Thank you."

His nod was solemn. "Tell me what I can do to help."

Just as she was about to share her possible lead with Hudson, Rebecca's phone rang. It was Hoyt Frost.

Rebecca's heart picked up speed as she answered the call. "How is he?" she asked in lieu of a greeting. When everyone turned to stare at her, Rebecca tapped the speaker button. "I'm putting you on speaker so everyone can hear."

"He's out of surgery." Frost's voice sounded raw with fatigue. "He's still not responsive and not out of the woods by far."

Much needed relief flooded through her. "But the surgery was successful?"

Frost sighed. "Yeah, I think so. How are things at the station?"

Rebecca glanced around at what was left of their crew. Greg Abner's feet were up on his desk while Viviane seemed ready to jump out of her skin. Hudson was solid, though the shadows under his eyes were a reminder that he was supposed to be home not sleeping because of his baby, not a murder case.

"Actually, I'm not sure. I came across something this morning that could potentially be a huge break in the Cassie Leigh case." She licked her lips, unsure of how to ask the question weighing on her mind. "Frost..."

"Do you need me?"

She exhaled her relief on a long puff of air. "Yes. I need as many hands on deck as I can get for the next few hours. Consider it an unofficial APB."

"On who?" Life crept into his tone.

"Owen Miller."

There was a collective pause, not only on the line but with the three people in the room with Rebecca. Frost spoke first. "How's that?"

"I'll explain it when you get here. He's the new number one. Will you come?"

Rebecca could almost feel the tug of war the deputy was experiencing back on the mainland. He hesitated, but not for long. "Yeah. Give me thirty minutes."

"Thank you."

Rebecca ended the call and met Hudson's gaze. "Want to ride with me to the Millers's house?"

The tall deputy grabbed his hat. "Let's go."

35

Rebecca opted to take one of the three Explorers sitting in the side lot, Hudson following behind her in an Explorer of his own. The time to be more official was now. And, for the first time, she actually felt as if she was a real part of the Shadow Island force—even temporarily.

She couldn't help but wonder if Hudson and Frost would be as confident that the algae filled muck on Owen's boots was the smoking gun they'd been looking for. Once it was collected officially, a simple lab test might be enough to bring him in for official questioning and get a warrant to search his house.

And most important of all, get a DNA swab.

At the Miller residence, Rebecca was disappointed to find the place empty. Standing in the shade of a tree, she filled Hudson in on all she knew, something she should have done before jumping in the SUV and taking off.

The deputy listened quietly, only asking questions for clarification as she explained her theory about the algae as well as the type of boot she'd seen in Miller's closet.

Hudson took it all in before lifting a finger. "Miller could have gone out to the marsh as a lookie-loo after the body was found."

He was right.

"True. But look at this photo." She pulled an image of the boots up on her phone. "See the way the mud comes up over the toes?"

Hudson took the phone from her hand, pinching the screen to enlarge it. "Yeah. I see what you're saying." He handed it back. "You think he was kneeling and leaning forward?"

The guy was quick. "Yeah, exactly. Possibly even leaning forward to strangle a girl."

The young deputy stuffed his hands in his pockets. "Yeah. Possibly."

"Something else jumped out at me. Owen Miller works down at the docks, right?"

Hudson nodded. "Yeah, he owns a fiberglass company. Works on boats if I remember correctly."

"I know this might seem thin, but I noticed that Miller's worn long sleeves each time I've seen him. For a guy who works on boats, isn't that strange?"

Hudson lifted a shoulder. "Not really. Could wear the sleeves for sun protection. Besides, fiberglass gets all over the place. Could be he's used to wearing sleeves for that reason too."

Rebecca chewed her bottom lip. "Cassie had skin under her nails. Labs are still being run so we don't know who yet."

Hudson uncrossed his arms. "She was strangled manually?"

Rebecca nodded. "Big hands too. Wearing thick work gloves. The kind of gloves you might have if you worked in fiberglass."

Hudson's intelligent pale brown eyes sparked to life as they batted the theory back and forth. "And would require strength too. The kind of strength you'd get from working with your hands all day. Owen Miller isn't the sort of guy that spends time out in the marshes, but he is the sort of guy that likes to hang out at the beaches, staring at the spring breaker chicks that come up. I've seen him doing that more than a few times. And the fact that the victim was his son's girlfriend..." He shrugged.

"Someone was having sex with Cassie, and the only places she was known to frequent were here and school." Rebecca spread her hands. "If it wasn't Dillon, as everyone says..."

Hudson met her gaze squarely. "I think you're right. We go after Owen Miller then. Good call."

"With these pictures to show him of the algae mud linking him to the crime scene, that could be enough to get him to crack. Then, we can get a warrant to search his house since there's no one to let us in, and I don't think Mrs. Miller is going to allow me to do a walk-through a second time. Should we have Viviane dig up Owen Miller's license plate number and car model so we can track him down?"

That got her a smirk and a head shake. "Not quite. It's a small town, Ms. West. I know Owen Miller's vehicle."

"How about Frost? He's on the way."

"I'll let him know. As for now...you take the west coast, and I'll take the east. We're looking for a red pickup truck. A late model Ford."

"If you find him before Frost or me, don't immediately approach him. Get me and Frost on the line."

It was clear that Hudson didn't enjoy taking her orders, but he nodded all the same. Just as he was getting into his own Explorer, Rebecca called out to him.

"And hey, Hudson. Congratulations on the baby."

※

LOOKING at the island she'd known and loved as a child from behind the steering wheel of a police vehicle was surreal. She no longer saw the shops and buildings as the center of relaxation and fun but as a maze of sorts. Even the glimpses of the ocean between the buildings and the busier streets seemed less majestic. It was sad in a childlike way, but it also helped keep her mind sharp and on the task at hand.

Because it was mid-morning, the traffic on the roads wasn't bad. She spotted a few pickup trucks here and there, but none that met the description. She was stopped at a red light, examining a maroon Chevy parked in front of a barbershop, when her cell phone rang. She recognized the number as Frost's and answered.

"You on the island yet?"

"I am. Crossed the bridge about five minutes ago. More than that, though, I already stumbled upon something interesting. I don't have eyes on Owen Miller just·yet, but Alden came over last night...before..." Frost cleared his throat, and Rebecca's heart squeezed for him. "Anyway, he told me that Serenity McCreedy was sort of a missing piece to all of this."

"She may be. We don't quite know yet."

"Well, it seems she's back in town. Not only that, but it almost looks like she might be hiding or waiting on something."

Excitement buzzed through Rebecca's system. "Where?"

"There's an old surf shop about a mile after you get off the bridge. It's been boarded up for about five years now. I was passing by and caught sight of a car parked behind it. I wheeled back around and ran the plates just to be certain, and it's sure as hell her."

"Makes me wonder what she's waiting on." Rebecca chewed her bottom lip. "I don't want to let her distract us too much."

"Yeah, I'd say she's small potatoes at this point, but I think

I'll double back and see if she's still there. Worse comes to worst, I know where she liv...hey, hold on, West. I got an incoming. It's Viviane. One second..."

Rebecca waited, passing through the intersection when the light turned green. The thought that Serenity was back home and seemingly waiting for something behind an abandoned building was odd. Or was it? Maybe it was the girl's favorite hangout for all that she knew.

The line clicked in her ear as Frost came back on. "West?"

"Yeah, I'm here."

"Viviane's got the plate number for you. It's...shit..."

"What?"

"I've got eyes on Owen Miller, and he's pulling in right beside Serenity McCreedy."

Interesting.

Rebecca checked her GPS. "I'm less than three minutes away. Is there another exit from the business?"

"Yeah, on the west side."

Running all the options through her mind, she came up with a plan. "You circle to the west side of the building and make sure they don't exit that way. Stay back since you're officially still on leave. Call Hudson. He's on the east coast."

"Roger that."

"Frost..."

Several seconds passed before he answered. "Yeah?"

"I know I have no authority over you or anyone else, but please listen to me when I tell you, do not approach. Wait on me."

Another few seconds ticked by before a sullen sounding "Roger" came through the speaker.

If Miller was willing to kill to keep his secrets, Rebecca wasn't going to let another cop get hurt because of her case.

Emotion pricked her eyes, and she blinked it away. "Thank you."

36

I didn't have the money. I'd never intended on even getting it, and Serenity McCreedy was a damned fool for thinking I would.

I had another plan. An easier plan. I'd play things out as long as I could just to get to her—to maybe get as much information out of her as possible.

When I came to the old surf shop, I nearly expected her not to be there. I was starting to think Serenity was just as nervous as me. I sort of understood too. A pretty little thing like her, just seventeen and wrapped up in some sick and sordid scenarios with the Yacht Club.

And she knew I'd killed someone. Would she really be brave—and stupid—enough to go face-to-face with a murderer?

God...it still didn't seem real.

I had killed someone. The thought bounced in my head as I pulled my truck alongside her fancy car. The ease in which I'd taken a life surprised me, but it also showed me I *could* do it. If I had to, I would do it again. I could defend what was mine. And for now, I didn't think Serenity suspected that of me.

She was soon going to be dead wrong.

All my life, people had underestimated me. Even Cassie had underestimated how I'd react to her news.

True, Cassie had been an accident. I'd lost control, overwhelmed by emotions led by fear. In the heat of the moment, it had been a simple thing to take her life.

But now?

Could I murder someone with premeditation? Could I kill Serenity?

My cock grew hard.

Yeah. Yeah, I could.

My breathing grew heavy as I imagined squeezing the life from the girl, watching her eyes bulge, her body writhing under mine until she grew still, and her eyes went blank.

In those moments, I was like God, controlling the fine line between life and death. Kill or reprieve.

Which would it be today?

Parking my truck, I toyed with the question. Live or die?

I laughed, the sound louder than I'd intended because I already knew the answer. I was wearing gloves, after all. The same type of gloves I'd worn when I'd chased down Cassie. And just like those gloves, I'd have to burn these as well.

It might be daylight, and the sun might have given Serenity enough sense of security to meet me face-to-face, but she didn't know this place like I did. Didn't know the trap she was walking in to.

Leaving the truck running, I hopped out, keeping my expression carefully neutral. Serenity did the same, and just like I'd hoped, she followed me to the shadows of the building.

What she didn't know was that there was an abandoned

well just a few feet from where we stood. It would make a nice little grave.

No more leaving bodies to be found. I was learning. I'd be smarter this time.

The way she looked at me pissed me off, and I struggled to keep my gloved hands down by my sides. The little whore had too much confidence, too much aggression. Too much greed.

"Where's the money?"

I didn't even hesitate. "In the truck."

"Well, get it then." She wasn't quite so pretty when she snarled. "I don't want to get caught out here." She waved her hand dismissively.

At me!

"I know, but I think we need to talk." As I took a small step closer to her, lava boiled in my stomach. My palms were sweaty inside the gloves.

"Talk about what, you fucking creep?" She crossed her arms over her chest, causing her breasts to nearly cascade over the top of the tiny tank top she wore. "I know what you did. I know—"

Raising a hand, I very gently rested a gloved finger on the side of her neck, focusing on how the leather was close to the same color as her tanned skin. So lovely.

Something primal flickered in her eyes. Fear. She lifted her chin, though, attempting to be brazen. "What are you d-doing?"

My cock pulsed with excitement, knowing I was the one who caused the stutter. The confusion. The alarm ringing in her head.

Serenity whirled, but before she could even take a step, I'd caught a handful of silky long hair in my fist. It was blonde like Cassie's, and for a moment, it was Cassie's head clenched in my hand. My heart surged with a strange combination of grief and joy, but the feeling was destroyed by a high, shrill scream.

The sound came to an abrupt halt as I slapped her across the face. "Shut up, you little whore."

Wrapping my hand more fully in her hair, I pulled until she was like my own living arrow, bent so far backward that I was surprised her spine didn't break.

"Please..."

The sound of her begging, the sight of her tears, the feel of her lithe body under my hands was nearly my undoing. "Please what, my little whore?"

Before she could answer or make a sound, I tugged her upright, not stopping until her face slammed into the side of the building. The noise was actually a little disappointing, just a small, hollow thud, but the explosion of her thick warm blood was visually appealing.

Her knees gave way, and I let her sink to the ground, following her down. Straddling her body, my hands went exactly where they wanted to go.

And Cassie appeared.

Blue eyes instead of green.

Her hands coming up to touch my face, silently pleading for me to let her go.

She was so very beautiful. And so very alive.

I was filled with joy! Cassie wasn't dead. Why had I thought that?

Had it just been a bad dream?

Leaning down, I kissed her, tasting her sweetness as I loosened my hands. Her fingers moved into my hair, her nails scraping the scalp and...

Sharp teeth sank into my lip.

I howled, rearing back to find Serenity beneath me again.

The girl wasn't just a whore, she was a witch. Just like the witch from the cottage.

I had to kill her. Had to remove her from this earthly plane. My hands found her neck again.

Squeezed.

Squeezed.

"Shh," I soothed her. "It'll be over soon."

Her eyes, wide and searching, were like Cassie's staring at me from whatever place existed beyond this life. Her eyes were hurt, broken...searching for answers.

Answers that would never come.

37

Rebecca almost felt like she was being pushed forward by some great, invisible hand as she pulled up to the surf shop parking lot. Just as Frost had said, a red Ford pickup was parked there, not even remotely hidden. A silver Audi was parked beside it.

But where was Owen Miller and the girl?

As she took the two vehicles in, she spotted movement closer to the building. Jumping out of the Explorer, she rounded the hood just as Owen Miller slammed the blonde girl's head—presumably Serenity McCreedy—into the side of the metal structure.

Shit.

By the time Rebecca drew her sidearm, Owen was straddling the girl's body. His gloved hands were around her neck, and the young woman was fighting with all her might.

"Sheriff's department! Stop!"

Owen didn't move, didn't even act like he'd heard the order. His back was to Rebecca, which was a relief. It meant she wouldn't have to use her gun—something she was a bit reluctant to do after last night.

She ran toward the skirmish, and Owen didn't seem to hear her until she was right on top of him. As he started to turn his head, Rebecca grabbed him from behind. She wrapped her arm around his neck, his chin caught in the crook of her elbow.

What's good for the goose is good for the gander.

With a hard jerk backward, she pulled him up and away from the girl. He roared in anger and stumbled to get traction under him. As he scrambled, Rebecca slammed him hard against the side of the building. The wind rushed out of him as his body rebounded into her hands.

Pressing him into the structure, Rebecca twisted his left arm behind him, angling the wrist so that if he tried to escape, the pressure would make it feel as if his wrist was about to snap. He cried out as Rebecca brought his right hand around. She'd not thought things through very well, so she had no cuffs on her. But with the way his arms were pinned behind him, all she had to do was keep his wrists high on his back and he was going nowhere.

Owen Miller wasn't smart enough to realize this because he tried to buck her off, even though the movement must have been hell on his shoulders.

Rebecca braced with one leg and brought the other up against the back of his knee. His leg buckled, and he dropped like a stone. A quick shove bashed his face into the metal siding as he slid down.

Sidestepping while keeping her grip on his arm, making him scream in anguish, she stomped her heel into his ribs. As much as she didn't want to, she pulled her strike, using just enough force to knock the wind and the fight out of him.

Broken ribs would require too much extra paperwork. Stunned and struggling to remember how to breathe, he couldn't fight her anymore. She dropped one knee to his back, pinning him to the ground...a reminder of a similar move she'd been forced to make last night.

"Don't resist!" She glanced at the girl on the ground, who was dry heaving as she shakily pushed herself up onto one elbow. "Are you Serenity McCreedy?"

"Yeah." It came out in a choked groan.

Rebecca turned her head toward the sound of an approaching engine. Seconds later, she watched as Frost pulled his personal vehicle into the lot. She pressed harder against Owen Miller's back as he struggled once again.

Frost came around the building just as Deputy Hudson also pulled into the lot.

"No...please..."

Owen Miller's pleas were weak and fragile. They were the sounds of a man on the brink, of a man realizing a huge and insurmountable loss was on the horizon. Rebecca had heard this tone and desperation out of men before, and they almost always broke to pieces and spilled everything in an interrogation room.

Hudson and Frost rushed in to assist. Frost stopped to check on Serenity, pulling her away from the fray while Hudson slammed a pair of cuffs on Miller.

With their suspect secured, Rebecca pushed to her feet, breathing hard. She glanced over at Frost, who was helping Serenity get on her feet. The young woman was staring at the monster on the ground, and for a second, Rebecca thought she might kick the man.

And for a second, Rebecca thought she'd let her.

Catching her breath, Rebecca pushed her hair back from her face, surreptitiously checking her head for lumps or bruises. Together, she and Hudson hauled the broken man to his feet.

"Owen Miller, you're under arrest for the attempted murder of Serenity McCreedy."

And probably a whole lot worse.

38

On the way to the station, Owen Miller started sobbing, apologizing to his wife even though she obviously wasn't there. After that, he'd repeated the same question over and over again, a question Rebecca ignored.

"There has to be a way out of this, right?" Snot and spittle leaked from his nose and mouth, and Rebecca had been very glad she hadn't been driving her Tacoma. "God, it was all just a mistake. There's a way out of it, right?"

At the station, the crying continued. It had de-escalated into soft sobs, allowing him to speak with some coherence.

It was never easy to question someone when they were in the midst of an emotional breakdown, but Rebecca did her best. It was better to get it all out of him now before he collected himself and started asking for a lawyer. He'd only been arrested for the attempted murder of Serenity. Now it was time to nail him for Cassie's death too.

"Would you consider what you had with Cassie an affair, or was it just a one-time thing?"

"I was in love with her." He wiped some tears away with his cuffed hands and looked up at the two deputies with pleading eyes. "She told me after things started between us that she was feeling insecure and needed to prove to herself she wasn't a little girl."

"And sleeping with her helped with that?" It disgusted Rebecca to even consider it. She even thought she saw a grimace of disgust on Frost's face.

"She came to me first. She told me what she wanted. She said she wanted her first time to be with someone who knew what they were doing. And she said she'd seen the way I'd sneak glances at her when she was at the house to see Dillon." He glanced around then, frowning as he started to come out of his fog. "Should I have a lawyer with me?"

Rebecca ignored the question. So long as he didn't directly ask for one, it didn't count, and he'd already been read his rights twice now. "Speaking of Dillon, did he have any idea you were screwing his girlfriend?"

It was as if that single question opened a new box of just how disgusting the entire ordeal was for him. Rebecca could see something break inside of him, some huge chasm opening up inside that he'd managed to keep closed until now.

It wasn't the reality of what he'd done, or the names of the girls involved. No, in the end, it had been the name of his son. He cringed and let out a series of wet, sobbing gasps. "No. Dillon...poor Dillon. No, he didn't know."

Frost asked his first question without moving away from the wall. His steely eyes remained on Owen the entire time. "How many times did you sleep together?"

"I don't know. Fifteen or twenty? It was on nights when Dillon chose to hang out with his friends rather than her. She'd text me and ask if we could meet up. Her father is never home, so it was usually there. But there were a few times she came to me, to my house, or to one of the rentals we own. Or the old cottage. It was there..." His face crumbled. "It was there that she told me she was pregnant and how she had no intention of getting an abortion."

"And how did you respond?" The question wasn't necessary, but Rebecca had to ask it.

Owen looked up at Rebecca with disgust and anger in his eyes. It was a huge contrast to the absolute sorrow he'd been enveloped in since his arrest. "I lost sight of things. I thought of how it could ruin me, of what others would think. I thought of my son and my wife, and I lost my mind. I couldn't let her hurt them."

"Did you wear gloves when you did it?"

He only nodded, looking to his hands as if seeing them for the first time.

"So, you lost your mind over the pregnancy but still had the forethought to wear gloves before you killed her?"

To this, Owen Miller had no answer. Instead, he went on with his account. At this point, it wasn't so much about answering Rebecca's questions. She sensed he was talking to himself, trying to make sense of how it had all happened.

"We argued, and I slapped her. She grabbed her dress and took off crying. I stopped at my truck and got the gloves before going after her, and I guess I scared her. I caught up with her in the marshes and…and that was all."

Rebecca considered everything he'd told them, feeling this initial round of questions was over. She had no doubt he may have slipped out of logical thought for a moment that night. But the fact remained there were indicators of premeditation.

He'd stopped to put the gloves on. And he'd chased her through the dark and into the marshes on a stormy night.

He hadn't planned to let her go.

There were several missing pieces left to be fitted into place, but Rebecca felt sure her job was almost done. They'd search for Cassie's missing car, which Rebecca guessed they'd find at one of his rental houses. And she still needed to tell Owen's wife and son what he'd done.

Poor Dillon.

There were also remaining questions regarding Serenity. What was her connection to the Yacht Club, and did it tie Cassie to it as well? Why had Serenity and Owen been meeting? Why had he been trying to kill her? She felt these would be easy answers to get but now was not the time.

That was fine. She could wait. She had the killer and his willing confession. She'd done her job. The smaller details could come later and from someone else. The deputies could handle the victim report on their own after Serenity was released from the hospital. While she'd seemed fine, they all wanted her to get checked over by a doctor.

A knock on the interrogation door startled them all, and Rebecca decided a break was just what they needed. Leaving the sobbing man at the table, Rebecca nodded for Frost to join her out in the hall.

It was Viviane.

Rivers of black mascara ran down her dark cheeks.

Oh no.

Frost was the first to speak. "What's wrong?"

Viviane took in a deep breath. "The hospital called, and Alden's taken a turn for the worse." A new river of tears began to flow. "They said family and friends should get there as soon as possible."

Rebecca pulled the sobbing woman into a hug. "Go." She forced her own tears back and turned to Frost. "All of you go. I'll take care of everything here."

She'd never seen a man look so torn. "Are you sure?"

Rebecca waved them down the hallway. "Yes. You all are his family, so get the others and be safe." Tears burned at her eyes, and she cleared her throat. "Be sure to let him know we got Cassie's killer."

Frost nodded and took Viviane by the arm, and the pair raced down the hallway calling for the others to join them.

Doors slammed, and then a few moments later, engines started in the parking lot.

Then it was quiet.

Too quiet.

The silence allowed room for all the questions Rebecca had been harboring to swim to the surface of her mind...

They'd caught Cassie Leigh's murderer, but at what cost?

Had the kindly old sheriff paid the ultimate price for that justice?

And how would this tiny department recover from his loss?

Was that even her problem to worry about?

That question stopped her cold.

Yes. It is my problem because I'm the reason he's dying right now.

Her thoughts turned into a whirlpool, sucking her down into its depths.

How could she just go back to her little Cape Cod now and spend the summer sunning herself on the beach? But also, how could she not? Did she expect a department full of men who held her responsible for the death of their sheriff to open their arms to her, welcoming her into their ranks?

And was that what she even wanted?

Rebecca paced the small station for close to an hour, trying to settle her mind enough to do the paperwork that needed to be completed. At the very least, she could cross all the T's and dot all the I's so the guys wouldn't have to do that bit of grunt work after...

After the sheriff died.

Closing her eyes, Rebecca pressed the heels of her hands against her temples, hoping to squeeze the thought from her mind. It wouldn't go.

Was he gone already? Or would the spunky Sheriff Wallace possibly rally and surprise everyone by opening his eyes?

"Please, God, let him live."

Her phone buzzed in her pocket, making her jump. With a deep breath, she pulled it out and tapped on her notifications. It was from Viviane. Two little words reminded Rebecca that it didn't matter how hard she prayed. It was never answered.

He's gone.

Rebecca, alone in the station for the first time—the last time?—sank to her haunches and allowed herself to cry.

The End
To be continued...

Thank you for reading.
All of the *Shadow Island Series* books can be found on Amazon.

ACKNOWLEDGMENTS

How does one properly thank everyone involved in taking a dream and making it a reality? Here goes.

In addition to our families, whose unending support provided the foundation for us to find the time and energy to put these thoughts on paper, we want to thank the editors who polished our words and made them shine.

Many thanks to our publisher for risking taking on two newbies and giving us the confidence to become bona fide authors.

More than anyone, we want to thank you, our readers, for sharing your most important asset, your time, with this book. We hope with all our hearts we made it worthwhile.

Much love,

Mary & Lori

ABOUT THE AUTHOR

Mary Stone

Mary Stone lives among the majestic Blue Ridge Mountains of East Tennessee with her two dogs, four cats, a couple of energetic boys, and a very patient husband.

As a young girl, she would go to bed every night, wondering what type of creature might be lurking underneath. It wasn't until she was older that she learned that the creatures she needed to most fear were human.

Today, she creates vivid stories with courageous, strong heroines and dastardly villains. She invites you to enter her world of serial killers, FBI agents but never damsels in distress. Her female characters can handle themselves, going toe-to-toe with any male character, protagonist or antagonist.

Discover more about Mary Stone on her website.
www.authormarystone.com

Lori Rhodes

As a tiny girl, from the moment Lori Rhodes first dipped her toe into the surf on a barrier island of Virginia, she was in love. When she grew up and learned all the deep, dark secrets and horrible acts people could commit against each other, she couldn't stop the stories from coming out of the other end of her pen. Somehow, her magical island and the darkness got mixed together and ended up in her first novel. Now, she spends her days making sure the guests at her beach rental cottages are happy, and her nights dreaming up the characters who love her island as much as she does.

Connect with Mary Online

facebook.com/authormarystone
goodreads.com/AuthorMaryStone
bookbub.com/profile/3378576590
pinterest.com/MaryStoneAuthor